BEASTS & BROMANCE

THE RANGER'S MAGI, BOOK 1

BEASTS & BROMANCE

ESKAY KABBA

4 Horsemen
Publications, Inc.

Content warnings: sexually explicit content, discussions of sexual grooming, incidences of violence and death

TABLE OF CONTENTS

CHAPTER 1

The Overnight Shift

10:57 p.m.

Three more minutes until the start of his shift. His first solo shift. Christopher Jennings was staring proudly at himself in the old rusty mirror in the back of the Tank – what they called the Ranger headquarters because it was literally shaped like a water tank—on the bathroom door. Green top and bottom, the official uniform, brown utility belt with his radio and tranquilizer gun on his left and .38 holstered on his right, small pad and pen in his top pocket.

10:58 p.m.

Chris put on the cotton ranger hat that matched the brown strip, vowing to buy a real fedora at some point. He smiled. "Fuck yeah," he whispered to himself.

"Happy there?"

Chris was startled, having almost forgotten that he wasn't alone in the room. Bergina, his immediate supervisor and mentor, was ending her shift. He put on his most serious face. "I'm just happy to be serving the people," he said professionally.

Bergina laughed as she grabbed her satchel. "I'm going to get out of here. You have my notes: Eight campers officially in the woods. But keep an eye on that blue sedan parked on Pine Road. There is a couple in there that has been making out since my last round at 9 p.m. They are probably doing it by now. It's up to you if you want to stop them."

Chris, who enjoyed a good screwing now and then, said, "Nah." Bergina grinned.

He used his peripheral vision to glance at the clock. 11:00 p.m. on the dot. He contained his excitement long enough for Bergina to grab her sweater and say, "Good luck on your first night. Bye!" as she headed out.

He could have cried, he was so happy. Finally, after four years of getting his degree in forestry management, two years at the academy, and one year of basic training in the forest shadowing Bergina, he had become a park ranger in the same woods he had frequented as a boy. He knew every inch of Verdant, the 5,000-acre forest in a very small part of Drenova National Park. Chris and his mother knew every stream, every tree, and even the hidden paths that led to the mountains. He had not stepped foot in his beloved woods since he went off to college in Tirana and couldn't wait to explore again.

Chris thought of his mother. She had died almost seven years earlier, but it was as fresh a feeling as if it had happened yesterday. His heart ached. His beautiful mother, who would take him and his siblings to the forest at least once a month no matter the weather, because Ma Ami always said

Korçë, the city they lived in, did not leave room to breathe. *"And where else could you breathe but around the trees that have given us life?"* she would say with a bright smile. His African mother always had sayings and proverbs to share with them.

Sadness started to take over—his dark cloud, he called it—as he remembered his mother's most famous words to him: *"Choose life and love over sadness and death, always."* Today, he chose to focus on the amazing life he worked so hard to achieve, including his dream job.

Chris re-tied his black boots and pulled a chair out to the catwalk. He leaned it against the side of the tank and crossed his feet at the ankles. He looked up and began to count the stars. August 1st was going to be the beginning of great things for him, he could feel it.

◆

1:39 a.m.

Ciaran yawned. It was his first week back, and he still wasn't used to the night shift again. He could barely keep his eyes open. After a year of gallivanting the four continents with his younger brother Sean, drinking, smoking way too much weed, and having more sexual partners in one year than he had had in his entire twenty-seven years on earth, coming back to his daily routine was almost torturous. He absent-mindedly touched his chest, feeling the soft curves slightly growing on his once rock-hard body. *I'm down to a four-pack,* he thought to himself, and laughed internally.

To the world, he was humble, but inside, Ciaran knew his body was a sight to behold and he took pride in it. It was what attracted people to him. It certainly wasn't the fiery red hair, blue eyes, and brown freckles that dotted most of his face, although that did make him stand out for sure. No, what caught the eye of others was the shape of his body, his two percent body fat and muscles all over. And when he was in a tank top showing off his Kumoi, the tattoo of his beloved Japanese dragon on his back and shoulder, men and women flocked to him.

Ciaran yawned again. *Shit, I need to wake up*, he thought.

He started walking the perimeter of the Dragon Reservation of Albania. The DRA had six dragons in total, a manageable number, while a few others dotted the sky in the far-off mountains. No complaints, though; anytime there were seven or more, there was chaos. There were about a hundred men—no female Dragon Tamers since Chitra left a few years ago—who dedicated their lives, sometimes literally, to ensure the endangered beasts had a safe place, a place to live and die in peace away from the cruelty of humans. And humans were cruel.

Ciaran had been obsessed with dragons his whole life, but after coming face to face with one when he was fifteen years old, he knew he had found his calling. Once he knew he was done in service to the Magi military, he joined the DRA at nineteen and never looked back. He would live and breathe that life, for the rest of his life. Hidden safely in the Verdant Forest, they had found peace, and so had Ciaran.

He passed the sleeping London, possibly a thousand years old and blind, with brown flesh that was still pink in his rawest spots. How he even knew to come there, no one knew. He showed up on top of one of the cliff's edges, drinking from its natural springs, two years ago. Maybe he knew he wasn't strong enough to play and fight with the rougher, untamable dragons in the distance, but did not feel safe with humans. So, in the middle, he sat.

The twenty-nine-foot-long dragon with six legs and two enormous wings stayed up there for two days before Dale, the Ringmaster of the Reserve, was able to coax him into the valley with the other dragons. London and Dale had become pretty close since then. Dale named him, saying that he looked like he flew all the way from London to Albania. And even though the dragon had two Tamers, Dale was the only one he let ride.

London slept a lot, which was fine by everyone on the Reserve. It was probably the most rest he had gotten on this earth, so they let him.

Ciaran passed the newest one, blue-black reptilian skin with yellow eyes, barely a year old, that they had yet to name. Some git must have opened an egg and tried to keep it as a pet, and when it got too much for them, they dropped her off in a cage in the woods as close to the Reserve as they could get.

Ciaran shook his head. *Seriously, a bloody dragon in the middle of the woods with Commoner rangers all about. Who the fuck is that stupid? We will never know.*

Ciaran was still fuming about it. He was the one who found her in July before he officially resumed working at the Reserve again, and brought her in. The dragon was wild and always looking for a way out. Plotting. Seemingly untamable. She seemed to like him though, most likely because while everyone else stood back, he was the one that took her out of her cage and cleaned her wounds. She gave hell to the other Reservers; snapping her jaw at anyone who got too close in the last couple of weeks. But to Ciaran, she simply roared him away when she didn't want to be bothered. She was currently sleeping at the base of the hill, just before the field and compounds.

One of these days, she is going to sneak right through the field and off the Reserve. He laughed to himself at that thought.

He passed the two Irish Camouflias that came in together half a century ago, who they named Ben and Anna. Their silver skin camouflage with the colors of the morning horizon, the brownish gray of the mountains, or the night sky. Cami's were rare, and even rarer as pairs. They were the youngest on the Reserve before the Magnetite came, barely a hundred years old combined, and very playful. The story goes they were raised together in the Scottish Highlands at another much smaller Reserve, until their kind Magi owner died, leaving in his will they were to be sent to the Reserve to live out their lives. Both were sleeping, curled up next to each other like the lovers they were.

Hina, was their Japanese dragon. A long-necked, four-winged, two-legged, golden yellow dragon, Hina was the epitome of what Commoners visualized as dragons. She had a partner too, Kumoi, who was Ciaran's first dragon as a Tamer and who he mirrored his own tattoo from. They had been on the Reserve the longest; the rumor being that they were the first dragons there. Kumoi died about seven years ago from an unknown heart condition, but he was pretty mature in age, at least thirteen hundred years old. It broke Ciaran's heart, and he had vowed to take care of Hina since then. She, too, was sleeping.

Ciaran looked at Hansel, the third oldest dragon on the Reserve, at eight hundred and fifty years old. The Pigeondon could be feisty at times, but generally, he was happy to be there and the easiest of all the dragons. Pigeondons were direct descendants of cockatrices, with wings like chickens that could actually fly, but they preferred to walk everywhere. Stocky and big-chested in the middle and literal chicken legs on the bottom, Hansel was more bark than bite.

Hansel had taken a liking to London since he had arrived and they flew together at least once a day when London wasn't sleeping. They rescued Hansel from Siberia almost six years ago and Ciaran was a part of that mission—his first. Hansel was usually up at that time of night, but even he was asleep. Ciaran thought it was the medicine that Sarah, their Novo, Reserve Healer, gave him for his arthritis.

Sleeping dragons were usually a good thing, but it did little to help Ciaran's lethargy. The night crew Reservers were also milling around, keeping occupied until the sun rose, the dragons woke up, or trouble arrived. *And unfortunately for me, there is no trouble,* Ciaran thought as he stood at the edge facing the valley.

No sooner than Ciaran thought this, a loud horn blared, breaking through the silence. Ciaran turned to the front entrance, the only place the alarm went off that loudly. He began running toward it. Thirty other men came running up from different directions, including Dale, who was caught in the loo, pulling up his pants and yelling, "Sonofabitch, sonofabitch" repeatedly. Everyone had to run since there was no Wisp magic used in the Reserve unless it was Dale. Wisp'ing scared the dragons too much.

Vladimir, the newest nighttime Fixer, was running back up from the front entrance. Dale screamed, "What the bloody fuck happened? Is someone trying to get in?"

Vlad cried out, "No! It's the black one, or blue one, or—"

"Put your nuts back in your knickers and spit it the fuck out!" Dale screamed again, just as loud as the horn still going off.

"The baby dragon!" Vlad spurted out. "She... she got out! She snuck up on me and swiped at me... I thought she was sleeping, but she wasn't! By the time I stood up, she was gone! She went right down the hill and out the main entrance!"

The Reservers stood there with their mouths open. No dragon had gone out the front entrance into the woods before, as far as they knew. But no dragon had come in through the front entrance either, like she had.

Dale waved his right hand and the alarm immediately ceased. He turned to Ciaran to tell him to go find her, but the dragon tamer was already down the hill and out into the Verdant Forest.

CHAPTER 2

New Mates

1:56 a.m.

Chris had just rounded Marker 9 when he heard a noise. Knowing his training, he turned off his flashlight, froze on the spot, and let his eyes do the listening for him. Could be a wolf or a bear. Either way, he had to stay still. The forest was denser over there and he knew that was where the real wildlife hid, away from the people. He never got too close, and they never came out, so it was a non-issue; but every once in a while, something decided to wander from its habitat and the rangers had to deal with it.

He heard it again. Something was walking toward him. Chris slowly went down to a crouch and unlocked the strap on the left side of his utility belt where the tranquilizer gun was. Whatever was coming was coming from the northeast of him. He figured he would subdue it, bring it farther into the forest, then continue his rounds.

But what Chris saw coming toward him as his eyes adjusted to the dark literally made him drop to his knees and paralyzed every muscle in his body. *What. The. Fuck. Is. It?* Chris thought to himself.

The beast was at least ten feet tall, and Chris was a good 6'2" himself. It was so black but it was also dark blue. Chris couldn't figure out if his mind was playing tricks on him. It walked on four legs, but when it saw Chris, it stood up on two. Bright yellow eyes shone in the dark and stared at him. Mouth shaped like an alligator. Teeth bared like a wolf ready to attack. Leathery wings like a bat as long as a small plane. It took a moment for Chris to realize *it had wings.*

He thought, *this would be an appropriate time to shit myself.* Yet even his bowels locked up. He was terrified, but also in awe. He wanted to move, but his body would not budge. Even as he watched the beast open its mouth and electric-blue light seared from its throat, Chris continued to be frozen in astonishment.

In a split second, something—someone?—slammed their entire body against Chris, rolling him along by his shirt, just in time as the beast let out a roar, shot blue flames from its mouth, and the tree behind where Chris was kneeling went up in flames. That magnificent blue-black beast had spit magnificent blue fire from its magnificent mouth.

Ho. Lee. Shit, Chris thought, as his voice seemed to have left him.

Ciaran, who landed on top of Chris, locked eyes with him. He asked quietly, "Are you okay, mate?"

Chris nodded, although he felt anything but okay. Ciaran nodded back. Then Ciaran jumped up and ran to the dragon. He waved his hand that had something in it toward the tree, and the fire next to Chris suddenly ... *stopped.* The tree was badly burned, and he could still smell the burning bark, but that was it. It was like the fire had happened the night before instead of one moment before.

What. Is. Happening? Chris thought, wide-eyed.

"Now, now there," Ciaran said scoldingly. "You know better than to run away. I'm not cross with you, sweet girl, but you have to come with me now."

Chris, who was lying in the same place Ciaran left him, was shocked. *He's talking to it like it is a dog that got out of its fence.*

The beast eyed Ciaran with intent as he continued his casual conversation with it. "You know," he said, "I haven't given you a name yet. Maybe that will help you feel part of the family. Do you want a name, sweetie? No, not Sweetie? Okay, duly noted. Let me think of some names. Winnie? No. Hannah? No. Beatrice? Nah, you need a name that can be masculine or feminine. Like a Taylor or a Jamie. Or maybe a girl's version of a boy's name, like Thomasina? Wilhelmina?"

"Robetta," Chris called out of the darkness from the ground. He knew a Robetta in high school.

Ciaran glanced back at the ranger and smiled. He looked at the dragon and said, "Robetta, it is! We can call you Betta for short if you like that. Do you like that, Betta?" He put his stick away, and took a couple of steps toward it, speaking so softly, like he was talking to a newborn baby, barely audible, but Chris heard every word.

"Robetta, I won't hurt you. You know this. But I need to stun you a little to get you back, okay ol' girl? You'll just fall asleep and then you'll be home again."

She moved back down to four legs and grunted as he came closer to the side of her. He touched her gently and she grunted again, but did not back away. Chris watched as he slowly reached into his pocket with his other hand, all the while cooing the dragon now known as Robetta. Suddenly his hand went up and he threw a bright, yellowish, powdery dust as thick as pollen into the air. The dragon yelled as it coated her head, her eyes, her nose, and her mouth. He threw it in her face again and again. Robetta closed her eyes and didn't move again, as if in a deep sleep.

"Whew," Ciaran said. He turned around to search for the man he left on the ground.

Chris realized he was still lying where Ciaran left him when Ciaran came over and held out his hand to help him up. Chris took it and stood up.

"So, you're the new ranger?" he asked.

"And you're the ... beast whisperer?" Chris asked, still in awe.

Ciaran grinned. "Yeah, I guess so."

Chris looked over at the beast. "What is it?" he asked.

"A dragon. A Magnetite to be exact," Ciaran answered. "Class B. When she becomes fully grown in about ten years, her skin will harden like iron on her back and top coat of the hands and arms."

Chris scoffed. "Fuck off, what is it really?"

Ciaran chuckled. "Okay, what do you think it is?"

To this question, Chris's eyes went wide. "Are you serious? A fucking dragon? Like, *A Game of Thrones*, *The Hobbit*, *Eragon*, '*Puff the Magic Dragon*' kind of dragon?"

Ciaran grinned with all his teeth again. "You certainly know your classics."

Chris moved closer; he touched her scaly, lizard-like skin, her toenails as big as his foot. "She is beautiful," he said.

Ciaran watched him curiously. "Yes. And she is just a baby. She will grow to be about twenty feet. I have to get her back now, but first I need to..." He raised his rodulé.

Chris spun around, reached up his hand, and grabbed Ciaran's wrist, yelling, "DON'T!"

Chris had read and watched enough sci-fi to know what was going to happen next: his memory was about to be erased somehow. And he couldn't let that happen.

Ciaran paused, the *dulé* in mid-air as Chris held his wrist. Neither man gave any resistance as they held their arms up. They locked eyes.

Chris held Ciaran's gaze and said, "I swear on my mother's grave that I will not tell a soul that I saw her. Not a single person. I will take it to my grave that dragons exist. Do not take this from me, please. Please." His eyes pleaded.

And for some ridiculous, inexplicable reason, Ciaran believed him. He began to slowly bring his hand down and Chris let him go. As he lowered his wand all the way to his side, he asked, "Your shift ends at 7 a.m., innit?"

"Yes," said Chris. "How do you know?"

Ciaran ignored the question. "I'll come by at 6 a.m. We'll talk then."

And with that, Ciaran snapped his fingers, and Robetta levitated off the ground. He started walking into the woods, the dragon floating after him. Chris stared after them until the darkness swallowed them up.

He realized he had five more checkpoints to do. Chris began walking toward Marker 10, which was closer to the road. He stood there for a moment, only then realizing how fast his heart was beating. After a moment, he continued, methodically completing his rounds, all the while thinking of Robetta and the man she led to him.

———◆———

Chris did his second round about 4:30 a.m. a lot quicker but lingered around Marker 9. To his disappointment, it was quiet. He sat down to complete his logs at the table, but his mind continued to wander. *Dragons are real! And real people guard them.* Suddenly his dream job seemed trivial to what he wanted to do. *I want to be a dragon watcher*, he thought hysterically. He would need to ask that man when he arrived in the next thirty minutes how to get that job.

And who was that man, anyway? He didn't even know his name. But he remembered everything about him: pale skin, pink lips, red hair, brown freckles—that was how close he was to him. His body was rock solid. The side of Chris that was attracted to men was definitely fascinated by it, but the dragons intrigued him more.

Chris realized at 5:39 a.m. that he had barely written a word. "Okay. Focus," he said to himself out loud.

All quiet, he wrote at each marker. As he finished writing the words at Marker 13, his peripheral view noticed movement in the room. His head snapped up and Mr. Red Haired Rock Hard Body was at the entrance. It was like he appeared silently. All of a sudden Chris's mouth was dry, and he was nervous. He slowly leaned back in his chair and put his hands in his lap.

Ciaran, on the other hand, smiled. He strode in like he had been there before, sat down across from Chris, and put his muddy boots on the table, crossed at the ankles. He was wearing a different set of clothes; earlier he had on some kind of full uniform, a light brown coverall a maintenance worker would step into and zip up. Now he was wearing a blue t-shirt that showed his bulging muscles with the letters DRA in the corner, blue jeans, brown work boots, and a satchel across his back. For a moment, they stared at each other and no one spoke. Chris broke the ice.

"And how is our Robetta?" he asked casually. He put one hand on the table and drummed his fingers.

Ciaran smiled again. "Doing well, thank you. She woke up on the east side of the Reserve which pissed her off, but she's fine. Since we know she is going to try to escape again, we put a tracker on her. And we didn't know she could spit full fire yet. Babies typically develop that kind of power after year one, so we nipped that in the bud, too. She was older than we thought. Either way, I got my eye on her."

Chris nodded, as if he understood the basics of raising a dragon. They were silent again, watching each other. It dawned on Chris why Ciaran was quietly watching him.

"Sooooo… How many rangers have you erased their memories so they wouldn't know about the dragons they saw? Before me."

Ciaran smirked; he was beginning to like Chris's frankness. "Two so far. You would make number three."

"Has anyone ever resisted?"

"No, because I didn't give them the chance to."

"But you gave me a chance to. Why?" Chris asked curiously.

Ciaran paused, then said, "Honestly, I don't know. I guess you have an honest face."

Chris nodded again, then said, "And did my face get less honest in the light of day?"

Ciaran laughed. "No, I still trust you. But seeing a dragon is a big fucking deal. You're going to need to talk to someone about it at some point. Confide in at least one other person that you trust, and that's how it gets out. And that's a risk I cannot take."

Chris nodded a third time. "Okay. Then I'll just talk about it with you."

"With me?" Ciaran was surprised.

"Yes, with you. If I ever get the need to talk about dragons or whatever else I might find out, I will talk to you, my new best friend."

Ciaran couldn't help it; he grinned that wide grin, took his feet off the table, and leaned in, folding his hands together. "You don't even know my name."

"Oh, that was deliberate!?" Chris said mockingly. "I just assumed between subduing dragons and saving my life, you just forgot to mention it, like I forgot to give you mine."

Chris leaned in as well, crossed his hands at the table, and said, "I'm Chris Jennings. Half Senegalese, half Irish. I live in Korçë, and I'm one of the few Catholics there. I live in a duplex with my two sisters and my nephew. Mum's dead, Dad's in Vlore near the sea. I'm single and ready to mingle. Born in Ireland, raised in Albania right here in these woods, and until yesterday, I thought I knew all of its secrets.

"I'm not asking to visit the area; I'm not even asking about any others. I just want to keep the knowledge that there is one magnificent beast in this world that I touched and almost got killed by it. I'm not going to lie, mate, if you erase me, I may forget what happened, but you and I both know I will never forget the feeling that I experienced an amazing thing and that I'm missing something. And I will probably keep searching for it because that's how my mind works." He exhaled. "Please don't erase me."

"*Abscondo*" Ciaran told him.

"Huh?"

"When you hide a memory from someone, it's called *Abscondo*. It's Latin, meaning to conceal. I do it with my *dulé*." Ciaran took his wand out of his pocket and put it on the table. To Chris, it resembled a white stick with a black handle. "Short for *Rodulé*, which essentially is a staff, a cane, or in our case, a wand."

"What are you, some kind of wizard or sorcerer?" Chris said jokingly.

"Yeah, sure," Ciaran said sarcastically.

"Shut up," Chris said in disbelief.

"Okay. I'm not," Ciaran said seriously.

And Chris suddenly believed him. "Yes. Yes, you are," he said with a straight face. Ciaran did not say anything.

They stared at each other again. Chris leaned back again and said, "Well Mr. Maybe I'm A Sorcerer, can we make a pact?"

"I'm listening."

"I will keep your secrets and you don't have to *abscondo* my memory. In return, I will keep all the rangers out of your area for as long as I'm here, to avoid another incident. I won't ask any dragon questions, but I may ask about our Betta from time to time, just to make sure she is okay. And I especially will not ask about your stick or the fact that you might or might not be a wizard or sorcerer who knows or does not know how to do a lick of magic. Can we shake on that?"

Ciaran didn't say anything, mostly for effect. Because what Chris didn't know was that five minutes into their conversation, he had decided he wasn't going to use *abscondo* on him and conceal his memory. Right after Chris called him "my new best friend."

He took a couple of moments and stuck his hand out. "I'm Ciaran, by the way. Ciaran Beals."

CHAPTER 3

The Magus

Ciaran met up with Chris every night at Marker 1, except on the weekends, when Chris was off. They would patrol together and talk about their lives and families, Chris avoiding the one thing he desperately wanted to talk about. Since Ciaran's shift was from dusk to dawn, he was in the woods hours before and was able to take his break around 1 a.m. He convinced Dale that it was important to keep an eye on the new ranger, and Dale reluctantly agreed to let him.

Ciaran was a very interesting guy to Chris. He learned that Ciaran was the second oldest of five children, but one passed away over a year ago and his twin brother was still trying to find his way without him. He and his brother Sean had just returned from a cross-continent backpacking trip, but he would say little to nothing about what they did. Ciaran was born in Kingsbridge, England, and moved to Albania eight years ago at the age of nineteen to work with dragons. He spoke very little Albanian, enough to get by.

Ciaran learned about Chris as well. He was the second oldest of three children in the middle of two sisters. Chris was biracial and amusingly called himself a Black Irish. He had a father that he did not get along with and a mother who had been his whole world until she died suddenly of aggressive ovarian cancer. Growing up in Albania was tough due to his skin color, but he quickly made up for it by running track and being a champion in middle and high school.

Chris and Ciaran became fast friends. They would do rounds together, then head back to the Tank, drink beers, and play cards until around 3 a.m. when Ciaran would head back to the Reserve. For the first few weeks, they talked about surface stuff. Then one evening when it started raining on their way back, Ciaran waved his *dulé* behind Chris's back and magically the rain fell around them as if they had an invisible umbrella over them. Chris looked at Ciaran suspiciously when they were no longer getting wet, but said nothing.

When they arrived at the Tank however, Chris said, "I promised not to ask, and I haven't, and I never will. But. I will listen ... to anything you would want to tell me about being a ... wizard?"

"Magus," Ciaran corrected him. "A male magical human. The women are called Mages. We are a community of Magi, or Magicians. And the source you call magic, we call *the Vis*."

Ciaran sat at the table, and Chris did the same. "You have to understand," said Ciaran, "that I am breaking a huge law here in my world. Since the twelfth century, the Magi have taken a solemn oath to remain in secret from the world of the Commoners."

"World of the Commoners? The regular world? Sorry! No questions," Chris said quickly, crapping himself because he asked a question. He was happy that Ciaran answered him without an issue.

"Yes," Ciaran said, "The world of people without the *Vis* in their DNA. Commoners are humans without a magical bloodline."

Chris nodded. "So I'm a Commoner."

"Yes, you are."

"How many Magi are there in the world?"

"Who knows?" Ciaran said. "There are eight billion people on this earth, so maybe one-third of that, if I were to guess. Most of us live among Commoners. We go to primary schools, work, pay taxes. We attend events and pray in churches or mosques or synagogues, and you would never know that you were walking and talking with a Magus or Mage. At age ten we take the oath of secrecy and begin at Campus, a magical school that teaches us how to wield our power, our *Vis*. We're there until around sixteen or seventeen. Then we must do at least one year of Magi military service, learning the importance of enforcing the secret. By eighteen, we choose how we want to live, within a homogenous Magi community, or within a Commoner community, or a mixed society, while still upholding Magi laws.

"When we graduate, we declare our classification: witch or warlock. Witches are earthy; they practice spells and incantations, and make potions to better society, ours and Commoners. Warlocks are more mental, strategic, linear in how their use their *Vis*. If you don't declare, you're simply considered a Magician."

"And which are you?" Chris asked. "Because I'm assuming that men can be witches and women can be warlocks."

"You assume correct. I declared myself a warlock a long time ago," said Ciaran with a sigh. "Now? I don't know."

"Well," said Chris, "The work you do on the Reserve sounds more witchy than warlock. Bettering society and all."

Ciaran smirked. "Maybe. But I am trained as a mercenary. I still think like one, very strategic, two steps ahead of everyone else. So maybe I still am."

Chris acknowledged with a nod. "All head, no heart? That's the opposite of me, mate."

"We Magus have hearts. Even the warlocks."

Ciaran explained the circumstances that secrecy had been breached in the past, such as a Magus or Mage falling in love with a Commoner, or Commoners suddenly having children with magical abilities, awakening an old bloodline.

"That's the work my father does for the Magi Council, introducing Commoners into our society. At the point of revelation, we would have to bring them into our world, and they too would take an oath of secrecy, the *Vis Sacramentum*. But when mistakes happen, we just *abscondo* and move on."

Chris nodded. "I understand the seriousness of it all. And I meant it when I said I would not tell another soul. I'm glad you didn't consider me a mistake and *abscondo* me."

Ciaran smiled. "Well, I think I enjoy your company far more than I let on, mate. You remind me of the little brother that I just lost. And his twin, who is lost without him."

It was the first time Ciaran had mentioned family, other than demographics. Chris understood what it felt like to lose a family member. "Do you want to talk about it, friend?"

Ciaran looked away and took a sip of his beer. "No."

Chris nodded. "How about a game of gin rummy instead?"

He didn't wait for Ciaran's response before he rose from the seat and grabbed a deck of cards out of a metal cabinet. And Ciaran was grateful for his understanding.

———

As the leaves turned rich in color, so did their friendship grow deeper and richer. Ciaran opened up more about the Magi world. Ciaran came from a long, historical Magi family, but they didn't set themselves apart like other generational Magi families did. They interacted with Commoners frequently. His mother owned an apothecary and herbal shop in their town, but his father worked for the Magi Council as a Magi Ambassador, wearing many hats, but ultimately a liaison between Magi and Commoners.

"There is a strong divide and mistrust between Magi toward Commoners," Ciaran told Chris, as they played cards one night. "Those that know of us hunt us down. There was a significant sector of Magi who struck first, going against the nature of the *Vis* and killing for sport. It had gotten worse in the last couple of decades. They would go as far as killing other Magi who did not agree with their fascism and bloodlust. That civil war had been brewing for years. And by the time I came of age, I was caught in the middle of it."

Ciaran talked about being a *Veneficus*, a warlock, since the age of sixteen. "Black warlocks, *Nigri Veneficus* or NV, are mercenaries for the Magi Council. We hunted Magi criminals, *Caerulus Veneficus* or CV. They bore a blue mark on their body when they committed a crime against the natural laws of the *Vis*. Talindra, a powerful Mage, was their leader, and she literally had blue skin. That's how much dark magic she used and how much she killed without mercy. That great and bloody civil war, brother against brother, nearly destroyed my world. Once the battle was over, we won and Talindra was captured, but at what cost?"

"I've never seen anyone walk around with blue skin," Chris said in disbelief.

"Well, Magi aren't stupid," Ciaran retorted. "There are spells to remove pigment cells. But they can't regrow them, so it leaves blotches like vitiligo. That's how they pass among Commoners."

"Interesting," said Chris. "When I was in high school, I heard about a cult of serial killers right here in Albania that was being blamed for people disappearing and then reappearing in the woods in the weirdest places, just dead with no known cause. Then suddenly it died out, and no one was actually caught."

Ciaran confirmed, "Yes, there were CVs in this area. There was an outpost for it, close to the Reserve. They were always trying to find a way to get in and get control of our dragons, to use them for their evil deeds."

"Wow," Chris said, shaking his head. "There is magic all around us, and we simply do not know."

"As a Commoner, you wouldn't," Ciaran said. "For you, it's fantasy and make-believe. For us, it is real life."

"Thank God the war is over, though. For the Magi world and the Commoner world," said Chris. He got up from the table and went to the fridge to grab two beers.

"Yes. But there is still a lot of prejudice and hate and mistrust in my world, and that will take a long time to heal from, if ever," said Ciaran.

"No different than us. Like a lot of racism, sexism, and homophobia, if you ask me. Those aren't things people heal from quickly," Chris said. He handed Ciaran a beer and sat back down.

"Surprisingly, those things you mentioned do not matter in the Magi world. Power and blood rite is what makes the difference, no matter what color your skin is, what gender you are, or how you love."

"Really? Then maybe I should have been born a Magus," Chris said with a smile as he took a sip of his own.

"Actually, it has been noted that Africa is the birthplace of magic, and some Magi believed that the more melanin you have, the more powerful your potential could be. What if I told you that the slave trade was about magical bloodlines?"

Chris gasped. "You're kidding!?"

Ciaran shook his head. "Slavery in Europe was a way to harness power. The more magical individuals you had, the more powerful you were. In the fifteenth century during the slave trade, English Magus were purposely getting female slaves pregnant in the hopes they would have a powerful child. If they showed magical abilities by age eight, they would keep them. If not, they would sell them off. America continued the practice long after it was outlawed here."

Chris's mouth dropped. "That's fucked."

Ciaran agreed. "It definitely is. The things people do to keep their bloodline pure and powerful is nothing short of disgusting."

Chris played a card. "So it's possible that I could have some magical bloodline?"

"It is possible, yes," Ciaran responded.

"Maybe after I start having children I just might be passing down Magi genes from my African mama." Chris grinned. "How exciting would that be?"

He chuckled. "You never know. That's usually how it happens; out of nowhere, one of your children starts to do unintentional magic."

"That would be amazing. I've always wanted to be a father," said Chris, almost dreamily. "I'd be the best dad, better than my own father was to me. I want to have as close a relationship with them as I was to my mother, who was my very best friend. Honestly mate, I can't wait to be a dad. Before I turn 30, so I got a few years since I'm 26 this year."

"But first, we have to find a woman that will want to fuck you," Ciaran joked.

Chris shrugged and smiled slyly. "Or a man. My seed though."

Ciaran's mouth dropped a bit in surprise, but he quickly recovered. "Oh. Okay."

Chris cocked his head slightly to the side. "Is that surprising?"

"No," Ciaran said quickly. "I dunno. Maybe. You just never mentioned it in the months we've been hanging out, so I didn't know..." He trailed off.

"That I like boys and girls and everything in between?" Chris asked, amusingly.

"Well, it's not like it's glaringly obvious. Except the fact that you paint your nails black, but I just thought you were a little emo."

"I'm that too," Chris said and laughed a bit. But then he asked in a serious tone, "Are you okay with that, mate?"

Ciaran, feeling himself go slightly pink, said, "Why wouldn't I be? Like I said, those things don't matter. You like who you like, you love who you love."

"Well, I haven't loved anyone in a long time, but I do love sex." He smiled.

Ciaran laughed, really turning pink, always amused by his candor. "So you're bisexual."

"I'm pansexual," Chris corrected him. "I don't exclude any genders, any individual. As long as they have what I need at the moment."

"So how does that work?" Ciaran asked curiously. "You just choose a partner based on..."

"Good question." Chris was thoughtful. "Sometimes I need soft, feminine, wet. Sometimes I need hard, strong, tight."

Ciaran nodded and played another card. He wanted to ask more questions, but instead decided not to. So, Chris picked up on it and asked, "Do you want to know what it feels like? Being with a man?"

Ciaran chuckled nervously, trying to avert direct eye contact. "Not really. It's just... I've worked alongside men for the last twelve years, first in the military and then on the Reserve. I just can't imagine being with anything other than soft, feminine, and wet."

"That's because you've never had tight."

Ciaran looked skeptical. "I've had tight."

"Whatever you consider to be the tightest hole you've ever been in, multiply that times ten," Chris said with a straight face.

Ciaran's mouth opened in surprise again, and they looked at each other. Ciaran looked away first. Chris smiled. "You're turning red, mate," he said.

Ciaran rolled his eyes. "Fuck off." They were quiet for a moment. Then Ciaran asked, "So, your last relationship was with a man?"

"Technically, my last relationship was with a woman," Chris said. "About a year and a half long that ended earlier this year. But my last sexual partner was with a man. We've been on and off again for way too long. It just needs to be over at this point." He played a card.

"Was it because of him that it ended with her?"

"No, actually. That was all me fucking it up with my commitment issues." He laughed, and Ciaran chuckled. "But it doesn't help that I had someone waiting in the wings to pick up the pieces. That's done though. I'm getting too old to keep going back to him."

Ciaran nodded. The more they talked, the less he was embarrassed by the conversation. Chris had a way of making him feel at ease.

Chris asked, "What about you? You haven't mentioned a Mrs. Beals in the last couple of months."

"That's because Mrs. Beals is my mother," said Ciaran. Chris chuckled. "I'm single. I haven't been in a relationship for a long time, over three years now. She was a Reserver, the only female dragon tamer. We were together first as just something to do, and then exclusively for about three years until she left the Reserve to be with her family while the war was going on. She moved back to India with them."

"So you've been celibate for three years, mate?" Chris asked in surprise. "There's no way I believe that with you looking the way you look."

Ciaran started turning pink again. Chris was looking at him in a way he hadn't before. Or maybe he never noticed until now. Either way, he felt his chest steadily flush with heat.

"No. I have not been celibate," he confirmed. "I'm just not actively dating right now. I've had more than enough sexual partners during my trip because of my sexually charged little brother literally bringing girls home with him. And they would come willingly all because he is a Beals, one of the most famous surnames in our world. So I'm just trying to hang back for a bit. I wasn't celibate before, but I kind of am now."

"Sounds like you feel guilty about getting your rocks off."

"Not guilty. I just feel like..." Ciaran sighed and sat back. "I should have been a better influence on him, instead of letting him influence me."

"Well. Considering he watched his other half die, I think it was perfectly fine to let him do whatever the fuck he wanted to do to feel alive. And it was perfectly fine for you to do the same," Chris said as he played a card.

Ciaran looked at him as if he wanted to say more, but then didn't. So Chris changed the subject. "Buuuut, now that I know the Beals name will get us a knob slob, we're going to have to hang out outside of the woods, my friend! When's your next trip to London?" They both laughed.

"I'll be sure to invite you along." Ciaran looked up, and it was almost 4 a.m. He said to Chris, "Time to go."

They both stood up. "Hey, thanks for talking with me about Magi and all. About you," Chris said. "As usual, your secrets are safe with me. I mean that." He held his hand out for a shake.

Ciaran grasped his hand back. "Hey, Chris, want to see a magic trick?"

"What do you mean?"

Ciaran smiled, then disappeared in a puff of wispy smoke right before his eyes.

Chris's hand was still hanging in the air as the smoke disappeared. "Well. That's not something you see every day."

CHAPTER 4

Caerulus Veneficus

No topic was off limits, from the Magi Community to sexual escapades, with Ciaran talking about the former and Chris talking about the latter, all the while playing chess, checkers, and card games. Ciaran taught Chris other magical games, introducing him to some of his favorite card games and board games, which became incorporated into their daily routine. And they bonded over their love of chess. Chris finally got Ciaran to open up about his brother Shane, who would forever be 21. Ciaran had tremendous regret for not getting there on time to save his brother's life when he was caught up in a deadly battle two years ago. Those conversations were sporadic and was clear it wasn't something he wanted to talk about. But Chris was grateful for the openness all the same.

One day toward the end of November, they were in the middle of a very intense chess game when the alert went off at Marker 6. Chris jumped up and ran to the switchboard.

"What's that?" Ciaran asked in confusion.

"Someone pressed the emergency alarm," he told him. Chris picked up the dial and pressed the number 6. "Ranger Jennings, how may I be of assistance?"

A woman, obviously scared, said breathlessly, "He's going to kill me... Hurry... Please... Don't let me die." And then the line went dead.

"Hello? Hello!?"

"Chris..." Ciaran said softly.

They locked eyes, then simultaneously began to move. Chris ran out of the tank and Ciaran was right behind him, running into the northwest side of the forest to the marker. When they arrived, all was quiet. Chris noticed there were not even footprints of someone having stood there. He swung his flashlight around, but all he saw was trees.

He called out "Hello!" a few times, but no one responded. "Where is she?" he said softly to himself.

Ciaran sensed it as soon as he stepped into the clearing. "There was a Magus here."

"What?" Chris said, whirling around on him.

Ciaran held out his palm by his side and turned around slowly. Little blue lights began to appear around him. "You see these blue spots? It's a *Vis* signal of a CV. Something bad is happening, I can feel it. You should go back."

Chris scoffed. "You do realize these are my woods and this is my responsibility, right? I'm not going anywhere. You should go back to the Reserve."

Ciaran stopped turning. "No. You don't understand. You could get yourself killed," Ciaran said.

"That's kind of part of the job, Ciaran," Chris deadpanned.

"Not today it isn't," Ciaran retorted seriously. "Go back."

"No, you go back. I got this."

"Chris..."

"I don't need you to protect me, Ciaran!"

"I'm not leaving you out here to die, Chris!"

Something more than friendship passed between them as they stared at each other. Ciaran brushed it aside. "Listen, we'll go together. But stay close to me."

Chris scoffed again. "And you stay out of my way." He walked farther into the woods off the trail. Ciaran rolled his eyes at his arrogance but followed him.

They moved through the woods as silently as they could until they heard a man's deep voice chanting. Chris froze and Ciaran went into a crouch, pulling Chris down with him.

"I told you, it's a Magus," he whispered. "It sounds like he's doing an incantation. And I don't think it's one to con-jure kittens and rainbows."

"We need to get closer," Chris said and started crawling on his hands and knees toward the sound.

"Chrissssstopher!" Ciaran hissed.

But Chris was already ahead of him. Ciaran followed until they saw a faint orange light, and they followed it until they came to the outskirts of a clearing. In the clearing was a large rock with a wooden slab big enough for a human to lay across. An unconscious female whose skin was glowing orange was tied to all four corners of the wooden slab by her hands and feet. The man was in a long black cloak, walked around the woman, holding out his *dulé* and saying words Ciaran did not understand but knew were bad.

Before Ciaran could stop him, Chris jumped into action. He stood up and raced into the clearing with his .38 drawn and said, "Ranger Jennings here. Kindly step away from the woman before I put this lead in your arse."

The *Veneficus* raised his *dulé* and did a war cry at the same time Chris fired. But the man disappeared in wispy smoke and the bullet hit a tree.

"No fair," Chris said angrily as the smoke reappeared into the figure of a man.

The warlock raised his *dulé* again. Chris tried to fire his weapon, but it locked. "What the—" Chris looked at his gun, then looked up in time to see the flash.

Ciaran yelled, "*Obex*!" from the outskirts of the clearing as a yellow light came from the warlock's *dulé*. Ciaran had created a barrier between Chris and the spell that would have killed him instantly. Instead, the spell bounced off the blue barrier and hit a nearby tree, bursting it into flames.

"Get out of here, Chris!" Ciaran yelled.

Chris yelled back, "I'm not leaving you with this maniac, Ciaran!"

As the warlock sent a wordless spell toward Chris, Ciaran yelled, "*Obex*" again, walking into the clearing. The spell bounced off the barrier again, this time hitting the boulder, splitting it into two and sending the plank with the woman on top of it sliding to the left. The CV finally realized he was dealing with another Magus and set his eyes on Ciaran.

"Get the fuck out of here, Christopher!!" Ciaran yelled again. He started throwing a series of attacks toward the warlock. The warlock started throwing spells at Ciaran. Reds, yellows, blues, and greens lit up the night as the two Magi dueled, equally matched.

Before Chris could react, a rebounded attack hit the ground inches in front of him, sending him three feet into the air backward. He flew into a nearby tree, closer to where the woman was lying, and crumpled to the ground. Chris felt blinding pain knowing his skull split somewhere, but all he could think of was saving Ciaran.

He slid over to the woman first, feeling the twist in his right ankle. He groaned before he touched her neck to feel for a pulse, to make sure she was still alive. Then he pulled himself to a standing position and watched Ciaran and the Magus in a heated and fast-paced duel, colors ejecting from their *rodulés*, Wisp'ing out of the way, and darting behind trees. Chris looked down at a log near his foot and bent over to pick it up, waiting for his chance.

And then it came. One of Ciaran's protection attacks wasn't fast enough, and he was flipped backward by the other Magus to the ground, his stick flying from his hand. Chris had no time to think, lifting the log over his head as the CV lifted his hand and began to yell an incantation. He hurled it in the warlock's direction with all his might. The log bounced off the center of his back and he roared in pain as the curse was blown off course. The warlock looked in Chris's direction, who had fallen to the ground.

"Fuck a douche," Chris groaned again. He was dizzy and began to see spots.

As the warlock started calling out an incantation toward Chris, Ciaran took that opportunity to call out for his *dulé*. The *rodulé* flew out of the dark into his hand. As soon as it touched his fingers, he pointed it at the CV and cried again, "*Indocillis!*" Green light flew from his *dulé*. The warlock was instantly knocked to the ground, unconscious.

Ciaran quickly walked over to the warlock and murmured some words, and the Magus's limbs began pushing close to his body as if an invisible rope were tying him from ankle to shoulder. Ciaran then made his way to Chris, who had fallen over right after throwing the log.

He kneeled beside him. "You okay?"

"Bloody fucking brilliant, mate. Ugh," Chris groaned.

Ciaran touched Chris's head where he was bleeding. "That's really bad," he said.

"I'll live, thanks to you," Chris said. "She's alive, too, by the way. Also, thanks to you." Ciaran gave him a small, worrying smile. "What do we do now with a bad Magus and an unconscious woman under a spell?"

Ciaran searched the grounds for Chris's radio and handed it to him. "Call it in like normal. I'm going to press Marker 6 again, hopefully they will come faster." He hesitated, then said, "I can't be here, Christopher. I'm sorry. I will come check on you later, but for now, I can't be found here."

He walked over to the woman and murmured, *"Renodo"* to cut her binds from the plank. Once removed, he gently laid her on the ground next to Chris. Ciaran realized that the plank was actually a door with markings on it. He had never seen anything like it before.

"Listen," he said to Chris, "when they come, find Inspector Arslan. Tell Arslan he has to take the case. Say it like this: 'A little boy named Ciaran told me to tell you that you have to take the case'. And say it deliriously, like in a daze. But make sure he takes you seriously. It sounds confusing, and it's supposed to, but say it like that. You don't know anything else. Did you get all that?"

"Yes," Chris said. "A little boy named Ciaran said for you to take the case. Say it deliriously. And make sure he takes what I'm saying seriously."

Ciaran felt the urge to sit next to him, hold his hand, and run his fingers through his hair in reassurance. He kneeled down again. "Are you sure you are okay? Because if not, I will stay and... fuck it."

Chris shook his head. "No. Go do what you need to do. I will do my part."

"Okay," Ciaran said. Again, he had the strongest urge to give Chris a forehead kiss as Chris stared up at him. But he shook it off, thinking the adrenaline had gotten to him.

He took the door and glanced back at Chris before he puffed away in smoke, leaving Chris to stare up at the stars, thinking about how he now owed Ciaran twice for saving his life.

———————

Chris was only in the hospital in Korçë for one day. He had suffered a small concussion, needed stitches, and sprained his ankle, but the doctor put him out for five days, to Chris's annoyance. Chris thought about Ciaran every hour on the hour as he lay on his couch listening to music. He was anxious to get back to work, to talk to Ciaran, and to find out what happened. He felt off not having his best mate to talk to every night.

On his first day back right after Bergina left, to his surprise, Ciaran appeared at the door of the Tank. Chris could not contain his smile. "Hey! I figured—"

But Ciaran walked up quickly and hugged him. Another surprise. "Are you okay, mate?" said Ciaran with concern.

Chris smiled widely. "Peachy!"

They patted each other's shoulder. Ciaran moved away first and sat at the table. "Sit down with me."

"Of course, but I'm okay Ciaran. Really." Chris sat down next to him. "So. Tell me everything."

Ciaran explained, "What we encountered was a CV trying to do a necromancy spell. His girlfriend died during the civil war, and he was trying to bring her back. The woman we found was her cousin. The door had ancient markings meant as a literal doorway for her spirit to reenter the world into her cousin's body."

"Pretty creepy stuff," Chris said with wide eyes. He was fascinated.

"Yeah. Anyway," Ciaran continued, "Arslan did take the case, thank you very much for that, and covered it up as a psychopath's attempted rape and murder. His magic has been subdued and he will be transported to the closest Magi detention. Then eventually tried, found guilty, and taken to Claustra, the biggest Magi prison in Europe."

Chris continued to be in awe of this hidden world. "Magi prisons. Wow. That's a real thing."

"It sure is," Ciaran said. "And although your ankle is fine, I'm still going to patrol with you nightly in case you come against something like that again. You need a partner, and I'm your official one, so be ready."

Chris almost laughed at his seriousness. Nothing ever happened in Verdant Forest. But he was not going to deny the company, especially Ciaran's. Internally, he welcomed it.

CHAPTER 5

Heat

Ciaran started spending more hours at the Tank with Chris. He would arrive at 1 a.m. at Marker 1, and they would patrol all markers together, then head back to the Tank to eat and hang out. Chris started bringing dinner for two instead of just for himself and a case of beer for Ciaran's since he stayed longer. Ciaran sometimes brought dinner from The Atrium, a bar and restaurant frequented by Magi and Commoners. It was also connected with the apartment complex where Ciaran and other Magi lived. Ciaran told him that it was the only place of its kind in all of Albania.

"So, if Commoners go there, I can go there too, right?" He had fallen in love with their simple steak and baked potato combo.

"Yes. I will take you one day. We'll plan it," Ciaran said to Chris's delight.

More comfortable with Ciaran, Chris continued to talk about sex. He talked about his random encounters with strangers and one-night stands often and lamented about not having enough of it. He didn't know why he did it, what compelled him to talk about sex so much, why he couldn't help saying things like, "Shit, I miss the feel of a nice round, tight arse around my cock." Most likely it was to watch Ciaran turn pink with embarrassment and get uncomfortable.

But one night Ciaran asked him, "Why do you talk about sex so often?"

"Because I like having it," Chris responded and laughed. "And I haven't done it in a while. I've spent the last two years focused on my career and getting this position. But now that I'm here working full time, I'm starting to think about all the many people out there just calling for my tongue on them."

And like clockwork, Ciaran chuckled, turned pink, and looked away. But then he asked, "So how long has it been, really?"

"Four months, last July. But that was with my ex." It was Chris's turn to look away as he got solemn.

Ciaran said, "Doesn't sound like it was a good idea."

"It wasn't," Chris said as he got up to grab another beer from the mini-fridge. "And you? Your last real fuck?"

Ciaran said, "June 20th."

Chris laughed. "Why do you know the exact date?"

"It was the day before my birthday," he said, laughing as well.

"Oh, so birthday sex. Was it good at least?"

"Actually, yes." He laughed again. "Or maybe I just think so because it's been so long and maybe I miss it, too."

"Well, then, stop punishing yourself," Chris said as he sat back down. "Nobody is forcing you to be celibate but you, mate. I'm going to get you laid real soon; watch me." He winked at Ciaran, who blushed again.

One cold night in early December, Chris warned Ciaran, "The thermostat is broken in the Tank and it's stuck at 88. It's scorching hot in there."

As soon as they walked into the Tank after their rounds, the blast of humidity hit them. Chris said, "Told you," and started reopening the windows he had opened earlier while leaving the front door ajar.

He immediately started stripping down to his bare minimum of clothing, a tank top and his pants, no socks, or shoes. Ciaran started taking off his outerwear as well, pulling his work jumper down to his waist, and took his sweater and t-shirt off.

Chris gasped at Ciaran's back. "Ciaran! You have a tattoo. Of a dragon!"

"Oh yes, my first baby. His name was Kumoi." Ciaran lifted up his black tank top to reveal the dragon that spread across the top half of his back onto his right shoulder, so when he lifted up his arm, the dragon lifted up its wing. It was gray and red with an orangey glow.

"It's magnificent," Chris said softly, and he moved close behind Ciaran and touched it.

Ciaran's stomach jolted at the feel of his fingers and heat spread throughout his body. He wasn't exactly sure why, except that Chris's hands were softer than he imagined they would be. Chris traced the outline of the entire dragon slowly, his face so close that Ciaran could feel his breath on him. Ciaran could not find words; for some reason his mouth was dry.

Chris suddenly stopped touching him and said, "I'm going to shine it up. Take your tank top off and sit down."

Ciaran said, "Sure," although he was unsure what Chris meant.

Not that Chris was asking; he had already moved to his locker. Ciaran sat down at the round table and Chris came back over with a small bottle of almond oil, which smelled subtly sweet. Chris sat behind Ciaran and lifted Ciaran's tank top over his head, dropping it on the table. Ciaran did not resist. He felt kind of numb and confused about what he was feeling at the moment, and that confusion left him paralyzed.

But Chris did not notice, totally focused on the artwork. "I'm going to shine him up so he looks real. What's his name again?"

"Kumoi," Ciaran said.

Chris rubbed oil on his hands, rubbed them together, then proceeded to slowly massage Ciaran's shoulder blade and the right side of his back. Neither man spoke nor made a sound as Chris's hands moved on Ciaran's skin, up and down, side to side, on the body of the dragon. Chris then moved to Ciaran's shoulder and down his arm. He kneaded the top of his right shoulder, then came around to the triceps, biceps, elbow, arm, wrists, hand, and fingers, adding more oil at each interval.

Chris realized Ciaran had not moved, let alone stopped him from going beyond the dragon. But Chris couldn't help it; he had full access to the body he had only felt and never seen, and was transfixed on how truly defined Ciaran really was. He wondered what was going on in Ciaran's head, as he was slightly bent over, eyes open, but his mind was definitely someplace else.

Many thoughts were racing through Ciaran's head. The first one was how amazing Chris's hands were. The man could give an excellent massage. His skin was soft and his grip was firm. The second thought was how much he wanted—really wanted—Chris to keep touching him.

Which led him to his third thought: Ciaran realized he was growing an erection. And he was trying to figure out what that meant. Ciaran was lost in the sensuality and the sexual implications of it all.

Chris moved up from Ciaran's fingers, past his shoulder blades, back to the center of his back. He continued to massage Ciaran to his left shoulder, down his triceps, biceps, elbow, arm, wrist, hand, and fingers. Then Chris slowly made his way to his back again, the upper part, then the lower part. Chris sensed that something had definitely shifted between them. How much had shifted, he had no idea, but he knew he liked touching Ciaran, and he knew that Ciaran liked Chris touching him, too. He thought to say something, but he didn't know what, and he didn't want to break the silence.

As to not push it too much, he made his way back to the dragon. It was so shiny with silver glowing eyes and it almost looked alive. Chris resisted the urge to kiss Ciaran's shoulder blade and instead said a quiet thank you to God for making this specimen of a man and bringing him into his path.

"All done," Chris said quietly. "You should see him, all like new. C'mon."

Chris got up and walked to the mirror on the bathroom door, thinking Ciaran would follow. But he turned to see Ciaran sitting in the same position, slowly putting his t-shirt back on, then his sweater.

"I... I have to go," he said. "I just remembered some work I needed to take care of at the Reserve. Dale is going to kill me."

He stood up and automatically faced the door to avoid Chris seeing his obvious full boner. Ciaran zipped up his brown jumper and started walking toward the door.

"Alright then, Ciaran," Chris said, curious about Ciaran's reaction.

Ciaran stopped at the door and said over his shoulder without turning around, "I will see you tomorrow." Then he disappeared into the night.

Chris stood there stunned for a moment, then looked down at Ciaran's black tank top that he forgot to put on first. He absentmindedly picked it up and brought it to his nose to sniff. It smelled of Ciaran: sweat, dirt, another smell he couldn't place. Chris inhaled deeper and felt warmth start in his chest and spread throughout his body. Chris sighed out and sniffed a third time, becoming intoxicated with the smell of him.

And in that moment, it dawned on Chris just what that unspoken feeling bouncing around the room was. He knew he liked Ciaran as a friend, but now he realized how much he was actually attracted to Ciaran. How much he wanted him.

"Oh God," he said out loud, dropping the tank top on the table as if it burned him.

Chris found himself laughing and put his hand to his mouth to control his smile. And Ciaran liked him, too, possibly wanting him in the same way.

Ho. Lee. Shit.

Ciaran could not shake the feeling.

He went back to the Reserve and checked on Betta first, and he found Tommy his Tamer watching her. Dale moved Vlad to daytime, where he was doing much better, and Tommy, being a more experienced Tamer, knew how to keep an eye on a feisty dragon. He continued to walk the perimeter, then started jogging into the valley. But no amount of running could stop his thoughts from catching up with him. He slowed down.

Ciaran was not gay. "I'm not!" he found himself saying it out loud. He had been with plenty of women, too many for his own comfort level.

He was a strong, heterosexual, alpha male who loved the feel of a woman beneath him. It was all he'd known and all he would ever be. And yet...

He wanted to deny the intense attraction he was starting to feel toward Chris. *Too many late-night sex talks and drinking,* Ciaran reasoned to himself. He tried to brush it off, but a little nagging voice in him wouldn't let him. *It's more than that,* the voice said. *It's who he is: funny, brave, smart, and, yes, sexy.*

Ciaran had never thought he would think that about a man, sexy. But he was, and it was obvious to anyone that had eyes. His light brown skin, brown eyes, full lips, the bottom one slightly bigger than the top one, a small black mole on his cheek. And he found himself wondering what it would be like to kiss him. Ciaran broke into a run again. He tried to take his mind off of it, thinking about his dragons and dragon dung, anything but imagining Chris's full lips around his penis, which was what had snuck into his mind all of a sudden.

Ciaran ran and argued with himself. *Get a grip!* he thought. *It's only because I know he's pansexual,* he reasoned with himself again. And the fact that he talked about sex and his sex life a lot, almost in a braggadocios way.

Yeah, he told himself. Sexuality was fluid, and it was just his human side being fluid right now. He did not actually want to fuck Chris. Chris was his friend. His best friend right now.

Yes, you do, the voice said again. *You want him to take your full girth and deep throat it you want him to bend him over and see just how tight he is you want him to bend you over just one time so you know how it feels to submit to a man how it feels for him to enter you you want to lay him down and flip his legs far apart so you can enter him too...*

"FUUUUUUUUUCK!" Ciaran screamed out loud and stopped running.

He felt a little nauseous and began to dry heave as he tried to get his breath together. But he also noticed that his erection had never really left him, but instead got harder. It was so hard he was afraid to touch it. He leaned against a pillar of rocks and tried to calm down.

There is nothing wrong with being bi, or gay, he said to himself. *It's okay. It's okay and accepted, and I'm fine with who he is. It's just not who I am.*

As Ciaran walked back to the Reserve, he convinced himself that it was just a fluke incident and that there must have been some internal switch within himself that made him feel all those feelings, and nothing to do with Chris himself.

Maybe I do just need to get laid, he laughed to himself. *It would be too weird to be attracted to my best mate.*

CHAPTER 6

Disappearing Acts

12:45 a.m.

The next night Ciaran stood at the entrance of the Reserve, feeling nervous. Almost to the point of shaking. Ciaran turned around and went back up the hill to the compound. He was not ready to face Chris just yet. He just wasn't sure how he was going to react to being alone in a room with him again. And he was scared to find out.

1:32 a.m.

Chris glanced at his watch. He knew Ciaran wasn't coming, but he waited another eight minutes before moving on to Marker 2, slowly. He went back to the empty tank and opened the buttons on his shirt, since the heat was still broken. He got in the bed, closed his eyes, and thought about all the different moments he had had with Ciaran since that fateful night in August.

Admittedly, he had always had fleeting thoughts of being with Ciaran, but his number one rule was to not come on to straight guys. If he wanted others to respect his sexual fluidity, he would respect the rigidity of another. His number two rule was not to break in virgin males with sexual curiosity. Ciaran fit both of those restrictions.

But suddenly, Chris found himself wanting to break his rules, to push and see what Ciaran would do. There was a strong emotional and sexual attraction between them. He felt it, and he knew Ciaran did, too. And suddenly Ciaran's disappearing act tonight made perfect sense.

Chris must have dozed off because the next thing he knew Miche, the next ranger, was shaking him wide awake. After giving him the report, he stepped out onto the catwalk, squinting into the sun. That was when he saw him, leaning against his car. He realized he had never seen Ciaran in the light of day in the four months they had known each other. His hair, tied back in a ponytail, was even more fiery in the sun.

Chris felt internal flutters, and consciously kept his face neutral as he walked toward Ciaran. Likewise, the closer Chris got, the more Ciaran could feel his palms sweat, and he purposely grabbed his satchel strap with two hands and did a slow exhale.

"Hello," Chris said first.

"Hi," Ciaran responded. "Sorry about last night. It was really busy last night and I couldn't get out. Last night." Chris raised an eyebrow but didn't say anything. "I just mean it might be hard for me to get out and patrol some nights. But I am. I will ... tomorrow. Or tonight. Well. Tomorrow. It should be fine."

Chris let a moment pass as they looked at each other. "Okay," he said nonchalantly.

He gave Ciaran a quick shoulder squeeze and opened up his car door. He started the car and backed out of the space, amusingly aware that Ciaran was still standing there, holding onto his satchel. He rolled down his window and said, "See you tonight then... or tomorrow." He winked and drove off.

Ciaran stood there for a few moments to watch the car disappear down Pine Road. He inhaled and exhaled, surprised at how readily Chris accepted his spluttering words.

Over the next two weeks, Ciaran and Chris met up as usual, patrolled, and went back to the Tank, carrying out their normal routine. Chris kept the conversation light for the most part, talking about holiday plans and work issues as Ciaran's thoughts continued to wander when they were in close proximity, and more so when he was alone in his flat.

Chris would still throw out sexual jokes, like, "I'm definitely getting some for Christmas, and I plan on cumming twice in one night, calling it a Happy Chris-Mass miracle!"

And Ciaran would turn pink or turn away and casually deal another card or make another chess move. He couldn't tell if Chris was testing him or was really oblivious to what was stirring up inside of him.

Chris did notice that when he would go a little overboard with his jokes, Ciaran would suddenly get "busy" the next day or two, and he wouldn't patrol with him. When he would show up in the morning, apologetic, Chris would continue to act unfazed by it all. But in fact, it nagged him. A lot.

After a three-day disappearing act in late December, and Ciaran showing up at his car, Chris cut him off in the middle of his bumbling apology speech and said, "Could you stop apologizing to me already? I'm not your boss. I'm your friend. If you want to be here, be here; if you don't, don't. No pressure."

Ciaran was taken aback. "Um, right. Okay, yeah," he mumbled.

Chris chuckled at his awkwardness and started to get in the car, but then looked up and said, "Do you want a ride, Ciaran?"

"I think you know I can get myself home," Ciaran said sarcastically.

"Yes, I know you can get home by doing that Wispering thing—"

"Wisp'ing," Ciaran corrected him.

"Yeah, whatever mate," Chris said. "But I'm asking if you actually want me to take you home. Like a normal, everyday car ride that us Commoners do."

"Ah… okay. Sure. I'm in Barç, about a thirty-minute drive from here. Faster if you're … me."

Chris nodded. "I think I can manage a thirty-minute drive. Get in." And Chris got in the driver's seat, not waiting for a response.

Ciaran slowly walked over to the passenger side and got in, then gave Chris his address. Chris started driving, heading north. He started his Spotify playlist and began singing along. Ciaran couldn't help but be mesmerized by Chris and his ability to put any situation at ease. By the time they had pulled into his block, he had Ciaran singing with him at the top of his lungs, albeit with less talent.

Chris stopped in front of the Atrium Restaurant and Ciaran didn't want their time together to end. "Come in for breakfast," he asked, a little too eagerly, he realized right after the words left his mouth.

"Really, breakfast as foreplay?" Chris smiled slyly.

Just as smoothly as Chris put him at ease, the tension between them returned and made Ciaran feel awkward again. Ciaran's eyes got wide and his dick involuntarily spasmed as he looked at him, lost for words.

"My God, you are adorable when you are pink," Chris said. "Let's go." He parked in the nearest space as Ciaran inhaled and exhaled. He led Chris into the restaurant.

Phoebe greeted Ciaran with a warm smile and spoke in English "There's my guy. I thought you'd be here by now. Byreck to go, yes?"

"No, actually, I'm going to get a booth. I'm with a friend," Ciaran said.

"Oh!" Phoebe's eyes widened with surprise. Ciaran rarely ate in the dining area; he would typically take his food to go or at the counter. She gave Chris a friendly smile and led them to an open booth near the back window. Ciaran ordered his usual, and Chris ordered shawarma.

When she left, Chris watched Ciaran grab the saltshaker. He began to move it side to side, then switch hands and move it side to side again. He seemed really interested in making the salt move back and forth in the small glass.

Chris watched him for a moment before asking, "So why do I feel like there's something you aren't telling me? Or something you want to say but are afraid to?"

"There isn't," said Ciaran, avoiding his gaze. He flipped the small bottle upside down quickly.

"Okay." Chris waited.

"I just got a lot on my mind lately. Work stuff. Family stuff." Ciaran moved the saltshaker from one hand to the other again.

Chris nodded. "Okay. But you know you can talk to me, right? That's why I'm here, mate."

"I know," Ciaran said. "Some things I don't think you will get … about me. Some things I don't understand … about myself right now."

"Well, I know that feeling of thinking no one gets you, why you do the things you do, or feel the way you feel. I spent too many years trying to fit someone else's idea on what my sexuality should be, gay, straight, if I was too masculine, too feminine. When I stopped trying to fit myself into a box, I became free. I freed myself from my own internal struggle. And I've been happier ever since."

Ciaran was dumbstruck. He stopped moving his hands and looked up at Chris. *Does he know?*

"But that's me, my past struggle," Chris continued casually. "What about you? What internal struggle are you going through?"

"I … can't… not yet." He sighed, looking away again. "I have to know what it is, how to describe it, before I can explain it to anyone else."

"Okay. Well, don't wait too long. Don't let it tear you apart from the inside out," he said concernedly.

Ciaran looked Chris directly in the eyes and said, "When I'm ready, you will be the first to know. I can promise you that."

They stared at each other until Phoebe came over with drinks, breaking their eye contact.

The two spent the next hour eating good food and talking with Phoebe, who explained their family empire, thinking Chris was a Magus from the Reserve, just like Ciaran.

"Right next door to The Atrium is The Exchange, where Commoners change their currency and Magi exchange Sagems for euros, pounds, or dollars," she explained. Chris quietly deduced in his head that Sagems was a term for Magi money. "My father, Erle, runs the restaurant with me, and my daughter Elsie and my brother, Lewis, the cook, also works here. My mother, Esme, manages the residential part of The Atrium, that's where Ciaran lives. And my oldest brother Andy runs The Exchange with my sister-in-law Rosemary and their oldest son Lucas."

"And Commoners use all three businesses, alongside Magi?" Chris asked.

"Not the residence, that is Magi territory only," she clarified. "But the exchange and the restaurant are open for all."

"That's wonderful," Chris said. "You're on the right side of Magi history."

Phoebe grinned at him. "You should see the real atrium in the residence. I think you'll really like it."

"Maybe one day Ciaran would take me to see his place." Chris smiled at Ciaran.

Ciaran smiled back. "Yeah. One day mate."

For the week of Christmas, Ciaran changed his plans and decided to stay in Albania instead of heading home to England, and he and Chris decided to work the holiday. Chris's mother passed away two days before Christmas, and every year on Christmas Eve, he and his sisters got together to share stories and remember their beloved mother. Ciaran knew how hard it was going to be for Chris and wanted to be there for him.

Ciaran met up with him as usual at 1 a.m. in a knit sweater with a goofy-looking green dragon on it. Chris immediately laughed and poked fun at him. He greeted him cheerfully but it did not meet his eyes. Ciaran noticed how much quieter their walk was, and he realized how much he depended on Chris's energy to keep conversations going.

So Ciaran stepped up to fill the void and started talking about things going on at the Reserve as they patrolled: how much Tommy, his protégé, was being annoying as usual, running into Bruno, his arch-nemesis, at the beginning of his shift as Bruno was leaving and they exchanged snarky words to each other, how Ciaran was next in line to lead a dragon mission and he was excited about that, Sarah perfecting a potion to heal poison ivy faster, Dale being as bit less surly and he was beginning to think something was going on between him and Sarah, and the five new recruits with dreams of being close to dragons only to be slopping up dung, holding logs over their heads in the rain, and being told what big head and little dicks they have by Sven, the lead trainer. Ciaran predicted only one or two would make it to the end of their first year.

Chris chuckled at all the appropriate parts and gave mechanical "Yeah?" and "Wow's" when the story deemed appropriate. But Ciaran could tell he was struggling to hold it together.

When they got back to the Tank, Ciaran pulled out a pack of cards, while Chris pulled a six-pack of beer from the minifridge. Ciaran said, "New game."

"What?"

"We're going to play Blow Fish. It's like Go Fish but when you lose a hand, the cards burn your fingers." Ciaran explained the difference and they began the fast past version of the original game. Chris lost the first round, and it burned his fingertips.

"Fuck!" he exclaimed.

Ciaran laughed uncontrollably making Chris laugh as well. "Many of us lost fingerprints playing this game growing up," Ciaran said.

"Wonderful way to introduce me to your world, mate," Chris said stonily, making Ciaran laugh again. That made Chris smile.

After that, Chris paid more attention and won three out of the five games they played. It definitely took his mind off his mother for the next hour, and he was grateful for the distraction. Grateful for Ciaran. But melancholy was seeping in and Ciaran noticed.

After a full minute of silence, Ciaran said, "Tell me about her." Chris looked up. Ciaran said again. "Tell me about her. Your mum."

Chris sighed and leaned back in the chair. Ciaran watched his lips part as if to say something, then close. He squeezed his eyes shut and exhaled slowly. Then Chris got up and moved to lay in the bed. Ciaran found himself moving too, and lay next to Chris, resisting the urge to hold his hand but feeling it would be totally appropriate to do so. They lay side by side in comfortable silence. Then Chris began talking, and Ciaran listened.

Chris talked about his mother, Amina Fatu Thiene, born in Dakar, Senegal, who they affectionately called Ma Ami. He talked about her growing up in Senegal and her life there until her father received an embassy job and moved his family to Albania when she was twelve and her brother was sixteen. Her mother and brother moved back to Senegal when he turned eighteen, no longer wanting to be outside of their homeland. She stayed with her father in Albania until she enrolled in the University of Ireland on a scholarship and met and fell in love with Chris's father, Collum

Dougal Jennings, who was her roommate and best friend's older brother.

While Ireland was welcoming, their love was never fully accepted by his side of the family, and they made the decision to move back to Albania, to her family's home right after Chris was born, to take care of her ailing father. When he passed, he left the home to his daughter. Chris told Ciaran that she was an amazing cook, mostly French cuisine, and it was her art and passion as a head chef in a high-end restaurant in town.

The tears flowed freely as he talked. He was still very upset with his parents for keeping the diagnosis of cancer a secret for a full year before they told their children, and by then it was too late. But it could have been an extra year of hiking and fishing and spending time together that they missed out on, since Clarissa, his older sister, was going through a divorce and he and his little sister Charity were at University in Tirana. Chris spoke of their favorite moments together in the Verdant Forest.

He talked and talked until the sunlight began streaming through the windows. He told Ciaran how Ma Ami was not just his mother, but his best friend and confidant. That she knew his sexuality before he did, that she always knew what he was thinking and feeling, and was the only one to bring him out of his dark cloud. How it was about to be seven years, and it still felt like it was yesterday that he lost his first love.

Ciaran barely spoke, just listened, the sound of Chris's voice soothing him, his words making his heart break for him. He realized he missed the rest of his shift and Dale was going to be annoyed, but he didn't care right now. The only thing that mattered was Christopher.

When Chris stopped talking, Ciaran said, "Hey, walk me back to the Reserve." And Chris agreed.

They began walking mostly in silence, then Ciaran said, "I think she raised a brilliant son, and she is smiling down at you at all you have accomplished. Sounds like she was waiting for you to find your happiness and you're getting there."

Chris said, "Professionally, yes, I'm kicking arse, but my private life is in shambles." He found himself chuckling. "I think she'd wonder..." Chris stopped abruptly. Suddenly he felt lost, like he didn't know where he was.

He started turning around to walk away when Ciaran grabbed his arm. "Hold on there, Commoner."

Ciaran touched the center of Chris's back with his *dulé*, and Chris felt a cold feeling go through him. He gasped and shuddered a bit, then it was gone.

He turned to Ciaran and said, "What the fuck was that?"

"A spell aversion. *Oculi aperti, viderm Vis.* There are particular wards attached to the reservation," Ciaran told him. "Wards are used to keep Commoners and Magi alike away from an object or property. We have a twenty foot perimeter of wards around the Reserve. This particular ward is for Commoners. As we approached the barrier, you were in the beginning stages of dementia. The closer you go, the more you forget yourself. Who you are. Your memories. Your life. So I put a shield on you, so you can walk closer without interference."

Indeed, Chris realized he had never been that far into the northwest part of the woods where the trees were denser. They approached a tree that looked like three redwood trees stuck together.

Ciaran stood in front of the trunk and faced him. "Here's the entrance. In case you ever needed to know."

"Can I walk in now that the spell is shielded from me?" he asked.

"No," Ciaran said. "There are more spells and incantations attached here, for Commoners and Magi. We don't even let Magicians just walk in either. They have to be escorted by a senior official. If you touch it, you will just be touching a tree. But if I touch it..."

Ciaran put his hand out, and it disappeared into the tree as if the tree wasn't there.

Chris stepped up and touched the tree. It was indeed solid. He was fascinated again by the world of magic that was hidden in plain sight. He was thinking this as Ciaran suddenly reached out and pulled Chris into an embrace with both arms over his shoulders.

Chris slowly returned the hug, lifting his hands around Ciaran's back, surprised but grateful. Ciaran felt more of a desire to hold and comfort him, and Chris felt himself melting under Ciaran's touch and natural scent. They hugged for a full minute before Ciaran let go first. He walked backward into the tree entrance, watching Chris watch him disappear into nothing. Chris stepped up to the tree again and felt the solid wood on his hand.

———

Chris did not see Ciaran again until New Year's Eve, in the morning, at his car. Though not unexpected, since they shared a tender moment and he knew it would scare Ciaran, he was disappointed in Ciaran's ability to stay away from him for almost a week while Chris was finding it harder and harder when Ciaran disappeared on him.

What Chris was unaware of was that Ciaran watched him every day. He saw him come in when he started his shift at 10:45 p.m. struggling with wanting to be around him but being afraid of how he was feeling about him.

Ciaran was honest with himself: If Chris was a woman it would be a no-brainer; he would pursue it to see where it would lead. But Ciaran wrestled with thoughts of wanting to express his feelings of... *what was it? Attraction? Infatuation? Bicuriousity?* He asked himself these things several times a day.

But he also had another practical reason for not pursuing it: Chris had become a close friend to him and Ciaran did not have many of those, none of which were outside of the Magi community. And Chris was his best friend at the moment. If they were to cross some forbidden line and it went to shit, he would lose a friend. So was he willing to take that huge leap into the unknown for the almost imminent possibility that it would end at a loss at best, heartbreak at worst?

That was the question that nagged at him every day. And every day Ciaran had a different answer.

Unfortunately, the one person who could probably understand was the one person he couldn't talk to about it. Ciaran sensed that Chris was figuring it out and growing impatient with his disappearances. But he didn't know how else to clear his mind except to keep his distance. When they were together in the same room, the question lingered, and he knew it was coming someday. He could feel it between them. He knew Chris could feel it, too. Ciaran also knew what the answer would be: an unequivocal yes. But to step outside of the bubble was to face reality—it just wasn't that simple.

These were all the thoughts in Ciaran's head as he stood by Chris's car on New Year's Eve that morning, waiting for his shift to be over. Chris gave a wry smile as he walked over.

"Those bloody dragons again, keeping you busy, huh?" he deadpanned.

Ciaran looked sheepish. "You're working tonight?"

"Yeah. You?"

"Yeah."

An awkward silence ensued. Chris moved closer and Ciaran shifted his feet slightly away, but didn't back up. Chris pretended not to notice and said in Ciaran's ear, "Don't disappoint me."

He got in his car as Ciaran said, "I won't." And he meant it.

CHAPTER 7

Mental Chess

1:02 a.m.

Ciaran met up with Chris at Marker 1. They made small talk as they patrolled, chased some kids from the lake that was thinly iced over, and talked about previous New Year activities since they were both working that year. They went back to the Tank and brought out a game of chess.

Chris, who had been thinking about Ciaran in a sexual manner all day, decided to tease him a bit. "God, I miss fucking," he said out loud, looking directly at Ciaran.

Ciaran didn't say anything but felt himself grow warm as Chris continued, "I miss the feel of a warm hot mouth and long tongue on my cock. I need a nice, wet, hairy hole to dig into. It's been way too long for me."

Again, Ciaran did not respond and pretended to be concentrating on his next move. "What about you?" Chris asked.

Ciaran mumbled, "What?" still not looking up.

"Sex, Ciaran. Fucking? Do you even remember the feel of the last time you fucked someone? Or better, when was the last time someone fucked you?"

Ciaran was practicing his breathing as his heart started racing. He looked up and saw Chris had a sly smile. He realized Chris was after a reaction. "You asked me that already. Last spring, remember?" he said with a straight face. "Been a while for me, too." He went back to his chess pieces.

Chris continued to talk nonchalantly. "Yeah, that's just way too long. We should make a pact to get fucked in the New Year." Ciaran found himself laughing out loud. "I'm serious," Chris said. "We should just go bar crawling one weekend, find some ladies, and have at it. A pair of sisters would be nice. I'll take the one with the fattest arse."

Ciaran made a move, still chuckling at his friend's words. Chris continued to talk about his favorite sexual position. "Doggy style. Because when they are face down, arse up, man or woman, it all looks the same, and it's the most beautiful sight to behold. Although one hole is tighter than the other." Chris made a move. "Check. Can you guess which one?"

Ciaran, thankful for the opportunity to concentrate on his pieces again, didn't answer. Chris waited a few more seconds, then said softly, "Have you ever fucked someone in the arse, Ciaran?"

Ciaran felt his cock twitch, and he drew in a small breath, which he played off with a clearing of his throat. "No," he said simply and without looking up. He made a move and instantly realized it was the wrong one. "Shit," he mumbled. He glanced across the round table to see Chris staring at him intently.

"You should try it. At least once. A cunt is soft and warm and even the tightest cunt is still like a tight, wet pillow around your cock. But the arse, it's firmer, unforgiving in how it grips onto your dick, like a warm, wet suction that keeps grabbing you from the inside. And the deeper you go, the tighter it holds on until you explode. It's the best feeling in the world."

They stared at each other. Ciaran was perfectly aware of how hard he was at the moment, but kept his face stoic. Chris was more amused and was only about halfway there. This talk was more for Ciaran's benefit than his own.

"Check. Your move," Ciaran said.

Chris smiled. He looked down at the game and said casually, "Your face is red, Ciaran."

Ciaran was almost angry at himself for being so transparent. He decided to turn the tables. "Why do you always talk about sex, really?"

Chris chuckled. "I told you, because I like having it. And I'm not having it nearly as much as I would like to right now."

"But what about love? Relationship. Commitment. Don't you want that too?" Ciaran asked.

"I do," Chris said confidently. Then he sighed. "At least I think I do. I just have bad luck with love and relationships."

"Why is that?" Ciaran asked.

Chris leaned back in his chair. "I don't know. Maybe it's my fucked up daddy issues. I know he loved my mum and she would tell me all the ways he did, but I just never saw it. Maybe it's because very few people in my life have actual long, loving relationships. My older sister's marriage failed, and she is pregnant by another man, so she's going to have two kids by two different fathers. My little sister is a bisexual whore like me. We just don't know how to do relationships well. But we are fantastic lovers." He winked, looked down, and made a move.

Ciaran was not going to let up. "No one teaches you how to be in a relationship. You just go in with equal footing and open hearts, knowing you want the same things. Then you take that journey together."

"Well, maybe I haven't found someone who wants the same things as me," Chris shrugged.

"Well, what do you want? In a partner?" Ciaran asked.

Chris mumbled, "I don't know."

"Try. Think about it."

Chris leaned back again, thoughtful. "I want someone who sees me, the good and the bad. Someone who knows my whoring past and never brings it up and still wants to fuck me, anyway." He laughed. Ciaran didn't and waited for him to continue.

"I want a love that gives me a reason to get out of bed every morning. Someone I can cook for and give back massages and they would do the same for me without asking. I want someone who knows how to make me laugh when I'm sad, and calm me down when I feel like putting my fist through a wall. Challenge me when I'm wrong, encourage me when I'm on the right path. Someone that will take me sailing into the middle of the ocean to make love under the stars, just because. I want that unconditional, unequivocal ability to love someone and know I am theirs completely, and they are mine." He looked away and said, "That doesn't exist for me."

"Maybe it does," Ciaran said softly.

Chris looked at Ciaran in the eye almost angrily. "And what about you? What do you want, Ciaran?"

And in that moment, Ciaran knew that Chris knew his deepest desire. He looked down. "I don't know."

"I think you do know. I think you are just too chicken shit to say it out loud."

Ciaran looked up and laughed. "Chicken shit? Really?"

"Yes. Chicken shit."

"I'm not afraid to say anything out loud, especially to you," Ciaran said. "I'm just... It's a lot going on with me. I'm trying to figure it all out."

"Yeah? Well, maybe I can help you if you tell me what's been bothering you. Maybe we can work it out together."

"No, you can't help me with this."

"Oh, I think I can," Chris said smugly.

Ciaran was starting to get annoyed. "Whatever you think you know, you don't."

Chris folded his hands on the table. "Okay. I wasn't presuming anything. But I will say that you have always been straight with me. For five months, we have always been straight with each other, but lately, it's like you are hiding something from me and it's just ... bizarre. We're friends, right? Friends tell each other everything, so all I'm saying is, whatever it is, you can say it. No judgment. No snarky comments. I can listen and advise, or just be there for you like you have been for me.

"Or maybe... maybe you want me to start the conversation," said Chris. Ciaran looked at him for a minute. "Is that something you'd rather have? Me take the lead?"

They stared at each other. Then Ciaran said, "Not yet. But I will let you know when the time comes. And like I told you before, when I am ready to talk about what's on my mind, you'll be the first to know. Trust me."

Chris nodded, then looked around. "It's past time for you to head back and we never finished our game."

"Oh, I think we've been playing chess all night," Ciaran said.

Chris smiled. "Yeah? Who won?"

Ciaran did not respond, just smiled back.

Chris spent the month of January throwing out sexual innuendos to Ciaran during their time together. Ciaran knew Chris wanted a reaction out of him so he would laugh them off or ignore them. But inside, he wasn't sure if he wanted to throttle him or bend him over the round table. He was growing increasingly distracted at work by his thoughts as well. Even Dale, whose natural demeanor was surly, barked at Ciaran to get his shit together and to stop snapping at the new recruits. But Ciaran couldn't help it; his head was spinning and Chris was getting under his skin.

He started having dreams shortly after New Years which didn't help. They started innocently enough, Chris and Ciaran hanging out, and then suddenly one was on top of the other, pumping away. If Ciaran was on top, Chris would be face down in a pillow, while Ciaran penetrated with fury until he exploded inside of him. He could handle those dreams a bit better although he found them disturbing. No, it was the other ones, when Chris was on top and Ciaran was lying face up. Those dreams seemed to go on forever, as Chris moved slowly, passionately. And Ciaran would see and study his face: the shape of plump lips, the small black beauty mark on his left cheek, his brown eyes, the dark brown curls of his hair.

In the dream, his face was close enough to touch, but they never kissed, just stared into each other's eyes. And Chris never came; he moved in and out like the ocean until Ciaran woke up sweaty, like he was burning from the inside, and sticky from his own ejaculation like a teenage boy. The former dream made him feel powerful and in charge of his fate, but the other made him feel completely defenseless, as if he had given himself over to something inexplicable. The loss of control was what scared him.

So he endured Chris's sexual innuendos: "*Not even a finger in your bum? Never?*" "*That two males to one female bisexual threesome is the most amazing experience*" and outright explicit monologues, "*Sucking dick is an art form. There is a correct tongue-flicking, throat-compression combo that not many people are able to accomplish. And to be able to deep throat is all in the mind.*"

Those days he contemplated not seeing Chris, but he knew if he missed just one day of patrolling, Chris would win this never-ending chess match they were playing, calling him chicken shit again, and that Ciaran could not let happen.

CHAPTER 8

The Lamppost

February rolled around and Chris announced he was finding them dates for Valentine's Day.

"It falls on a Friday, and we're both working, mate," Ciaran reminded him.

"Okay. Sunday then. An after V-day pussy grab. So many lonely hearts and wet cunts available that weekend," Chris said excitedly. "Just leave it to me."

"So you want a woman, not a man?" Ciaran said before could stop himself, instantly regretting it when he saw the look on Chris's face, one of desire directed toward him.

"No," Chris said. "The man I want doesn't want me."

Ciaran looked away, needing to put some distance between him and the conversation. So he focused back on Chris's proposal. "Okay, fine," he agreed. "Find us dates and I will go."

"Really?" Chris said excitedly again. "Because I meant it when I said I'm getting laid this year. I also meant it when I said you were, too."

"Yeah, make plans, and I will be there."

Chris came back a week later and said, "Okay. I met these two nurses at the hospital where my sister works. They are also working Friday and Saturday but are available on Sunday. I told them we will have a whole Valentine's Day redo that day, with flowers, chocolate, and dinner. I also told them I got a hotel room in case they didn't want the night to end, and they agreed!"

Ciaran was not paying attention to the game they were playing and burned his hand on a card. "Ow!! Room? Just one?" he asked.

"Don't worry, you prude, double beds," Chris said, shaking his head.

"And they agreed to fuck you, who they just met, and fuck me, who they never met?"

Chris smiled. "I'm pretty convincing."

Ciaran looked unsure, and Chris saw it. "Oh, don't back out on me now. We are so close to getting our nobs slobbed!"

Ciaran chuckled, but his mind was still on the one room. "Why not two rooms, though? No privacy. We'll be able to hear and see each other."

Chris looked at Ciaran in the eyes and said with a straight face, "Maybe I want to hear how you sound when you moan."

Ciaran was not prepared for the boldness of that response, and his mouth dropped open. Chris laughed a loud belly laugh and said, "Christ, you should see your face."

"You're an arsehole." He shook his head and scoffed, but noticed his heart was beating fast.

"Listen, if you really want privacy, we will get two rooms, no big deal. I just thought it would be fun. Plus, I get the sense they are kissing besties, so I am kind of hoping they give us a show."

Ciaran did not speak right away; he was focused on slowing down his heartbeat. Then he said, "Okay."

Chris smiled widely. "Excellent."

The following Monday's overnight shift before Valentine's Day, Chris and Ciaran did their normal routine of patrolling, beers, and games, this time Monopoly. Chris had not dropped one sexual joke all week, so Ciaran relaxed a bit. Then Chris brought up the dates.

"So, we're going to meet at Mountain Grill, and you're in charge of the romantic shit—flowers and chocolate."

Ciaran laughed. "Why me?"

"Please. We both know you're the romantic one out of the two of us." Chris looked at him slyly. "I have one goal."

Ciaran laughed again. "This is true. Okay, I've got it."

Chris continued, "Afterward, we'll head to the International Hotel in Korçë. Drinks at the bar until they decide when they want to go up. If they decide."

"And if they don't?"

"Then we go home with blue balls and cottonmouth." Chris laughed. Ciaran didn't, but seemed thoughtful. Chris asked, "What's on your mind?"

"Nothing," Ciaran said. Chris didn't say anything, but waited. Then Ciaran said, "It just seems like a waste if they didn't want to go, that's all."

Chris decided to push Ciaran further than he had before. "We don't have to waste it. We could go up to the room ourselves."

"And why would we do that?" Ciaran said sharply.

Chris glared at him. Then he scoffed. "Okay." They were quiet for a moment, but Chris couldn't help himself. "It must be fucking exhausting being you," he said.

"Come again?"

"I mean, the amount of mental gymnastics you must do on a daily basis. It must be fucking exhausting."

"Fuck off," Ciaran mumbled.

But Chris said loudly, "No, you fuck off!"

They glared at each other. Chris asked, "What do you want, Ciaran?"

"What do I want about what?"

Chris's eyes narrowed. "What. Do. You. Want. Kir. Ran."

Ciaran stuttered, "I'm... I'm not... no... no... we... we're not... no... doing this... not today."

"Okay, then when?" Chris asked boldly. "When would be a good time to do," he gestured his hands around, "this?"

Ciaran didn't answer; instead leaned back in his chair and closed his eyes. Chris started again. "What do you want, Ciaran?" Silence. "What do you want, Ciaran? What do you want—"

"AAAAH, fuck off already!" Ciaran yelled, opening up his eyes. "Don't you think if I knew what I wanted I would have..." He trailed off. Ciaran sighed deeply, looked up, and stared at the ceiling. "You should probably cancel the dates. I'm sorry."

"And do what instead?" Chris asked. Ciaran did not answer. "What do you want, Ciaran?"

"Back off, Christopher," Ciaran said, frustrated.

"No. What do you want, Ciaran?"

"What do YOU want, Chris!?" Ciaran yelled at him.

"Do you really want me to answer that?" Chris said calmly. Ciaran did not speak, unsure. Chris said, "I want you to be honest with yourself first, then be honest with me."

Ciaran said sarcastically, "And you think if I unburdened myself, all my problems will go away?"

"No," Chris said seriously and leaned in. "But I think you will feel less fear." Again Ciaran didn't answer. Chris continued, "I think you know what you want. I think you are scared of what will happen if you go for what you want. But you should know by now that I won't leave you out there by yourself. You've walked with me almost every day for six months, since you saved my life. You know who I am. Let me walk this walk with you."

Ciaran stared at him in disbelief. "You're right. I do know who you are. And I know you don't know what I want. Bloody hell, I don't know what I want. But I know that *you* are not looking for what I'm looking for. So how could you walk this walk with me?"

It was Chris's turn to be silent, realizing that Ciaran might be right if it was a relationship he was seeking, and not just a physical one. But it was the closest Ciaran had come to confessing how he felt about him, and it left him speechless. The last thing Chris ever wanted to do was hurt him, and crossing that line with his best friend would surely end up in Chris messing up their current friendship.

Ciaran suddenly stood up. "I gotta go."

He grabbed his jacket and headed out into the cold, forgetting he had the ability to disappear. Chris wanted to call out after him, but he didn't.

That Tuesday night, Ciaran did not come to the tank or meet him at Marker 1, nor was he at Chris's car on Wednesday morning. Chris was annoyed, but he was equally glad that they started putting things out there. He was tired of the merry-go-round of unspoken feelings that they were on.

Either someone needed to get off or they keep going around together, but this standstill was not going to happen anymore, he thought to himself angrily all day on Wednesday. Chris canceled the dates under the guise of "My buddy went out of town, sick grandma, ya know?" without a promise of a rain check.

On Wednesday evening at the start of his shift, he walked Bergina out and stood on the catwalk looking out. He thought he caught a glimpse of wispy smoke by the edge of the woods, but wasn't sure.

When Ciaran did not show up for patrol again, Chris had resolved in his head he was not going to let him off the hook anymore. He was going to confront Ciaran the next time they saw each other, and he was going to get his answer, one way or another.

Ciaran felt his nerve wavering. Chris's words struck a chord deep within him and the challenge was too great to ignore. He knew the next time they saw each other, he would need to give an answer, but he still wasn't sure what that answer would be. So instead he spent the next couple of days borderline stalking Chris, watching him at the start and end of his shift from just beyond the line of trees.

On Thursday morning, Chris stepped out ten minutes before the end of his shift and Ciaran had to quickly disappear at the edge of the woods, just as he did the evening before, hoping he was not seen.

Unfortunately, Chris did see him and laughed at the absurdity of it all. *So, a game of cat and mouse is in pursuit,* he thought.

So that Thursday evening, Chris arrived twenty minutes before the beginning of his shift. He parked under the lamppost, got out of his car, and waited, leaning on the driver's side door.

"Ciaran," he called out. "I know you are here, mate."

Ciaran, who was a couple of yards away behind a nearby tree, felt his heart come out of his chest. But it was time. So he bravely walked out.

Ciaran stopped under the lamppost, put his hands in the pocket of the coveralls, and looked at Chris.

"Where have you been?" Chris asked.

"Around. Thinking." Ciaran couldn't avoid Chris's intense gaze even if he wanted to.

Chris nodded. "I thought I saw you yesterday. And this morning."

Ciaran did not respond. Chris walked over to him and stopped about a foot from him under the lamppost. Ciaran was prepared for the "What do you want?" barrage of questions that were sure to come. But he still wasn't sure what he would say.

Chris was ready to confront Ciaran as well on what he knew to be true: that Ciaran had real feelings for him. But the vulnerability in Ciaran's eyes made Chris want to take a different approach.

"Tomorrow, actually tonight at midnight, is Valentine's Day," Chris said.

Ciaran was thrown off by the statement. Obviously, they both know that. He let Chris continue.

"You know, I've never been kissed on Valentine's Day."

Ciaran noticed that Chris was moving very slowly toward him, staring into his eyes. He did not speak. He stared back at Chris as his mouth went very dry.

"I mean, I've been kissed obviously. Just not romantically. I've never been a romance kind of guy and I've never had someone want to be romantic with me. It would be nice for once if I could be that guy, you know. The guy who gives or gets the sweet romantic kiss on Valentine's Day."

Ciaran held onto the inside of his pocket a little tighter, but otherwise, he did not, could not, move.

"You're a romantic kind of guy, aren't you, Ciaran?"

Ciaran did not move or speak.

"Do you think you could do me this favor?"

Even if he wanted to run away at that moment, he couldn't.

"Would it be alright if I showed a little romance on Valentine's Day?"

His feet felt like they were stuck in quicksand.

"A little Valentine's Day kiss for a best mate?"

Ciaran suddenly realized how close Chris had gotten. So close he could see the black mole on his left cheek, he could stare at the brown in his eyes under the light of the lamppost, see how his bottom lip was slightly fuller than his top lip. He could feel his breath on his face and heard him say so softly it was almost a whisper, "Can I kiss you, Ciaran?"

Ciaran looked into Chris's eyes before he instinctively closed them and slightly lifted his chin. Chris followed suit with a slight angle. Their lips touched, softly at first, then with a little more pressure. Ciaran opened his mouth and pulled Chris's bottom lip gently between his two lips. Then Chris slowly pulled away.

"Thank you," Chris said softly. Ciaran opened his eyes, still afraid to speak, lips still slightly parted, when Chris pulled his own from them.

Chris moved back a little and softly whispered again, "Thank you for my Valentine's Day kiss."

He slowly backed away, watching Ciaran watch him. Eventually, Chris turned around and walked up the stairs into the Tank without looking back, leaving Ciaran under the lamppost.

Ciaran realized he had been standing there for a few minutes, then became horrified to realize Chris could still see him standing there like an idiot if he wanted to just by looking out of the window. That thought wiggled him out of his stupor and he began to have feelings in his legs again, just enough to Wisp.

But Chris was not looking out of the window. He was too busy being stunned himself and he had a smile on his face he could not get rid of, for various reasons. For one, he was proud of himself for making the first move; two, he was surprised that Ciaran let him, he had to know what was coming; three, Ciaran had absolutely kissed him back; and four, the realization that he was not alone in his feelings, that his suspicions were confirmed, and that Ciaran had feelings for him, too.

CHAPTER 9

Nervous

Ciaran stumbled into the Reserve looking harried. He struggled to take off his outerwear, then realized he needed it on, and began to redress, barely noticing Dale watching him at first with impassivity. But as Ciaran's agitation at his clothes continued, Dale watched with actual interest.

When he finally succeeded in putting back on his coverall, Ciaran stood for a moment, lost in thought. A line had been crossed, that he knew for sure. *But what happens now?*

Dale watched Ciaran as he stood before a mirror. "Hey, Ciaran?"

"Hmmm?"

"Are you pretty enough for your dragon babies today?"

Ciaran looked up, confused. "Huh?"

"Take your arse back to work, that's what!" Dale barked.

Ciaran rolled his eyes and headed into the grass opening toward the valley. His head was spinning. *What now?* he kept thinking. *We can't just go on patrol and pretend like he didn't kiss me. That I didn't just let him kiss me, but I sort of kissed him back. Not sort of. Actually kissed him back.*

Somehow Ciaran thought it would be different kissing a man, rougher maybe. He found himself chuckling. *Of course, a kiss is just a kiss. It could be as hard or as soft as you made it to be. And Chris's lips were very soft. Sex is probably similar...*

Oh, God... sex! Does this mean we will have sex now!?

Ciaran worked himself into a tailspin over it. *I have no idea what I'm doing. How much of it transfers from sex with a female to sex with a male?* Ciaran was now trying to recall all the conversations where Chris was educating him. *Doggy style, sure. But what about missionary, do men do missionary? Is it anatomically possible?* Ciaran had never thought about it until that moment. *What about oral?* He vaguely remembered Chris's monologue about how to do fellatio excellently. *I'm almost certain to screw that up. I've never sucked anything bigger than a tit. What if I choke and throw up?*

All kinds of horrifying thoughts of him messing up sex with Chris circled his head as he checked on each dragon, ensured their supplies were stocked, and talked a little with Tommy. They were running low on dragon claw shavings; Ciaran would make a note to the day team to collect some. *What if he didn't like the kiss?* The Novos needs more dragon dung for the garden. Ciaran would tell Khalid, the dung coordinator, in the morning. *What if my cock is too big for him? What if his is too big for me??* London had been looking paler lately. Ciaran needed to put him on the list for a checkup sooner rather than later. *What if we do it and I realize that I actually prefer sex with women? What happens then??*

By the time he looked at his watch, it was ten minutes past 1 a.m. and Ciaran panicked. There was no way he was going out there to patrol. He wasn't even going to the doorway. He knew it was decision time, and he needed to delay it a bit more. Instead, he went back to the breakroom for the veal soup they offered. But Ciaran couldn't eat either. He instead paced the room, thinking.

It was undeniable at this point. Ciaran had feelings for Chris. Strong, intense, emotional, sexual feelings for Chris. The question for him was, *do I go all in? With a man? With a Commoner? And if I do, what will my family say?* He had already broken Magi law and would have to answer to that at some point. But would his family accept him being with a man? Was Ciaran even gay? If so, he was already terrible at it. Chris would literally have to teach him the ins and outs from lovemaking to handling discrimination. *What would my mother say?*

Ciaran was so lost in his thoughts he failed to see Dale enter the room. "Aren't you supposed to be patrolling?"

Ciaran jumped at the sound of his voice. "No," he mumbled. "Not tonight."

Maybe never again, the way the conversation in his head was going.

Ciaran continued to pace, sit down, shook his leg until he had to get up, and pace again. Dale was watching Ciaran with great interest now. It was apparent to him that something shifted in his "friendship" with the ranger, and frankly, Dale wondered what had taken them so long.

After the fourth pace-sit-shake-pace combination, Dale pulled up a chair and sat in front of Ciaran during the shaking stage. Ciaran stopped shaking his leg. "What?"

"You tell me," Dale said. Ciaran didn't answer; he instead turned away. "It's okay, you know," Dale said.

Ciaran did not look at him. "What is?"

"Everything you're feeling. It would be crazy if you weren't confused, debating the pros and cons of it all."

Ciaran wanted to pretend that he had no idea what Dale was talking about, but it was the closest he had come to hearing someone other than himself on the issue.

Dale continued, "For the record, no one in our world will give a horse's arse. We care more about bloodlines than where or who you stick your prick in, in case you didn't notice."

Ciaran, still looking away, said, "I have no idea what I'm doing. I've never been so clueless about myself in my entire life. What if I fail?"

"It's not a fucking test, Ciaran. No one is grading you on your love life. Shit, if that's the case, I've failed three times already, and that's just counting my marriages, not the string of broken hearts I've left along the way. No, you only fail if you never try in the first place. Spend your life wondering if he was the One, and you were too pussy to find out. Since when is an old fool like me telling a young dragon like you about bravery?"

Ciaran knew Dale was right. There was something about Chris that drew him in. The connection from the moment they met grew into a spark, then an attraction. And the kiss tonight sent it into overdrive. He wanted to know. He needed to know. And he would be kicking himself if he ran away from it all.

He was still trying to figure out when and where he should make his move when Dale barked, "Why the fuck are you still sitting here with me? Get the fuck out of here!"

Ciaran smiled and stood up. Dale continued his berating, "Oh, and take a shower before you go. You smell like shit. Literal dragon shit. And don't come back here until you sort this shit out. Can't have you distracted on the job, dying on my watch, yeah. Who else is going to tame Robetta? Not that half-wit cunt Tommy that follows you around like a lost puppy. Not me, that mean dragon bitch. No, you can't die here, so do what you need to do, and come back tomorrow, ready to act like you have some goddamn sense."

Ciaran laughed at Dale's attempt to cover up his fatherly mentoring with spite.

Chris did not expect Ciaran to come out for patrol. He actually did not expect to see Ciaran for the next week, maybe two. He sat at the table with his feet up and his eyes closed, reliving the barely kiss again, smiling at Ciaran's reaction. He was trying to figure out whether he should leave the ball in his court or make another move the next time he saw him when Ciaran appeared outside the Tank door.

Chris was startled by the sound of the door opening and fell backward, crashing the chair he was in onto the floor. Shocked, he stood up quickly and called his name. "Ciaran!"

Ciaran was wearing street clothes like he did at the end of his shift. "Yeah, sorry I missed patrol. I was ... figuring stuff out."

He came in and closed the door behind him, took a deep breath, then turned around and walked to the round table.

"So, what were you trying to figure out?" Chris was suddenly aware of how fast his heart was beating.

"Us," Ciaran said simply.

"What about us?" Chris asked.

"How we feel about each other." Ciaran started walking around the table toward him.

"What do you mean by that?" Chris started walking in the same direction away from Ciaran, but kept eye contact with him. Ciaran noticed and stopped walking. Chris did as well.

"You kissed me," Ciaran said factually.

"I did. You kissed me back," Chris said just as factually.

He paused. "Was that a test? To see if I would?"

Chris shrugged a bit. "Didn't really put much thought into it, mate."

Ciaran's eyes narrowed at Chris's attempt to shrug off what was happening between them. He started walking again and so did Chris, around the table.

Ciaran had a realization. "Am I making you nervous, Christopher?"

"No," Chris said unconvincingly.

"Why are you running from me, then?" Ciaran stopped walking and realized he was now on the other side of the table, and Chris was near the door.

"I'm not running. I'm walking like you are." But truthfully, he was a little afraid of what Ciaran might do if he caught up to him.

"You look nervous."

"I'm not nervous. I'm just ... surprised to see you, is all. I didn't think I would see you for a while."

Ciaran started walking again, slower, and Chris followed suit. "You thought I would be chicken shit again."

Chris chuckled. "Yes, well... maybe a little."

"Well, maybe I don't feel like being chicken shit anymore. Maybe I'm ready to tell you what's been bothering me these last couple of months. Do you want to hear it, Chris?"

And suddenly Chris wasn't so sure he did. He knew things would change between them once Ciaran confessed his feelings, and suddenly he wasn't sure he wanted things to change. Chris was really good at fucking up relationships, and at that moment, he realized just how much he cared about this one.

Ciaran sensed his trepidation. "You asked me a few days ago to tell you what I want."

It was Chris's turn for his mouth to go dry. He just nodded. Ciaran laughed. "Look who's chicken shit now?"

Chris stopped walking abruptly and Ciaran did as well. They were standing again where they started, Ciaran on the side of the table near the door, Chris on the side of the table near the bed.

"I'm not scared, I'm not chicken shit, and I'm not nervous. It's just... okay, maybe I'm a little nervous. This really is a lot. For both of us. I never wanted to pressure you; I wanted you to just ... know what you wanted. And I would spend some time trying to figure out what I wanted."

"Was I right? Do we want different things?" Ciaran asked quietly.

"No," Chris said right away. "I don't think so. Well, maybe a little. Maybe we will approach it from different angles and meet in the middle. I don't know. I told you I'm bad with these things."

And Ciaran understood. While Ciaran was worrying himself for hours, months really, about the sexual aspect of a relationship with Chris, Chris was worried about the emotional part, feeling something real for another person that went beyond sexual intimacy. Worried more about how their relationship would end up, if he would fuck it all up with his commitment issues. Worried about hurting Ciaran in the long run and losing his best friend.

And suddenly, Ciaran was completely at ease with his decision.

"I trust you, Chris," he said. "I trust you to help me figure out the parts of all this that are new and confusing for me, if you trust me to help you navigate the stuff you aren't so good at. Neither of us has anything to be nervous about."

Chris paused, then said, "Listen, mate. I just need you to be absolutely sure. Because once we cross that line, there is no going back, yeah. Are you ready for that? Because there is no going back for either of us, Ciaran."

Ciaran quickly circled the table and took Chris by the back of his head. He kissed his best friend on the lips, pulling his bottom lip, then putting his tongue in his mouth. Chris moaned and returned the kiss with enthusiasm, reaching up and touching Ciaran's face, licking his tongue, and pulling in his top lip as well.

Ciaran broke away first, looked Chris in the eyes, and said, "I'm ready."

CHAPTER 10

Instinct

They kissed again, and the minutes ticked away. Ciaran, unsure what to do with his hands, kept one hand on Chris's head, slowly running his fingers through the bottom of his loose curls. Chris knew he had to take over. He put his hands on Ciaran's waist and pulled him closer so they would feel each other's erection, then reached in between them and gently caressed Ciaran's. He felt Ciaran draw a short breath into his mouth and his penis twitch between his fingers. But Ciaran did not flinch or pull away. Chris took that as a sign to move forward.

Without breaking his lips apart, Chris unbuckled Ciaran's jeans, zipped down his zipper, and reached into the hole in his boxers to run his fingers up the length of his penis in one swift motion. Ciaran pulled back first to make an audible gasp, lifted his head back, and closed his eyes. Chris used this break in kissing to go for it. He dropped to his knees, pulling Ciaran's jeans and underwear to his thighs and grabbed his cock, then completely took him in his mouth, holding onto the shaft, sucking halfway down, and pulling up with a pop sound.

Ciaran moaned loudly, then he looked down at what Chris was doing. Chris continued the same motion and Ciaran continued to moan in pleasure, his dream coming to life as Chris's full lips pressed hard on the way down, pursed out, and tightened around him on the way back up to the head, taking him deeper and deeper every time. He could not believe how immensely pleasurable it was, arguably the best blow job he had had in his life. Ciaran knew that if Chris kept going like that, he would not be able to keep standing.

Chris likewise underestimated the length of Ciaran's cock and was afraid to embarrass himself by gagging accidentally. As Ciaran slid down to sit on the bed, Chris let go of Ciaran, kneeled between his legs, and kissed him again. Ciaran, hands slightly shaking, started unbuckling Chris's belt and zipper. He noted Chris wore boxer briefs with a buttoned center and freaked out briefly in his mind. But then he used common sense, took both hands to pull the top down and lift Chris's penis out. He started stroking Chris the way he stroked himself when he was alone and he found he didn't hate doing it. Quite the opposite. And Chris's moaning with his tongue in his mouth made it ten times better.

Chris broke from the kiss and leaned into Ciaran's neck, sucking, kissing, and licking it, breathing in his soapy scent. *Ciaran took a shower before coming over. He knew all this was going to happen,* he thought excitedly.

Chris alternated between kissing and sucking Ciaran's neck from the right side to the left, sucking his ears and kissing his lips and tongue in between, moaning softly as Ciaran stroked his already hard prick. The sensuality of it all was driving Ciaran crazy, and he stroked Chris harder and faster. Then Chris looked Ciaran in the eyes as he unbuttoned his own long-sleeved work shirt and wiggled out of it, leaving his white tank top on. He moved Ciaran's hand off him and bent down again, putting his face toward Ciaran's lap. He took a deep breath, relaxed his throat, and took Ciaran all the way in, again startled by the length but ready this time, and ended with his nose touching Ciaran's pubes.

"FUUUUCK!" Ciaran called out and instinctively grabbed Chris's head with both hands. Chris deep-throated Ciaran three more times; each time Ciaran responded with a hearty, "FUCK!"

Chris pulled Ciaran's pants and boxers all the way down, thankful his boots slid off easily as well. Then he reached up and pulled off Ciaran's sweater and long-sleeved shirt in one swoop. Ciaran was as naked as the day he was born right before him. Before he gave Ciaran a chance to think about what was happening, he kissed him again, and used one hand to pull down his own underwear and pants, yanking off his tank top, too. Then he sat on the bed next to him and pulled Ciaran by his meaty arms on top of him.

Ciaran reacted instinctively. He kissed Chris and positioned himself between Chris's legs, grinding his genitals against him. Chris took the pillow from behind him and lifted himself slightly to put the pillow underneath his midsection, elevating himself. They kissed fervently. Chris managed to get the rubber band from Ciaran's hair, so his red mane fell around his face, and he massaged his scalp.

Ciaran was already in ecstasy, every sense in his body was awakened. He smelled Chris's clean-scented aftershave and felt the roughness of hair beginning to grow on his chin and above his lips. He listened to Chris's soft deep moans of "hmmm... hmmm... hmmm" so rhythmic. He tasted beer and mint that he must have had before Ciaran came over on

Chris's tongue. He could feel Chris's hardness against his own on the lower part of his belly. And when he opened his eyes to see his own feeling of ecstasy and desire on Chris's face, he knew it was time.

Ciaran unlocked his lips and waited until Chris opened his eyes. They looked at each other for a second. Then he pushed his body lower than Chris's and lifted up his legs into an up-and-bent position so that his hole was visible. He sat back on his legs, spit a couple of times in his hand and used it along with his pre-cum to stroke himself, then spit a few more times and stroked the outside of Chris's anus.

Chris gasped but did not break eye contact with Ciaran. More spit. First one finger, then two, then one again. More spit again. Ciaran watched Chris try to control his breathing, failing miserably. He no longer had short deep moans, but uncontrollable gasps in between erratic moaning. He wanted this, badly, and that excited Ciaran. Watching Chris lose control was so unbelievably sexy that Ciaran's erection was starting to ache. He stopped stroking and leaned over between Chris's legs and guided himself to his hole, entering him very slowly.

Chris was right. It was the tightest hole Ciaran had ever been in, and he found himself gasping. He wanted to see how far this rabbit hole went, but knew he needed to take his time, for the both of them. Chris gasped too, then bared down. Ciaran's head went in and they both took a moment to pause. Then Ciaran pushed on. The deeper he traveled, the more Chris audibly moaned and arched his back, the tighter it molded around Ciaran.

When he was about eighty percent in, Chris cried out, "Aaah!"

Ciaran paused. "Do you want me to stop?" he asked with concern.

"No," Chris panted. "Just… don't go… all the way… in… right now…" Chris looked at him in the eye. "Your cock is big."

Ciaran smiled. "Indeed. It is."

Ciaran kissed him gently, sweetly, pulling out most of the way, then pushed in about halfway, then pulled up again to the head. He moved and Chris moved with him. Chris held onto Ciaran while Ciaran held onto the headboard rail in front of him with one hand and Chris's arm with the other. They breathed in sync, but moaned at different intervals. Ciaran couldn't think of anything other than how tight and deep and filling Chris felt around him. He had never felt sex like that before, and it made him feel like howling at the moon.

His orgasm quickly rose, and he started feeling the waves coming fast and strong. He tried to slow it down by slowing himself down. He wanted the feeling to last longer, although he had no idea how long they had already been in that position. For once, neither of them were keeping time. Ciaran found himself inching deeper than the agreed-upon length, grinding faster and Chris getting louder and more audible with his moaning as he held on and took the pounding.

Ciaran tried hard to stay conscious and in the moment, trying to tell himself to hold on a little bit longer, but without warning, everything went numb except his groin, which involuntarily spasmed. He let out a deep moan and could not stop cumming. He could have blacked out with how intense it felt, how good it was to release inside of Chris again and again and again and again with nowhere for his sperm to go, leaking out as he collapsed on top of him.

Chris felt every moment of Ciaran's buildup and release, his cum warming up his insides, and he was elated by how amazing it felt to have his best friend inside of him.

Neither moved for a moment. Chris could feel Ciaran's fast heartbeat through his chest, and he started to gently stroke his back, lightly rubbing his fingertips up and down. He knew Ciaran was going to have a reaction, he just didn't know if it was going to be "That was great!" or "I feel disgusted with myself." So he waited.

Ciaran was also stalling, using the moments to try to gauge how Chris was feeling. He stupidly thought now that he should have used some kind of lube. *Of course, the anus does not secrete like the vagina and the drops of spit did nothing.* He also thought about how hard he came and how Chris hadn't at all, and what a selfish person he was. He didn't want to be the first person who moved, but his erection was getting softer by the minute, and that position was getting increasingly uncomfortable. And he knew he was crushing Chris with his body, too.

Ciaran sighed and rolled off Chris onto the side of the bed and looked up. No one spoke for a couple of seconds. Then Chris started laughing. Ciaran looked over at Chris and his laugh became infectious, so he started chuckling himself.

Chris yelled, "Ciaran Fucking Beals! I can't believe that just happened. I just got fucked—FUCKED—by Kir. Ran. Fucking. Beals!" He sat up and laughed, wiping tears from his eyes. "I'm fucking buzzing right now!"

Ciaran punched him in the shoulder playfully and laughed as well. "Shut up. My God, you are such an arsehole."

Chris, still laughing, moved around on the bed until his back was on the wall the bed was up against, and his one leg hanging over, while the other was bent with his foot on the bed. Ciaran moved to sit next to him, awkwardly at first, then made a conscious decision to relax and put his head on Chris's shoulder. Chris put his hand on Ciaran's thigh and leaned over to kiss his head and sighed. Again, no one spoke.

Then Ciaran asked, "Was … that okay?" Really he wanted to know was, was he okay, satisfactory, for Chris.

Chris sensed his real question in the air and squeezed his thigh gently. "That was better than okay," he said. "That was bloody brilliant. Fan-fucking-tastic." He paused, then said, "And I don't want that to be the last time."

Ciaran nodded. "I don't either."

"So. Are we really doing this? I mean, all of it, not just the sex part?" Chris asked.

It was Ciaran's turn to sense the question Chris was really asking, and he didn't want to hesitate. "Yes. I mean, I don't want this to be just about sex, either." He let a moment pass, then said, "I want to see if this could really be something."

"I want that, too," said Chris. "I've never really wanted to before. But I really want to try, with you. I … like you, Ciaran. And not just as a friend."

Ciaran lifted his head to look at Chris. There was a seriousness and vulnerability in his eyes that made Ciaran want to kiss him, reassure him. So he did. He kissed him lightly on the lips. "I like you too. So yes. We are doing this." Chris smiled. Ciaran asked, "Do you still have date plans?"

"No. I canceled the dates and the reservations. You told me to!"

Ciaran laughed. "That's okay. We can find something else to get into on Sunday," he said knowingly. "You plan it."

Chris understood. They were actually dating. A couple. "Okay. I will take you to one of my favorite spots in the city, not far from where I live."

"Okay," said Ciaran.

"Okay!" Chris said with a smile.

They kissed again, gently. Then Ciaran put his head back on Chris's shoulder. He reached his hand down and held Chris's hand that was still resting on his thigh, and entwined his fingers with his. They squeezed simultaneously, then released pressure but kept their fingers together, silently reliving the moments since Ciaran walked through the door.

Chris was lost in how passionate Ciaran's kisses were. Kissing was not Chris's thing, but Ciaran made him want to kiss him. He could tell Ciaran loved his full lips, the way he would pull and suck on them. Truthfully, he would have been okay with a little kissing and a lot of groping, maybe giving Ciaran a blow until he came. He did not expect to go all the way... or maybe he did. It happened so fast he couldn't tell who took off whose clothes first. It was probably him. But Ciaran did get on the bed first, so what was that a sign of, if not wanting to go all the way? Either way, once they started, it was like a train running full speed ahead and there was no way to stop it. The sexual tension between them exploded.

Ciaran was lost in thought as well, of the anal sex he just had. Chris was absolutely right. It was the tightest hole he had ever been in. With all the sexual escapades he had while hanging out with Sean, he never thought to enter the other way. The tightness of it all was ... unbelievable. A part of him wished he had something to compare it to, but a bigger part of him was glad he didn't. Something about it being his first time with Chris made it special, sacred. He began to wonder how it would feel the other way.

And then he remembered. "You didn't come!" he said out loud.

"Hmmm?" mumbled Chris, his own thoughts getting interrupted.

"You didn't come at all."

"I know, it's okay." Chris smiled. "I will come another time."

"No." Ciaran sat up, but didn't let go of Chris's hand. "I know you, Chris. We didn't just spend the last six months talking about how much you love sex, for you not to actually have a go at me, too. C'mon, mate."

Chris laughed him off. "No, Ciaran." Ciaran didn't budge. He stared at him intently. "NO," Chris said more seriously. "We've done more than enough for our first time, and you're not ready."

Ciaran was surprised. He assumed Chris would jump at the chance for some anal action. "Chris, I don't know what you mean by 'I'm not ready.' I told you I was, and not just for part of it. For all of it. ALL." Chris shook his head and tried to turn away, but Ciaran made him look at him. "I am absolutely certain there will be pain, but I'm not afraid of it. Because I'm not afraid of you. I know you will take care of me."

But Chris was actually afraid of it, being on that side of it. He had never deflowered a man before and his only deflowering of a woman was his first time as well. Chris's first time was absolutely awful, so he could not imagine hurting Ciaran in that way. And he all but said so.

"Ciaran, I don't think you understand how terrible it is to be broken in. At best, you will want to scream too loudly. I'm not kidding. And it's not the time or the place."

Ciaran read between the lines. "Are you afraid to do this? You've never actually broken someone in before, have you?" Chris did not respond. "Ha! Of all your randos and one-night stands, flings, and relationships, none of them were anal virgins? None??" Ciaran was amused.

But Chris said seriously, "No. I purposely do not go after straight men or men that have not been exposed to anal sex or being gay, really. It's a huge turn-off if I have to do all the fucking work and hold their emotional shit through it all, and most likely after. Plus, they are usually shitty lays."

Chris just realized what he said as Ciaran's eyebrow went up, still amusingly. "Oh shit, Ciaran, I didn't mean you or us. Honest!"

Ciaran laughed. "I didn't think you were talking about me. But I do hope I wasn't a shitty lay, because you certainly weren't for me."

"Well, I don't know. I haven't laid you yet," Chris teased.

"Then do it," Ciaran said seductively. Chris said nothing, just shook his head. Ciaran tried again, "Chris, I want to do this, now. Not just for you, but for me. You won't hold any of my emotional shit because it's my decision and mine to carry." He leaned in real close and whispered, "Let me feel you inside of me, Christopher Jennings. Please?"

Chris could not help it. His penis twitched, and because they were still naked, Ciaran saw it out of the corner of his eye. He let go of Ciaran's hand, reached over, and began to stroke Chris, surprising himself again at how much he liked doing it.

He leaned into Chris's ear and whispered, "Break me in, fuck me slow until you come inside me."

Chris's cock did a huge twitch in Ciaran's hand, and Ciaran knew Chris would not say no again.

CHAPTER 11

Pain and Pleasure

"Okay," Chris said. "Okay, but we do it my way. And we might not get there, and that's okay too. I'll just put it in and we'll see what happens."

Chris jumped off the bed and started looking around, mumbling to himself, his semi-hard penis bobbing in front of him. He kneeled down to his pants, pulled out his keys to the safe under the switchboard, and pulled out a bottle of brandy and two small glasses, setting them on the table. Ciaran watched in interest as Chris crossed to the other side of the Tank to his locker. He pulled out the bottle of almond oil, came over, and placed it on the floor by the bed. He motioned for Ciaran to stand up as he filled two glasses halfway with brandy.

"Drink this." He gave Ciaran his glass and quickly drank his own. Ciaran barely drank the first glass when Chris had already poured himself another. "You're taking too long, mate, drink up." He pushed Ciaran's glass to his mouth to drink faster while he swallowed his second glass whole. Ciaran swallowed in one gulp, letting it burn down his throat. Once done, Chris filled his glass halfway again, and said, "Drink." Ciaran drank the next glass quickly. Chris started pouring him a third glass.

"Really? I have to be drunk for this?"

"I'm not kidding. Drink," Chris said seriously. Ciaran sighed and downed his third glass in a row of brandy.

"One more," Chris said. He poured another one for Ciaran, and he drank it. Ciaran's body was starting to feel very warm.

"Okay." Chris clapped his hands together and gave a nervous chuckle. "Lie down face down. No face up. No... no, face down. Yeah."

Ciaran wanted to laugh, but Chris had such a look of seriousness mixed with anxiousness that he did not want to make him more uncomfortable and call the whole thing off.

Ciaran lay down on his stomach, used his hands and arms as a pillow, faced the wall, and closed his eyes. Chris's heart was pounding. He poured a bit more for himself and drank it in one gulp. He clapped his hands again, rubbed them together, and sat on the edge of the bed. He noticed he was trembling slightly as he grabbed the oil and rubbed it in his hands.

Relax, get it together, he told himself.

He reached over, massaging Ciaran's back, starting with the beloved dragon. He kneaded and massaged all the way from the nape of his neck and around to the shoulders. Chris massaged his whole back, still enamored with how perfect his physic was. He admired Ciaran's soft reddish blond hairs and freckles everywhere. He concentrated on his lower back and the groove between it and the tailbone, giving him a deep tissue massage.

Chris spent the next hour giving Ciaran the best massage he could ever muster. Ciaran lay so still that Chris thought he fell asleep, but as Chris moved to massage his buttocks,

Ciaran clenched up a bit, then relaxed. Chris pretended he didn't notice and kept on massaging down to his outer and inner thighs. He massaged down to his calf, took some time kneading out the knots, and behind his ankle to his heel.

Ciaran was completely relaxed, but awake and alert. Chris used the oil more on his way back up, concentrating on his inner thighs. He opened his legs apart just enough for him to sit at the bottom of the bed near his ankles and continued to massage the crease between his groin and thighs. Chris took notice of the reddish-blond hair on his balls as well and had fleeting thoughts of licking them. Instead, he poured oil down his butt crack and massaged it from the top of his crack, up underneath the bottom of his cheeks, back to the crease between his groin and thighs. Then he slowly crept his thumb over, circling his anus with the flat part of his thumb.

Ciaran clenched up at first, but did it less and less the more Chris did it. The first time he stopped clenching, Chris slipped his thumb inside and massaged in a circular motion, and Ciaran let out a low moan. Chris poured more oil, and kept going in and out and around, circling the rim on the outside, and then slipping in to circle around the inside past the first ring, stretching him out until he could get his whole thumb in there without Ciaran clenching. Then he slipped his index finger in and did the same.

Every time Ciaran relaxed, Chris would take another step. After the index finger, it was his middle finger, then the index and the middle finger together, pouring more oil every time. Ciaran had not made a sound since the first short moan, but his breathing became erratic. When Chris upped it to three fingers, Ciaran let out another low moan, but nothing else. Chris was fascinated by his resilience and he was aware of how hard he himself was at this time. His penis was throbbing and ached to be inside, but he knew he needed to hold out just a little bit longer....

Ciaran was beside himself with how aroused he was. His own penis was rock hard again, as if he hadn't just cum about an hour and a half ago. He kept trying not to tense up, but it was an initial reaction every time Chris added another layer to stretch him out. Between the brandy and the massage, however, his body was more relaxed than it had ever been and all of his pleasure senses were heightened. By the time Chris got to three fingers, he knew what was coming next, and he was so excited he thought he would cum on himself.

"Lift your knees in like you are about to do a yoga pose," Chris said quietly.

Ciaran slowly lifted his knees into his stomach, bottom high in the air. He felt Chris positioning himself behind him. He put one hand on Ciaran's anus, alternating between the index and middle finger, and then entered three fingers, and massaged his own cock. After a couple of strokes, he knew he had stalled long enough. He grabbed the oil again and put an unreasonable amount of oil on his own penis and smeared the rest on Ciaran's already glistening ass crack, inside and outside his anus.

Chris took a deep breath and put the tip of the head slowly in Ciaran. Ciaran let out another small moan, as Chris did as well. Chris paused, took the head all the way out, then pushed it back in a little farther. Ciaran moaned again; he couldn't stop himself as he felt like he was being split open. Instead, he buried his face in the pillow as his cock deflated. Chris did this routine a third time, pulled all the way out, then slowly pushed in a centimeter farther, and again Ciaran moaned, but this time instead of tensing up, Ciaran pushed back and Chris felt the head slide all the way in. Chris paused to give Ciaran a moment, then slowly pulled back out, then pushed back in again. The head went in much easier as Ciaran did not tense up, but rather allowed Chris to go farther and farther in, little by little.

Ciaran was completely lost in the moment. He felt pain that made his eyes water and also felt pleasure like he had never felt before. The fullness of it was indescribable, especially since Chris kept hitting a pressure point inside of him, and it almost made him forget the pain. Almost. But Chris's moving so slowly was also driving him crazy. Each time Chris pulled all the way out and pushed in, taking a bit more down with him, it literally took Ciaran's breath away. Every time he felt like he couldn't feel fuller, Chris would push deeper, making room he didn't know he had. He couldn't control his moaning even if he tried.

Chris, on the other hand, was trying to stay present and not get lost in how tight it was. He was consciously pleading with his body not to cum yet, and it was a struggle. Ciaran's moans were not helping either, as it made him want to go deeper and faster. Chris started noticing Ciaran moving along with him, moving at a slightly faster pace, but Chris needed to control his orgasm, so he grabbed Ciaran by the waist and made him slow down.

But Ciaran's cock had begun to rise again. And he felt like he was going to explode and needed to release. Now.

After ten more minutes of the slow crawl, Ciaran lifted himself up with a loud moan onto his hands and knees, taking Chris by surprise. Chris continued the slow strokes, pulling all the way out and all the way back in as he tried to ignore Ciaran's moans that were audible, loud, and sexy.

"Chriiiissss," Ciaran moaned.

Chris stopped moving inside him. He leaned all the way over and felt Ciaran's dick practically drooling in pre-cum and rock solid. Again he marveled at his length at full erection, skin stretched tight. He started penetrating again slowly, holding onto Ciaran, stroking him with more speed than he was moving at the moment. By the ninth or tenth stroke, Ciaran pushed back on Chris and let out a loud, "Aaaaaah!"

Ciaran's orgasm and ejaculation came so fast and strong he had no idea what hit him until his body froze and he started spazzing for the second time that night, cumming all over Chris's hands and the bed.

"Ho. Lee. Shit," Chris said out loud.

He was still only a little more than halfway inside of Ciaran, stunned that he had made him cum so hard, and so soon. He intended to let Ciaran catch his breath, but the moment was too great to pass up, and he began pumping again, a little more speed, but still not as fast as he wanted to be. And he stopped pulling all the way out; no need for that anymore.

Ciaran started moaning louder, fists clenched on the bed. Chris became aware that anyone within earshot could probably hear him, but he did nothing to stop him. Chris held onto Ciaran's hips and moved like the ocean waves whose tide was just coming in, moaning himself. He wanted to change positions to see Ciaran's face, but Ciaran seemed to be enjoying the current position too much.

And Ciaran was. The pain was nowhere as Chris moved deeper and deeper inside of him, continually hitting that pressure point, now pleasure point, that Ciaran had no idea existed, that was again literally taking his breath away. He felt like he barely lost the last erection when he noted he was hard all over again. Chris tapped Ciaran's legs and motioned for him to stretch out so he could lay flat and Chris could lay on top of him, then he began to pound him, forgetting the

Ciaran was an anal virgin, or maybe no longer caring since he now needed his own release.

Ciaran was aware of Chris's tight hand on his shoulder as he dug deeper and deeper with each stroke. Chris's now hard thrusting involuntarily moved Ciaran's hard cock against the mattress. Ciaran was getting fucked from the inside and stroked from the outside. The sensuality of that sexual experience was immeasurable, and he could barely contain how loud he was.

Chris began moaning in sync with his "hmm, hmm, hmms". Chris was trying to keep one part of his brain conscious still because somehow he knew Ciaran was going to cum a third time that night. So every time he felt his own potential build-up, he would slow down or change up his stroke. Ciaran was not aware of why Chris was doing this, changing up his short quick strokes to long hard strokes to circular motions; he thought Chris was teasing him and blowing his mind on purpose. This went on for an eternity until Chris hit that pleasure point too many times in a row and Ciaran felt the waves of orgasm fast approaching once again.

Ciaran yelled out, "I'm ... ah ... gonna ... ah ... cum ... ah ... again ah ah ah!"

And Chris, who had been pumping to get that last bit of himself into Ciaran, thrust all the way inside so he was pelvic bone deep and ground against his prostate. Ciaran thought he was going to die and be reborn. The pleasure was almost blinding and he let himself get swept away by his orgasm, which hurt him and freed him, all at the same time. He exclaimed loudly, and cum exploded from his untouched penis, with nowhere to go but to spread out across his midsection and the bed.

Chris was on the verge of his own orgasm, but stopped moving completely. His aching penis pulsating angrily at him, still bone deep inside of Ciaran. But because he felt the intensity of Ciaran's orgasm, he had to stop and ask, "Are you okay?"

Ciaran, trying to catch his breath in between, said, "Did... you cum... yet?"

"No."

"Well, hurry ... the fuck ... up... don't know ...how much ... more ... I can ... take..."

Chris smiled, then slowly pulled all the way out and Ciaran moaned at how empty he felt. Chris moved off the bed, then positioned Ciaran so that he was leaning over the side of the bed and Chris was standing behind him. He pushed Ciaran all the way down and spread Ciaran's cheeks wide, noticing how red his hole was, making him excited.

Chris had no intention of holding back this time. He added more oil and told Ciaran, "Bite the pillow." Then he buried himself all the way inside in one motion.

Ciaran let out a yell, but Chris ignored him, grabbed his waist, and fucked him hard. Chris surprised himself by not cumming right away, realizing he must have chased it off with all the stops and starts. *No matter*, he thought, *I'm coming for it, literally.*

It was Chris's turn to be vocal and audible with his moans and grunts. He went a full eight minutes before he started to feel the growing heat in his center. "Fuck yeah!" He found himself shouting while thrusting away. "Take this prick, take every inch of this cock up your arse. You fucking love this shit, don't you? Love this cock in your arse, huh? Huh?"

As the heat inside him intensified, he looked down and watched himself disappearing in and out of Ciaran's freckled arse and lost track of time and space. He came so hard he found himself slamming five hard thrusts with each spurt, yelling, "Aaaaaaaahh!" He collapsed on top of Ciaran, then slid to the floor and lay on his back, panting. He felt dizzy and wonderful.

Ciaran stayed in the same position, leaning over the bed, also trying to catch his breath. He managed to crawl up the bed, lay straight on his stomach, and looked down at Chris on the floor. Chris looked up at him and smiled. "Sorry," he said breathlessly.

"For what? Fucking the shit out of me?" Ciaran smiled back.

Chris grinned. "Yeah... that..."

Ciaran reached his hand down and Chris took it. He pulled Chris's hand back up to him and kissed his fingers. Suddenly Chris wanted to be right next to him, so he got off the floor and onto the bed. He lay on his side while Ciaran lay on his stomach and they kissed softly for the next couple of minutes, pausing to take it all in, then finding each other's lips again.

Eventually, Ciaran lifted his arm to look at his watch. "5:39 a.m.," he said out loud.

Chris nodded, but neither of them moved just yet. Ciaran had arrived at the Tank a little after 2 a.m. so they had been at it for hours from the first kiss until the last. Ciaran's whole body was aching, and he had never felt so alive.

They lay there touching each other, kissing, wanting to close their eyes and sleep but knowing they couldn't because Miche, the first-shift ranger, usually came in by 6:30 a.m. They watched the sunrise until Chris said, "We got to go." It was Ciaran's turn to nod.

Chris helped Ciaran put on his clothes first, then found his own. Ciaran went to sit on the chair at the round table, but his bottom betrayed him with pain, so he opted to stand instead and watched Chris. Chris changed the sheets, putting fresh ones on the bed and the soiled ones in a bag so he could take them home to wash. He put the brandy back in the safe and his oil, which barely had any more left, back in his locker.

At 6:20 a.m., Chris pulled Ciaran in for another kiss. "No regrets?"

"Absolutely not," Ciaran said right away. He kissed him back and said, "I will see you tonight, for patrol." He gave Chris one last peck, turned around, and disappeared in a wisp of smoke.

CHAPTER 12

Taming The Beast

Ciaran's mind stayed consumed with the events that had happened in the last eight hours, give or take. His bottom was on fire as he sat in the tub soaking and he welcomed it, as it was a constant reminder that what happened really did happen. He closed his eyes and slid farther down, lightly touching his penis.

So unbelievably tight.

That was a whole experience by itself. He could still taste Chris's tongue in his mouth, tasting of beer and mints. He could still feel his mouth on his neck, feel Chris's penis swell inside of him—that thought made him gasp out loud. He never thought of how much he would actually enjoy it.

Not just enjoy it. Full-on ejaculate more than once. He never expected to feel that way from anal penetration. Chris only talked about what it felt like to be the giver, not the receiver. *He's been holding out on me,* he thought with a chuckle. The first (second!) time he came, he understood Chris had gotten him off. But that last time was internal. It started deep, grew intense, and completely overwhelmed him. He didn't even know the male anatomy could do that.

After soaking for well over an hour and almost falling asleep in the tub, Ciaran came out, body still aching. He drank five milliliters of a healing elixir and took 800 mg of Motrin. If that didn't do the trick, nothing would. He lay down on his bed face down and closed his eyes, remembering Chris's face as he thrusted and gyrated inside of him.

Ciaran had only one thought before sleep took over—*we are doing it again, tonight!*

Chris, who thought he was coming home to be at peace with his thoughts, walked into a loud house instead. Charity was arguing with his five-year-old nephew Rudy about putting on socks that matched and then his sneakers so she could take him to school.

"And why is this not happening upstairs in his apartment again?" he asked, annoyed.

"Because Clary needed some rest. She said the baby is giving her insomnia, and she didn't sleep well last night. I brought him down here to make him some breakfast so I can get him off to school," Charity explained.

Since it was Friday, he knew Charity was off, which meant instead of going back upstairs after dropping Rudy off at primary school, she would come right back to his apartment downstairs and crash in the spare bedroom. Or worse, crawl into his bed. For once, he wished his sister had someplace else to go. He didn't want to talk to anyone; he just wanted to lay down and relive every moment, possibly rub one out, but that wasn't going to happen. He sighed, grabbed the wrapped plate of breakfast she made for him, and started eating with his hands, watching the drama in front of him. After much protesting from his young, stubborn nephew, Charity managed to usher him out the door to do the five-minute walk to school.

Chris stripped and stood in the shower, leaned against the wall, and let the water hit him. In less than nine hours, he went from being extremely annoyed with his best friend to fucking him. The getting fucked part was incredible. It never occurred to him that Ciaran would have an anaconda for a dick. He didn't look the part, average height of six feet, nice muscular build. In his experience, muscular guys usually weren't walking around with large equipment.

He would have been perfectly happy sucking Ciaran off until he came, but he realized he underestimated it, and was not going to choke on it being the "experienced" one between them. So his only play was to let Ciaran fuck him, and it wasn't a bad idea at all.

He smiled to himself. Even with that, Ciaran had the upper hand. The penetration hurt going in and regardless of it being drier than he would have liked, Ciaran was already hitting his spot without being completely in, and he had to make him pull back a bit. Chris thought maybe they did too much for the first time, and then thought maybe they didn't do enough. There was still so much to explore, positions, oral. He had no idea the sleeping dragon he awakened by giving that first kiss. And Chris liked the kissing, the touching, the passion of it all.

He found himself touching his growing erection, remembering those first few moments and Ciaran's astonished face as he repeatedly took him in his mouth, when he heard the door slam.

Shit, Sis is back, he thought. He switched the water to lukewarm to cool down his erection and quickly washed, then wrapped a towel around himself and slid into his room, which was closer to the bathroom. He put on a white t-shirt, underwear, and gray sweatpants, then lay on the far side of the bed, and waited.

A few minutes later, he heard her knock on his bedroom door, then it opened without waiting for a response. She plopped herself down on the bed next to him and sighed. "I swear I'm that boy's dad. She should just put my name on his birth certificate."

Chris "hmm'd" but didn't say much else as Charity went into a tirade about their older sister and how she again couldn't believe she got pregnant by a guy she had known for less than three weeks. "I mean, isn't she supposed to be the responsible one?"

Chris agreed in all the right places, but his head wasn't in it and Charity could tell. *"Quoi de neuf?"* Being ten months apart, they were as close as twins, and she could read him well.

So he told her, "Remember my friend, Ciaran? The conservationist that patrols with me at night that I told you about?"

"Yeah?"

"Well... something happened ... between us..."

Charity sat up and looked at him. "Chrissy, you didn't!"

Chris didn't answer, but a smile crept up on his lips. She hit him in the arm forcefully. "Oy! I didn't do anything he didn't want!"

Charity groaned and lay back down. "I thought you said he was straight."

"He was. Until last night. And this morning." He laughed, and she hit him again. "Ow!"

"You're such a slut," Charity said. "I thought you said he was a really good friend."

"He was. He *is*," Chris said. "We are still friends, we are just … more than friends now."

"So fuck buddies." She scoffed. "I hope you know what you're doing."

He paused, then said, "We're actually going to try to make a go of it."

Charity sat up again and gave him a look. "I know," he said. "Crazy. But. I like this one. And I haven't really liked someone in a long time. And I think he really likes me too. At least he likes me enough to want to date me, not just fuck me. I mean, I don't want it to be all about sex, and I know he doesn't, so we are going to try to see if this could be something, you know?"

Charity looked at Chris intently and said, "He must have a big cock." Chris pushed her all the way off the bed.

She laughed, then got right back on the bed and lay next to him, still laughing. When it died down, Chris said, "His dick is pretty big, yes." He smiled.

"Ha! I fucking knew it!" She laughed again. "There is no way you would be giving it a go if he was a shitty lay, you whore you." They both laughed. Then she said, "Growing up, huh? Go on, make a go of it then. A real one, Chris." She gave him a knowing look. "Take it seriously. Put yourself out there. One of us needs to be in a healthy relationship." Chris nodded.

Charity then said, "So? Don't hold out on me. Tell me everything. How big is he?" Her eyes went wide with amusement.

Typically they shared their conquest stories with each other, but he didn't want to, not this time. "Maybe later," he replied. "I just want to hold on to this myself a little bit longer."

Charity sucked her teeth, channeling her African mother. "You must really like this one. So when's the next romp?"

"Maybe tonight. Maybe Sunday when we go on our date."

Charity groaned. "Uuuugh, you aren't taking him to Nemo's are you?"

"Yes," Chris said, laughing. "He might as well start his journey to the other side there."

7:30 p.m.

Ciaran thought of nothing else as he took a quick shower that evening, ate dinner, and got ready for work. He went through the front doors of The Atrium instead of the restaurant portion, so he wouldn't have to talk to anyone. He Wisp'd from the alley right to the Reserve entrance. His stomach leaped as soon as he landed, although logically he knew Chris would not be in the woods for several hours.

But Ciaran was nervous anyway. He wasn't sure if he was going to find him at the beginning of his shift or later on for patrol. He didn't want to look desperate, but he also wanted Chris to know he was okay. And he wasn't sure what, if anything, was going to happen tonight. The healing potion did the trick; he didn't feel any pain in his bottom at all, and he was ready to feel Chris inside him again, tonight if possible, but he wanted to play it cool.

Ciaran entered the Reserve and went through his daily routine, glancing at his watch every hour, then every couple of minutes. At ten minutes to 11p.m., he knew he needed to at least see him; the anticipation was too great.

10:45 p.m.

Chris came to work with nervous energy. He parked and looked around, half expecting Ciaran to appear in front of him. He sighed and walked up the stairs into the Tank where Bergina was. She started talking about filing that needed to be done, archiving that needed to be uploaded, all the grunt work that falls on the overnight staff to give them something to do rather than sleep. He was only half listening, anxious for her to leave. At 11 p.m. on the dot, when she finally did, he walked her out to the catwalk and watched her get in her car and drive away. He stood for a moment in the February cold.

Ciaran's cloud appeared right at the bottom of the steps, and he was surprised to see Chris at the top. He tried to have a normal walk, but felt clumsy and awkward. Chris was also surprised but tried to play it cool. As much as he wanted Ciaran to appear, he did not actually think he would.

When Ciaran reached the second to last stair, he looked up and said, "Hey."

Chris smiled. "Hey."

They looked at each other for a moment, then Chris leaned over and kissed Ciaran gently on the lips, took his fingers, and led him inside. Once the door closed, they kissed more passionately. Chris backed Ciaran against the door and held onto his hips, pressing against him. He was already hard. Ciaran mimicked Chris and held onto his waist as well.

Then Ciaran remembered. "I… I gotta get back," he whispered. "No one knows I left."

Chris sighed and stepped back, but still held onto Ciaran. "I'll see you in a few hours, then?"

"Yeah."

They held on a few moments more, then hugged. Ciaran let go first and opened the door, disappearing right on the outside.

12:59 a.m.

Ciaran still had on his work uniform, so when Chris walked up to Marker 1, he knew Ciaran wasn't staying all night. Ciaran gave him a light kiss, sweet and kind. They began walking silently at first, each lost in their thoughts. Then Chris broke the silence.

"So I got a place set up, where we can go. This gastropub I frequent from time to time. We can go on Sunday since you work tonight. If you still want to go."

Ciaran smiled a little. "Yes. Of course. Did you want to meet at The Atrium?"

"Actually, my flat is closer, walking distance really. Comes in handy when you're sloshed."

Ciaran chuckled. "Okay, give me the address." Chris did. "7 p.m. okay?"

"Sounds good."

Ciaran started talking about Ben and Anna, how they had been fighting lately like a married couple who hate each other from time to time, and they had to pull two more Fixers in to manage them. Now they had one lead Tamer and five Fixers each, as opposed to the one-to-three ratio the other dragons had. Ciaran had left Ben sleeping and Anna restless, and they were trying to keep her away from him. Chris, who still didn't understand the dynamics of the workforce there, listened mostly.

"I know I should be there to help but…" He let the words linger and Chris smiled.

"You don't have to stay tonight."

"You don't want me to?" Ciaran asked, more alarm in his voice than he intended.

"No, I *do* want you to. But Bergina gave me a shitload of work to do, so I understand if you can't, and I can make myself busy. We both are technically on the clock."

"That is true. We have to be mindful of that," said Ciaran. "I won't stay long. We'll just make the most of the time we have."

"Yeah. I'd like that." They walked along quietly again with an excited nervousness in the air.

When they got back to the Tank, they both removed their shoes by the door immediately. Ciaran zipped down his uniform completely to reveal a shirt and sweatpants he had underneath. And Chris already knew what he was going to do.

"Sit on the edge of the bed," he told Ciaran. Ciaran promptly complied.

Chris kneeled down in front of him and slid in between his legs, pulling Ciaran's neck down for a kiss. After a few moments, he slid off his t-shirt over his head, licked the base of his neck, moved down to kiss and nip his nipples, moved back up to find his mouth, and kissed him again. He started rubbing Ciaran through his sweats, and Ciaran let out a deep moan. He kissed and stroked Ciaran until his imprint got bigger and bigger, then he let go. He grabbed the sides of Ciaran's sweatpants, and with Ciaran's help, pulled his sweats all the way down and off.

Chris started stroking Ciaran again, getting a better look at it than the night before. It was tan with freckles, slightly darker than the rest of his body, with the head being the pinkest. He could see the line where he was circumcised, and it had a slight curve upward, barely noticeable. And it was long as fuck. A little girth, but not much as the length made up for it. He saw why he was overwhelmed the night before. But Chris was determined to be the beast tamer today.

He looked at Ciaran and smiled slyly. Then he relaxed his jaw and throat muscles and took Ciaran completely in his mouth until his nose touched pubes, then sucked hard on the way back up.

Ciaran let out an "Aaaaah!" Very few people were able to do that for him, so it was unexpected.

Chris did not let up for five more deep throats until his mouth filled with saliva and he poured it all on Ciaran's penis, then began stroking again. He leaned Ciaran back slightly and bent his head all the way down to put Ciaran's full testicle in his mouth, gently swished it around, and completed the task with the other testicle. Chris licked back up the length of Ciaran's long and very hard penis.

If Ciaran thought he was going to play it cool, that went out the window the first moment Chris went down on him. Ciaran had officially died and went to cock-sucking heaven. He responded with loud "fucks, shits, aaahs, and uuughs," and put his hands on Chris's head not as a guide, as Chris clearly did not need one, but to steady himself. He knew he was not going to last long at all.

At one point Ciaran fell backward on the bed and Chris took it as an opportunity to swing Ciaran's legs onto the bed so he could position himself over him. *Better for deep-throating anyway*, he thought, and continued to push all the way down and suck all the way up. He knew what he wanted, and Ciaran was going to give it to him.

Ciaran knew what he was going for as well and was not going to deny him. He started grabbing Chris's curls with both hands and bobbing his head faster and faster, moaning louder. When Chris could feel that Ciaran's hardness had reached its full max, he lifted his head from Ciaran's grip, put one finger in Ciaran's puckered hole, and started stroking him faster. He waited until Ciaran gave him eye contact and said, "Cum."

It was as if Ciaran's body responded to Chris's command. He immediately felt the beginning of his orgasm as Chris stroked. And right before Ciaran exploded, Chris stopped stroking and deep-throated Ciaran again.

Ciaran's eyes crossed. He saw stars and growled, bucked upward and came forcefully. Chris felt it right down his throat and swallowed, then swallowed some more as Ciaran's cum kept pulsing out of him, with his lips wrapped so tight around the shaft that not one drop would get loose. When Ciaran finally stopped cumming, Chris slowly pulled back off Ciaran's cock and sat back. He watched Ciaran, who was lying there breathing heavily, both hands over his eyes.

"Fuck, Chris!" Ciaran exclaimed. "What the fuck? Where the fuck did you learn how to do that!?"

Chris smiled and said, "It's magic."

Ciaran opened one eye and looked at Chris through his fingers, and Chris laughed. He closed his eye again and Chris watched him.

Chris started touching Ciaran's body lightly, his thighs and the crease between his thighs and balls, the damp and wild reddish-golden hair that surrounded his genitals. He ran his hands over his abs, over and over again, touched one nipple, gave it a small pinch, touched the other, and did the same. Chris hovered over him and touched his neck and Adam's apple, then traced his finger over his lips. He was only semi-hard, but growing by the minute. Ciaran still had his eyes closed, but had moved his hands to the top of Chris's head, enjoying the sensual touch.

Ciaran moved his hands to Chris's hips and grabbed both cheeks, moving his body against him. He said, "Take off your clothes."

Chris stood up and started to strip and Ciaran watched him. Ciaran surprised himself with how attracted he was to Chris's body. Nothing about it was feminine but it was the sexiest thing in the world to him at the moment. When Chris had only his white socks on, he got into the bed and Ciaran turned to his side to give him room but also to face him; it was his turn to appreciate Chris's body.

Ciaran touched his skin, admiring his shade, a perfect cup of coffee with cream and sugar in it, except for his nipples, which were a chocolate brown, along with his penis and testicles. Chris wasn't hairy like he was; there was little hair on his chest but it was soft and curly like the ones on his head and arms. He had no tattoos, unlike Ciaran, and barely a blemish on his body except a birthmark on his thigh, a misshapen triangle, and the mole on his left cheek.

Ciaran ran his hands along his nipples, gave each of them a slight pinch, and ran his hand down his abs and stomach. Chris didn't have a six-pack, but it was flat and firm. He had some roundness to his pecs that Ciaran found he liked as he traced it with his finger. He moved farther down and put his finger in his belly button, which was neither an innie nor an outie, but a perfect combination. He reached down and touched his penis, which was leaning against his own. Chris was clean-shaven, the skin smooth along the creases between his thighs. His penis wasn't as long as his, but was certainly thicker than his own, toasted almond at the head, milk chocolate all the way down. Ciaran began to wonder what his milk would taste like.

He reached down a bit farther and touched his testicles. Ciaran had never touched another man's penis until yesterday, and it was his first time touching a man's balls, too. He expected them to match his own in girth, but they were looser than his. *Probably due to the fact he is much more experienced than me,* Ciaran thought. The thought embarrassed and excited him.

Chris wondered what Ciaran was thinking as he explored his body, but his face was unreadable. Ciaran continued to be curious about the male anatomy and wanted to make Chris feel as good as he made him feel. But didn't know how to until Chris said softly, "Turn over."

Ciaran looked up at him. Something about the way Chris was taking control was an experience he didn't know he liked or needed in his life, but it was everything right now. For the second night in a row, he happily submitted and gave Chris control over him. Ciaran lay flat on his stomach.

Chris got off the bed and went to his bag, pulled out a small bottle of lubricant, and came back to sit on Ciaran's legs. He did the same routine he had the night before, massaging Ciaran's butt cheeks first, then inserting his fingers one at a time, but at a much faster pace. He used the lube liberally and made sure he got it all in there, first with his thumb, then with his index finger, then index and middle finger. Ciaran moaned, and he wasn't sure if it was out of pleasure or pain, but he didn't clench up once, which was a good sign.

He put lube, much silkier than oil, on himself and stroked himself while he fingered Ciaran. When he was ready, he opened Ciaran's cheeks and smoothly inserted himself inside. Ciaran moaned, but again did not tense up, and instead pushed back on Chris as he slid into his tight, but open, hole. Chris sighed and gave him one long stroke to see how deep he could go. Ciaran was still tight, but the lube helped more than the oil had, becoming slippery after a couple of slow strokes.

Once he was all the way in, Chris went to work. He stroked in and out, up and down, back and forth, sideways and circular, all for his own pleasure. He could tell which strokes Ciaran liked best based on his moaning, and Ciaran liked a direct up-and-down motion, whether fast or slow, as long as it hit that sweet center of his.

Chris was mostly focused on his own orgasm unlike yesterday, and he tapped Ciaran to move to a face-down, ass-up position, so he was able to go deeper. He pounded Ciaran with short strokes, increasing his speed as Ciaran buried his face in the pillow, held on, and moaned. As Chris began to feel the heat in his center, he did nothing to stop his orgasm, instead, he did the opposite and pounded harder. He barely made a sound as he exploded inside Ciaran, letting the shock waves go through his entire body before bringing him back down to reality again.

Ciaran, who was conscious of every feeling today more than he was yesterday, felt Chris's penis pulse and his warm cum coat his insides. He collapsed, taking Chris with him, then stretched his legs. Chris exited but lay on top of Ciaran, his soft groin getting softer by the minute sitting in the crack of Ciaran's ass, Chris's arms over Ciaran's, fingers entwined.

Neither spoke, feeling each other's heartbeats as they were thoughtful, Ciaran again wondering whether he was satisfactory, and Chris in bliss at what kept transpiring between them. They lay there for a while, neither wanting to break the silence or the moment.

Suddenly there was a vibrating sound and red sparks in the room. "Oh, *shit!!!*" Ciaran exclaimed and sprang up. Chris had to balance himself so he would not fall off the bed.

"I'm sorry. So sorry! It's an alert; something's wrong. I have to go!"

Ciaran dressed in record speed, leaving his t-shirt behind but jumping into his underwear and sweats, then into his work uniform. He started running toward the door, his *rodulé* still spitting out red sparks in his hand, then he ran back in and gave Chris a kiss.

"Tomorrow at 7 p.m. right?"

"Right," Chris said, bewildered.

He kissed him again and ran out, disappearing in the doorway.

CHAPTER 13

Nemo's

6:49 p.m.

Chris was ready. He felt surprisingly calm, none of the first date jitters he thought he would feel. He knew that Ciaran would probably be really nervous, and he wanted to put him at ease. He had already kicked Charity out and banned her from coming back until tomorrow. The house was spotless, especially his room where he had diffused some essential oils: lavender, Spanish rosemary, and lemon, his special combination for lovemaking. Almond oil and lube bottles were underneath his pillow in anticipation of what may happen after dinner and drinks.

Maybe I am a little romantic, he thought to himself with a smile.

6:59 p.m.

Ciaran appeared in front of the address he was given. He went up the stairs and realized he was looking at two doors and had no idea which door was Chris's. He moved from one side to the next, trying to decide which bell he should ring first, when the door on the left opened and Chris was standing there.

"Hello, hello," Chris said cheerily.

"Oh. Hi."

Chris reached behind his door to grab his leather jacket and scarf and stepped out. He led the way, and they walked about ten minutes quietly toward the riverfront, then turned a corner into the busiest part of the area. There were still a few shops open and well-lit restaurants.

Chris turned down the first alleyway to another smaller pub off the path. Ciaran immediately noticed the pride flag but also noted another flag: Brown, yellow, and black stripes with a bear's paw on the side. Ciaran was confused about what that flag was. In between the two flags was a sign that said, NEMO's, with a whale in the O. Chris opened the door and led him inside.

It was loud and looked like a sports bar filled with men. The first part had a long bar with stools on one side, two-seater tables around the other side, and a pathway in between that led to the back where tables and booths were for restaurant seating. There were TVs in the back as well as the front and a live football match was playing. Ciaran watched Chris nod at the bartender, a burly, hairy guy who pointed toward the back. Chris led him to the host.

"Chris, I heard you got yourself a table today," the host said with a smile.

"Don't worry, I'll go back to my regular bar stool by next week." He winked and the guy laughed, leading them to a booth.

It was crowded back there as well, but not nearly as loud as the front area. Tables and booths were filled with obvious dates, while others looked like two guys having a beer. Ciaran wondered what he and Chris looked like.

The waiter came over and Chris ordered some appetizers and beers. Before Ciaran started picking up the saltshaker nervously again, Chris started talking.

"So what happened last night with the," he lowered his voice, "red sparks thing?"

"Oh right," Ciaran said. "Ben and Anna. We'd been keeping them apart and somehow she broke free of her Tamers and woke Ben up, which made him very angry and they started fighting. They called me back to step in because Ben will only let me ride him since Jesse was out sick; that's his lead Tamer. Anyway, I got him to take flight and get out of there for a few hours."

Chris was amazed. "You. Ride. Dragons?" he whispered.

Ciaran smiled. "Well, yeah. It takes a lot of trust to build up for a dragon to allow you to ride, but once he or she does, it's the most amazing thing. Better than being cloaked."

"Cloaked?" he asked.

"Yes, we have certain cloaks that allow us to fly short distances. Farther out than a Wisp, which is approximately sixty kilometers on average. Some Magi can go longer. A cloak can get you up to two hundred kilometers or so."

"Whoa," Chris said in awe. "Do you have one?"

"Yes, but not here. Back home in Kingsbridge. I have no use for one here."

"Okay. But back to the dragons. How many of them trust you to ride them?" Chris asked.

"Right now, almost all of them. Hansel lets me ride him, but Hansel is easy, anyone can ride him. That's usually where we start dragon riding lessons, with Hansel. Then Kumoi until he died. I call Kumoi my first baby although he was well over thirteen hundred years old, I think, but he let me ride him, and then Hina. Ben and Anna were next and Ben never let anyone ride him but me for a while, until I did a warm hand-off with Jesse. Betta will only let me ride, no one else. I am trying to hand her off to Tommy, but Tommy is… well, awkward at times and she senses it. Only London I don't ride, but London won't let anyone touch him but Dale, let alone ride him. He has no Tamers, just a couple of Fixers who feed and monitor him."

"Tell me what that means, Tamers, Fixers? What's the difference? We never really talked about how it all works."

Ciaran smiled. Talking about the Reserve and dragons was the best way to put him at ease, and he knew Chris was doing that. "Everyone starts out on dung. We call them Dungers or Shitheads, naturally."

Chris laughed. "Naturally."

"All new recruits wear a special suit and go into the valley to schlep dragon dung and live in the barracks for a full year. They aren't allowed to interact with the dragons until they start training. Khalid is the Recruit Coordinator—that's the official name but we call him the Dung Coordinator, or Lead Shithead." They both chuckled. "Along with supervising their work, Khalid teaches them about the history of the Reserve, discipline, hard work, and teamwork. The dung gets packaged, sold, distributed, and shipped to Magi all around the world for gardening or elixirs or whatever else. It's how we make money to keep the Reserve afloat. Dungers also work the ground, keeping things clean, neat, and orderly.

"As early as six months, they can join the trainee line if Khalid feels they are ready, but he can keep them there as long as he feels necessary. Technically, when they start, they're trainees, but they still schlep dung until they become a Fixer, so they are still Shitheads to everyone else. A Fixer is someone who works closely with the dragons, taking care of all their needs, what every Dunger aspires to become. Sven teaches the trainees about how to relate and tame dragons, and perfects their incantations. I'm his Assistant Trainer and the Senior Lead Tamer, and I teach them dragon safety, and to respect the dragons. With me, is the first time the trainees really get close to them and only under my watch. I do it in small groups at dusk when they are at their calmest.

"Sarah, our Lead Novo—that's like a healer or a medicine keeper—takes the trainees early in the morning to go over healing potions, tonics, herbs, and how to care for dragons. And all three of us kind of haze them a bit, see what they are made of. They can stay trainees and Dungers for up to three years, or until Sven or Dale or I decide they can move up to becoming Fixers, or Bruno picks his Hunters or Sarah picks them for Novos. But they have to do at least one full year of training under Sven, Sarah, and I before we can move them into paid positions, the Fixers."

"Wait, so they are schlepping shit for anywhere between one to three years, maybe longer, before they even get to touch a dragon, and they don't get paid for it!??" Chris asked incredulously.

"No," Ciaran said definitively. "You don't come to the Reserve for the money. You come for the dragons."

Chris thought about it. "Okay, yes. I see that. You wouldn't have to pay me either for a chance to be near a dragon. And then get to care and ride them? Yeah, I'd be schlepping shit too." Ciaran laughed. "So then you pick them to become Fixers. What do they do exactly?"

"Basically, they care for all the dragons collectively. They make sure the dragons get fed breakfast, lunch, and dinner, their area is clean so they don't get diseases, play games with them or take them airborne so they get exercise and enough sun, monitor their naps so they aren't sleeping too much or too little; really just whatever they need to make sure their lives are comfortable and happy. They do this with all the dragons until they get assigned to just one. But they might not ever get assigned to one, or they might choose not to be assigned to one but to have a relationship with all of them. That was Tommy before I assigned him Betta."

"So Tommy now controls Betta," said Chris.

Ciaran shook his head slowly. "You do not control a dragon. No one controls them. The mistake that people make, especially those who want to use dragons to do harm, is thinking they can control any dragon, even the Class A ones. We are cultivating a trusting relationship with the dragons so that we can care for their needs and they can live a better life. But the valley and the mountains are their domain. And we must never forget that."

"Wow." Chris continued to be fascinated by this world. They quieted as the appetizers had arrived and they dug in. They waited until the waiter was completely gone before Chris started asking more questions. "So, how quickly did you move up?"

"Pretty quickly," Ciaran said. "We all did. Khalid and Sahid, the twin brothers, Jesse, Felix, and I all started the same year at Campus. Together we joined the Magi military, *Conditus* division, which is special forces, and learned advanced combat and tactical *Vis*. And then the five of us left at nineteen and came to the Reserve together. I learned all I could from Rufus, the Dung Coordinator. before Khalid took over three years ago, and in six months, we were all tapped to begin training. But then we all went in different directions. Felix went over with Sarah and became a Novo and gardener, then her second-in-command Novo. Sahid went under Bruno and became a Hunter, which surprised a lot of us except his brother, obviously. You would think they would both want to be as close to the dragons as possible. Hunters are the complete opposite; they stay out in the woods, gather food for the dragons, and operate like security for the Reserve. They will also kill a dragon without a second thought if they need to, to protect the life of a fellow Reserver or human."

"Wow! I mean, I get it, but... wow."

Ciaran nodded. "Bruno leads them and he will kill a human for shits and giggles. Fucking arsehole," he grumbled.

Chris laughed. "So you won't be sharing beers any time soon?"

Ciaran glared at him, making Chris chuckle. "Bruno hates me. And I equally hate him. And that's the way it will always be between us."

"Hmm... Okay. Duly noted," Chris responded. He asked, "So where did your other friends go? Khalid stayed with dung the whole time?"

"Well, no, he went on to become a Lead Tamer. Then Rufus was having health problems and wanted to retire, so he trained under him on all the Dung Operations and took over. Jesse and myself are still Lead Tamers."

"Obviously, you were assigned to Kumoi when you first became a Fixer, then a Tamer."

"Not right away, but yes, he took a liking to me early for some reason, maybe because of my red hair that matched his red skin. I was a Fixer by the time I was twenty, and put under Kumoi, and was his second-in-command Tamer until he died. Then I was Ben's Lead Tamer until right before I went away for a year, and when I came back, I switched to our Betta. Or, better said, no one could tame her but me, so I took over and handpicked my second-in-command Tamer and three Fixers."

"Tommy's your second, then. Your son."

Ciaran laughed. "Yes. It was time. He's only twenty-two himself, but yes, he's kind of been under me since he got on the Reserve at seventeen. He's always either saying or doing awkward shit, or he's hyper and annoying. But he's a good lad."

The waiter came back and took their orders. The skinny blond man said to Chris, "So, does this mean it's over between you and me?" He winked at Ciaran.

Chris laughed. "It never started, Twink." The waiter laughed out loud and walked away.

"Twink?" Ciaran asked.

"His real name is Roel, but they call him Twink because... well, look at him."

"I don't get it," Ciaran said, confused.

Chris chuckled. "Okay, here's your crash course on gay stereotypical titles for males, mostly based on looks and body types. You're ready?"

Ciaran chuckled back. "Okay."

"We have Bears, Jocks, Otters, Twinks, Drags, Daddies, Hunks, Chubbs, Muscles, Femmes, and, err... I guess Transgender males. They're men, too."

Ciaran laughed. "Holy shit."

"Yes." Chris laughed with him. "Not all gays are alike."

"It's a whole world I've never been privy to," said Ciaran.

"Sort of like me and your Magi world, I assume," Chris said back.

"Too right," Ciaran agreed. "So, where do you fall in?"

Chris smiled. "I don't believe in labels."

Ciaran laughed. "Naturally."

Chris laughed as well. "Plus, I'm not gay; I told you, I'm pansexual. Men excite me. Women excite me. People excite me." He shrugged.

Ciaran asked, "So I know what the pride flag is, but what's the other flag on the entrance?"

"It's the Bear flag. Nemo," Chris pointed to the bartender, "is the owner with his partner Richard. He's a Bear—big, burly, hairy gay man. Richard was a Twink—really thin, young-looking gay man with no hair anywhere—but he's put on some weight. They are complete opposites, 14-year age difference, but they have been together for over twenty years. This is the only males-only gay bar in this part of Albania. It's a place specifically for men to be in the company of other like-minded men. Sometimes patrons side-eye fem-boys and transgender males if they are too flamboyant, which I think is stupid, but whatever, I don't own the place. When I feel like I just want a place to hang out, I come here. When I want to be around everyone else on the Kinsey scale, I have other spots."

Ciaran nodded slowly, smiling. "Can't wait to experience all that with you."

Chris smiled. "And I can't wait to ride a dragon with you!" he whispered excitedly.

Ciaran laughed. "Highly unlikely." Chris pouted playfully. Then Ciaran said, "We're not going to run into an ex of yours here, right?"

Chris laughed. "Highly unlikely. I don't shite where I eat. At least not anymore."

It was Ciaran's turn to be fascinated as Chris talked about this world he knew nothing about. He had been introduced to Nemo's by his friend Rem when he was 16 and had been coming there ever since. Nemo had been like a father figure to him, where he came for advice about relationships or just being pansexual in general. They moved on to other topics. Their food came, and they ate and talked. It had always been easy for them to relate to one another, and tonight reminded Ciaran of that.

Toward the end of their meal, three men came in talking about the game yesterday, Chelsea versus Manchester United, and Ciaran's ears perked up being a Manchester United fan himself. They argued loudly and Ciaran found himself chiming in. Soon they were all talking and arguing so loudly about the penalty shot that turned the game around that Nemo himself had to come into the dining area.

"Shut up and watch it. We recorded it," Nemo announced. Everyone cheered.

He turned the TV on and suddenly all of the TVs in Nemo's showed the same game. Ciaran, who had gravitated toward the center of it all, looked back to find Chris toward the back, standing and talking with the waiter named Roel called Twink.

He mouthed to him, "This okay?" Chris nodded and raised his glass. Ciaran smiled and turned back to his new football friends.

By the time the game was over, it was nearly midnight, and Ciaran was a little drunk and singing his football club songs. He looked around and didn't see Chris at first. As he moved through the crowd to find him, another tall blond-haired man grabbed his hand and started flirting with him. "If you aren't here with anyone, Manchester, take me home with you," the man said seductively.

Ciaran's eyes went wide, and he froze. He actually had never been hit on by a man before and did not know how to handle it. Before he could think of a response, he felt an arm around his waist from behind him and heard Chris say, "He's here with me."

The guy moved on. Ciaran was again taken aback by how easy and good it felt to have Chris take control. He also realized this was the first time Chris had touched him all night. It sent a chill through him.

"Are you ready to go?" Chris asked, still holding onto Ciaran's waist.

"Yeah," Ciaran responded.

They grabbed their jackets. Chris shook Nemo's hand on the way out and they stepped into the cold night.

CHAPTER 14

Arcanos Susurros

12:03 a.m.

On the way to Chris's house, Ciaran absentmindedly reached for Chris's hand, and entwined in their fingers, wanting to touch him. Chris felt warmth in his chest at how sweet the gesture was, but said nothing and held on. There was hardly anyone in the road as they walked in silence. The cool air felt good on Ciaran's face; he had not realized how hot it had been in there. He also realized he was a little tipsier than he wanted to be. But he felt good just being with Christopher.

When they got to his steps, Chris turned to Ciaran and asked, "Are you coming in tonight?"

Ciaran was surprised at the question. "Of course," he responded automatically.

Chris nodded and led him inside. They entered a short hallway, where Chris took off his jacket and shoes and Ciaran followed suit. They walked into the open living room, dining room, and kitchen area. Ciaran took off his sweater, leaving on his long-sleeved shirt, and took off his socks, then sat on the arm of the couch, but found himself sliding inside it.

Chris went to the kitchen while Ciaran got a good look at his place. The wall unit in the living room consisted of a large TV and stereo underneath it and bookshelves on the side. Ciaran rose out of the chair to get a closer look. There were textbooks and journals about wildlife and forestry, and dystopian novels like *The Hunger Games*, *Divergent Series*, *Lord of the Rings*, and *Children of Blood and Bone*. He also had a section of movies, with a whole row of Disney cartoon movies. Ciaran reminded himself to tell Chris that Walt Disney was a Magus.

There were pictures in the unit above the TV, so Ciaran stood up and went to look at them: A picture of an attractive dark-brown-skinned woman and an equally attractive white man who Ciaran assumed were Chris's parents in their youth; and a photo of two women mid-laugh, one very light-skinned with curly black hair in a ponytail, the other more brown-skinned like Chris's complexion. The latter could have been Chris's twin sister, the former a lighter version of Chris's mother.

Both women were astonishingly beautiful. Chris's almost twin had hazel eyes, the same as his father. Her hair was in a headband pulled far from her face, and her curly hair was kinkier like Chris's, standing up in contrast to her sister's falling straight down. He realized as he stared at her photo how truly attractive Chris was. He looked over at Chris making tea and smiled. He turned his attention back to his sisters and noticed both of them had the same small black mole on their faces, the lighter one on her nose, and Chris's twin on her left cheek, again identical to Chris. Ciaran could have looked at these two women all day, but he moved on to other pictures.

There was a picture of a small child he assumed was Chris's nephew as a baby, as right next to it was a school-aged boy in a picture, probably taken recently. An old track team photo, Chris in the center. Another photo of a blond-haired guy and a brown-haired girl, with Chris again in the middle, his arms around both of them. A picture of a dog.

Ciaran walked over to the kitchen area just as Chris was pouring the two cups. "How do you take it?"

"Milk, two sugars."

Chris made the two cups and handed one over to Ciaran. They stood side by side and sipped. Ciaran, who was feeling less inhibited, heard the words tumbling out before he could stop them. "Why haven't you touched me all night?"

Chris's eyes went wide, and he looked over, half startled, half smiling. "What?"

Well, I might as well continue, inebriated Ciaran told himself. "I just meant, other than holding my hand just now, you barely touched me all night. Not even…"

He wanted to say, a kiss, but stopped himself. Chris put his cup down on the counter and moved to stand in front of Ciaran. He was reminded that he was taller than Ciaran as he put his hands on his waist.

"I didn't realize I hadn't. But I guess you're right. I don't know why. Maybe I just wanted you to be comfortable and I don't know where you fall with public displays of affection." He leaned closer, putting their foreheads together. "But I'm touching you now."

Ciaran put his cup down, lifted his hands to Chris's neck, and initiated the kiss between them. It was soft and warm and tasted of tea for both of them. Chris moved his hand to the lower part of Ciaran's back and pulled him closer. They kissed softly and sweetly. Chris broke it off first.

"Come on," he said and took Ciaran's hand to lead him to the back bedroom. He closed the door and turned to face Ciaran.

Before Chris could come closer, Ciaran took out his *rodulé*, pointed it upward, and said, *"Arcanos susurros."*

A stream of yellow sparkles went from the tip of his wand to the ceiling, and it spread out like ripples. It coated the entire ceiling and all the way down the four walls to the floor, then connected again underneath their feet before it disappeared. Chris watched in awe, aware that this was the first time he had actually seen Ciaran do magic with his wand, save for his duel with the bad warlock.

"Whaaat was thaaaat?" he said, still astounded as he looked around.

"It's Latin for Secret Whispers. Noise is contained right here."

"To soundproof the room from loud noises coming out?" Chris asked. He gave Ciaran a knowing look.

Ciaran shrugged. "In case we need it. I know you have family upstairs."

Chris came closer to Ciaran, took off his shirt, and put his hand on the center of his bare chest to feel his heartbeat. He stepped back, took off his own shirt and tank top, and came forward to embrace him, chest to chest. They held each other for a long moment, open to the possibility of where the journey would lead them, no longer afraid because they would sojourn it together.

Chris let go first. Ciaran watched Chris unbuckle his jeans, and Ciaran started to do the same. They left their clothes on the floor and Chris backed Ciaran up to the bed.

Ciaran sat down first, then scooted topside. Chris followed him, crawling in between his legs, and kissed his lips.

When Ciaran made it to the pillows, he lay down and Chris leaned over him, licked the inside of his mouth and neck, then moved farther down to kiss his chest and lick his nipples. He used his tongue to travel downward to his navel and the tip of his member as Ciaran moaned. Chris put his mouth on Ciaran's penis and sucked and licked gently, then he moved farther down to his balls and licked him gently there. He could tell he was driving Ciaran crazy by his moaning, erratic breathing, and the way he was squirming. His plan was to drive Ciaran even crazier.

Chris lay flat on his belly on the bed between Ciaran's legs and lifted his thighs all the way up so that Ciaran's knees were in his chest. "Hold them up for me, will you?" he said softly, and Ciaran did.

Chris licked his lips first, then gently licked the outside of Ciaran's anus. Ciaran let out an "oooooohh shit!" Chris did it again and again, then put his mouth on his hole and tongue kissed it like he tongued Ciaran. Ciaran's moans got louder and louder.

Chris put two fingers in and pulled them out, licked some more until Ciaran said breathlessly, "Unless... aah... you want me... to aaah... burst..."

Chris smiled. "Reach under the pillow and pass me the lube," he said, and he raised himself up to a seated position.

Ciaran laid his legs down and grabbed the lube to hand to him. Chris lubed himself and lifted Ciaran's legs up again, but wider this time, and lay in between him to enter him. Ciaran, still not used to this feeling, gasped, then moaned as Chris entered him fully in one motion. Chris would give a few slow strokes, kiss him, then give a few more strokes.

Facing Ciaran was new for both of them, and he loved watching Ciaran's face scrunch up in pleasure.

Without stopping his steady strokes Chris moved Ciaran's right leg over to the left and kept thrusting into him sideways, then decided Ciaran needed to turn all the way around and pulled out to position him on his stomach, making Ciaran gasp again at the emptiness. It was only for a moment, as Chris reentered him and fucked him hard from behind.

The sound of ass slapping cheeks and Ciaran's loud "ah ah ah" were driving Chris mad with ecstasy, but he knew he didn't want to come just yet. He again motioned for Ciaran to flip to his back and put a pillow underneath him. Chris pushed Ciaran's legs back into his knees and grabbed his waist to fuck him hard and fast, then slow and circular, then hard and fast again.

Ciaran's mouth was a frozen o as he moaned and Chris started talking dirty. "You like this cock? I know now. Love this prick fucking your tight muscle arse."

And Ciaran, amazingly found himself agreeing, "Yeeeeessss... fuck yeeeeessss..."

Chris changed Ciaran's position once more, putting his legs on his shoulders, and fucked him hard and fast again with a purpose. Beads of sweat on Chris's forehead dripped down the side of his face, while a trail of sweat went from Ciaran's neck down his chest. Ciaran again tried to keep up by jerking himself off, but it was too late. The pressure had already built up and Chris came hard with a grunt, filling Ciaran up. He gave himself a moment to regain his thoughts, but he was far from done. Chris was incredibly horny.

He pulled out, found the lube, and coated Ciaran's cock before he got on top, surprising Ciaran completely, and positioned himself over him. They both groaned with pleasure as Chris slid all the way down until he was seated in Ciaran's lap. He looked down at Ciaran and smiled widely, and Ciaran found himself smiling widely as well. Chris leaned over him, holding himself up by his arms, and started moving and gyrating his hips back and forth.

Ciaran immediately felt the tight grip on his cock, shuddered, and yelled out, "FUCK!" No woman had ever ridden him like that. Nevertheless, he knew what to do: he held Chris's bottom with both hands, but allowed him to dictate all of it. Chris riding his dick was the best thing to ever happen to him in his entire life, he suddenly decided.

Chris could feel Ciaran stiffen completely inside of him and the more he grew, the harder he ground against his prostate. He moved back and forth faster, purposely hitting his spot over and over until he felt the orgasm he was waiting for. He closed his eyes and let out a low groan as his anal orgasm sent spasms through his body over and over again. He couldn't stop; Ciaran made it so easy to rub against his spot and he kept hitting it over and over again climaxing until his untouched penis exploded on Ciaran's stomach with translucent cum.

Chris's orgasm had him clenching so hard that he knew Ciaran was going to release. Ciaran held Chris's waist down and pushed his own midsection as far up as it could go as he came inside of Chris, making Chris cry out from the pain and pleasure of having all of Ciaran fill all of him up. Chris rolled off him and moved to his side, putting his head between Ciaran's arm on his upper shoulder.

Ciaran, once again, could not believe all that had transpired. Three days ago, he was basically a virgin in all this, and now he was literally getting flipped around and fucked sideways. He started laughing, and Chris, on cue, started laughing as well.

When it died down, Chris said, "I wish we had gotten some water for this journey we just went on."

"Do you have a glass here?" Ciaran asked.

"On the dresser." Chris pointed.

Ciaran sat up and reached out his hand, calling out, "*Cedo.*" The cup rose from the dresser and flew into Ciaran's hand. He circled the glass rim with his finger and said, "*Sitio.*" The glass filled with water. He took a sip, then handed it to Chris, who had sat up.

"That's literally the most magic you personally have ever done in front of me, Gandalf," said Chris, astonished.

Ciaran shrugged. "No reason to hold myself back now. You licked my arsehole."

Chris broke out in loud laughter. He drank the water, then said, "I thought you needed your *rodulé* to do magic."

"Technically, you don't," Ciaran said. "The magic is inside of us. The *rodulé* is a conduit to ensure the magic gets channeled properly. Many people aren't able to tap into the magic without it, because that's what they have been taught, that they need it to be powerful."

"But you can?"

"Well, Sean and I learned a few tricks on our travels. There are many people, nations, and cultures around the world who have never touched or created a *rodulé* and have powerful magic, so we learned from a few of them. But I barely scratched the surface. I can make things come to me from a short distance, so I perfected retrieving my *rodulé* above all else, as long as it's close by. And to retrieve water at all times."

Chris passed the glass back to Ciaran, who drank again, then he stared at it and slowly let go of the glass. It hovered in front of him. "*Expletus,*" Ciaran said softly. The glass traveled back to the dresser along with his *rodulé.*

"Why Latin?" Chris asked with interest. "There are millions of other languages in the world. But magic and Latin seem to go together, even in the fantasy books."

"Don't really know," Ciaran said with another shrug. "I never went into Scholarly to learn all the ancient secrets. Scholarly is what we would consider higher education after Campus is completed at age sixteen. Historians and researchers of the *Vis* are there and some never leave. Think of a combination between a university and a medical facility, that's Scholarly. It's separate from our Magi Council, the ones who decide our laws and regulations, monitoring magical trends, but often they work together in the Magi community. I just know that at some point Latin was considered the common tongue in more established societies and that is what was taught at Campus. But again, traveling around the world helped us to understand anyone's common tongue will suffice. It's about the intention behind the words. I could have said, 'I thirst,' instead of '*Sitio*,' and the outcome would have been the same. But the language is ingrained in me."

"Fascinating," Chris responded.

Ciaran smiled and pulled Chris back down in the same position, Ciaran on his back and Chris in the corner of his arm and shoulder. They lay in silence, feeling comfortable in each other's arms.

CHAPTER 15

Chris's First Time

Ciaran's mind was swimming, and he needed to ask some questions. "Chris, can I ask you a few things ... about ... sex?"

"Of course," said Chris, wondering.

"I'm just curious... where you learned it all. Clearly, you are more experienced than I am. I mean... the blow job was ... fucking *incredible*. I'm not just saying that. Fucking. Incredible. We've talked about sex, but not about you, not really." He paused. "You weren't bragging. You've had many partners. I know this now."

Chris sighed, then moved outside of Ciaran's arm to lay on his back on the bed and stared at the ceiling. Ciaran immediately reached for him, putting his hand on his chest.

"No judgment at all," said Ciaran softly. "I'm pretty sure my brother has slept with over a hundred women at this point, so I'm not going to be shocked or scared away by anything you tell me. I just want to know you, understand all of you." He kissed the part of Chris's skin that was closest to his mouth.

Chris was silent for a few moments, and Ciaran waited. Then he sat up and started talking. "You have to understand that when I lost my mum, I kind of lost my mind too for a time. I just needed to feel anything other than grief. So the next couple of years after that I slept with ... a lot of people. Mostly women, if you can believe that."

"I believe it," Ciaran said, again thinking how incredibly attractive he was.

"So there were a lot of one-night stands. A handful of relationships along the way, but none I took seriously. I picked up a few things, what works for one person, what works for another one, and I learned to read body language. I can always feel when someone is about to cum. It's like I almost feel their energy. So anyway, that's why I'm so good at it, I guess. I've had time to practice and perfect my skills."

Ciaran gave him a reassuring squeeze. "How many actual relationships?"

"Hmmm... A girlfriend and a boyfriend in high school at the same time..."

Ciaran laughed. "Naturally," he said, making Chris laugh as well.

He continued, "Rem, who was... I don't know if I could even call it a relationship, but it was my longest partnership thus far. We're always on and off. Then a summer fling, right before Uni, with a beautiful Irish boy with black hair and emerald eyes. I was seventeen and Jack was two years younger than me, so I taught him more than he taught me. But he definitely taught me about the simplicity of ... love. Then in college two women, two men, not at the same time... I think? No, Nico and Samara were before my mum died. Abu and Natalis were after. Natalis was my longest relationship, almost three years, and I thought she was going to be the one, but she wanted a commitment that I wasn't ready to give. I was cheating on her left and right, so I never took our relationship seriously. I was an arsehole and broke her heart, repeatedly. That's probably my biggest regret; I should have let her go a long time ago.

"After that, I slowed down and focused on my work and my career. Still dealing with Rem until he disappeared on me or cut me off like he always did. Then I met Onyeka, the prettiest thing you'd ever lay eyes on. Her mother was from the UK, her father was African American and Japanese, and she was bisexual. I met her in a club and it started out as a one-night stand that we just couldn't let go of. She matched my sexual energy, and she loved threesomes. Her favorite thing was to watch me get fucked by a man while she masturbated, then I would fuck her right after."

"Whoa," Ciaran said with wide eyes. "She sounds like someone right up your alley. What happened?"

"What always happens." Chris shrugged. "She wanted more. She wanted me to meet her army dad and English mum. She was in love. I was ... enamored and comfortable." Chris shrugged again. "That's not true. I think I did love her. But she wasn't my ... person, my forever, you know what I mean? So after about a year and a half, she got tired of waiting and we got into a huge fight about whether we were moving in together and that was that."

Ciaran reached up and caressed Chris's nipple with two fingers. "And then Rem again?"

"If we're talking relationships? And then you." Chris pulled him closer and rubbed Ciaran's back.

Ciaran was quiet for a moment, then asked, "Who is Rem to you?"

Chris tensed. He did not want to talk or think about Rem; it always brought out a range of emotions. But then he sighed and decided to tell his best friend.

"Remington was … my first real male sexual partner and a dominating arsehole. Someone who every time I try to wash my hands of him, he comes crawling back to my hole, literally. And like an idiot, I let him in."

That scared Ciaran a little to hear, but he didn't let on. Instead, he asked casually, "Is it over?"

"It has to be," said Chris in a hollow voice. "It is emotionally detrimental to my health." Ciaran did not like that answer, and Chris could tell by how quiet he got. He began rubbing Ciaran's arm. "It's been almost a year since I've seen or slept with him," Chris said reassuringly. "I don't think about him at all."

Ciaran was quiet for a few moments. "Tell me about your first time," Ciaran said.

"Why?"

"Because I want to know."

Chris laughed. "It was awful."

But Ciaran didn't let it go. He needed to know before he got any deeper with Chris how deep Chris was in with Rem. He wanted to know everything. "Tell me. How did you meet him?"

"Oh, well… that." Chris took a moment, then said, "He was a 25-year-old coach of a rival school's track team. I was fifteen."

Ciaran's eyes bulged, but he didn't say anything. Chris continued.

"There aren't a lot of African people in Albania, in case you didn't notice. So when you see each other, it's like an instant connection. I was the fastest on the four-way relay. Rem approached me after the meet; a dark chocolate, brown-skinned, baldheaded man. He said he wanted to train me personally. He came by my house and introduced himself to my parents and put together a training schedule for me.

Dad loved the idea, but Mum always said there was something that she couldn't put her finger on about him. But, of course, I begged to have this gorgeous brown godlike man train me. I did have a girlfriend at the time and we were doing it. Jesika was who I actually lost my virginity to just a couple of months before meeting Rem. But I had not been penetrated by a male, so naturally I had all kinds of fantasies of this being more than just training.

"But for the first few months, that's all it was. I was in training every day, two afternoons a week with my own school track team, three nights a week with Rem. He pushed me to my limits and made me better, disciplined me, no more junk food or pot, weight training, endurance training, all of it. I never thought he looked at me as anything other than his pupil until one night I was running and caught a charley horse. After yelling at me about how I wasn't hydrating enough or eating clean enough, he sat me down in the middle of the empty field and massaged my calf. Then went up to massage my thigh, then through my shorts to massage my cock. I was shocked, but he looked me right in the eyes the whole time he was doing it, daring me to say something. I was scared and excited and I didn't last long at all. He then put his mouth on me and licked it clean. I didn't even know people did shit like that at the time. Then he told me to go home, just like that. I thought about it all night and ended up rubbing another one out, as my fantasy just came true.

"When I saw him again two days later, he never acknowledged it, just business as usual and put me on the track. But two hours later, at the end of practice, he says, 'Tell your parents that you're coming to Tirana to the campus for the whole weekend. I need to see you on a real track.' I knew immediately something was going to go down, but I played it cool, gave them the story he gave me. Dad didn't flinch. Mum said okay, but her eyebrows were raised."

"Were you still fifteen?" Ciaran asked.

"No, it was late November, so I had just turned sixteen by that time," Chris said casually.

Ciaran nodded slowly, although inside he was screaming in rage for him. But let Chris continue.

"Rem picked me up Friday after school and took me to his off-campus apartment. He taught physical education classes at the university as well, so he had access to their facilities. As soon as we got there, we dropped off my bag and headed to the field to train for a few hours, then headed back. I was starting to think nothing was going to happen at all. But then he ordered pasta, surprising me because that's junk food to him, and we brought it back to the room. Then he started asking me personal questions that in the two months I'd known him he'd never bothered to ask: Do I have a girlfriend? Yes. Do we have sex? Yes. Have I given her anal? No. Does she do blow jobs? Not really. Have I ever had a real blow job? Yes. With my boyfriend. I volunteered that info. But no anal? No. So he asked if I had ever given a blow job. Yes. Then he said, 'Give me a blow job.' And I agreed, but I probably should have asked to see it first. One, it was the biggest, blackest thing I have ever seen, and two, I was out of practice being that my boyfriend had left the country five months before that. So it ended up with me on my knees until I gagged and thew up pasta chunks everywhere."

"Aaaaaah, Chris!" Ciaran exclaimed. "That sounds awful."

"Oh it was," he said. "And just wait, it's just going to get worse from here on. He made me clean my shit up, wash my mouth, and do it again on my knees." Ciaran's eyes went wide again as Chris nodded at him. "I knew better than to gag the second time around. When he came, he pulled out of my mouth and came on my face, then put it back in my mouth so I could taste it, then told me to go to bed without washing my face off and that we had training at 5 a.m."

"What. The. Fuck." Ciaran could not close his mouth.

"Hold on there, Ciaran, this story is far from over," he said sadly. "So, Saturday morning he made me blow him again, then we went on a 7k run. We stopped for breakfast, came back to the flat and he told me to take a shower. When I came out, he had me lay down, and he blew me and it was fucking amazing, but also kind of mechanical. Also, he wouldn't let me cum in his mouth, just all over myself. Then he told me not to get dressed but to wait for him and went to take this ridiculously long shower. He comes out and rubs baby oil on his body, stroking himself and he's all chocolaty and glistening, so I'm stroking myself, too, thinking, okay, this is it, this is going to be fantastic.

"He turns me over on all fours and starts eating my arse and now I'm hard all over again and so open and this is the closest he has come to actually kissing me, so there's that. So he fingers me a little, licks me a lot, and maybe he thought that would be enough because then he just rubbed baby oil on my bum, rubbed a little on his cock, and just tried to slide it in like I wasn't a fucking anal virgin. I screamed so loud and scooted away from him. He was calm and said, 'What the fuck are you doing? This is going to happen, so get your arse back here.' So I did, but now I was scared of the pain. He added more oil and ...''

Chris sighed. "It was fucking awful. I had real tears streaming down my face. Once he got the head in, it was better, not great, but it didn't burn like fire. He fucked me until he came and I was bleeding a little. He had me clean myself up and rest. I fell asleep, woke up some hours later, and he ordered more food. This was to appease me, I know, but I didn't care."

Ciaran was stunned. He was beside himself at how much of a predator and asshole Rem was. But he said nothing.

"After we ate he was like, 'You ready to go again?' I sure as fuck wasn't, but I wasn't going to tell him that. By that point, I knew that his asks were really commands. So we did it again. It hurt just as bad, but it went easier. And I learned that the less I tensed, the less it hurt, so I tried to just relax and take it and I started feeling it a little, but it still was more pain and roughness than I was expecting, and it just fucking sucked. It didn't help that it took him longer to come that time, either. Then he went to take a shower, leaving me to question if I even still liked men after all this. He sends me to take a shower and then we go walking around campus. I didn't even know how I was walking, my bum hurt so badly. I didn't know what we were talking about, either. I just remember thinking, *It cannot be this bad all the time, no man would do this ever.*

"We stopped, had dinner, came back to the room, and I was terrified we were going to do it again. But instead, he put in a porn video and gave me a beer, told me to watch. This wasn't my first time seeing men sexing other men in a porno and I was completely aroused again. I watched it with different eyes. I noticed all of the sensuality of it and realized I wasn't getting any of that. I saw him watching me and somehow I found my voice. I said to him, 'Can you slow down the next time, please? This is not fun for me.' He laughed, but then he said, 'Okay.'

"He came over to me and kissed me for the first time, played with my nipples, and stroked my dick like he actually liked me. He started giving me a blow job, but I told him I didn't want to cum that way. So he pushed my knees up to my chest, lubed up, and entered me instead. It was the first time I wasn't on all fours like a dog in heat. He did it slowly, and it was less painful than the first two times combined. His strokes were gentler, and I started to feel real pleasure in all this. I was able to relax and take it without crying and pay attention to what I was feeling. When he moved faster, not as hard as before but not slow either, every time he hit my prostate I thought, *Okay now I get why men do this.* And when he came, I felt all of it, from his swell to his pulsating release and then my guts all warming up. I thought, *Fuck yeah, I like this shit.*" Chris laughed, and Ciaran smiled faintly.

"The next morning he woke me up, and it was slow and the gentlest he had been with me so far, holding me, kissing my neck. It was just a nice morning, you know? We got up and did a 7k and actually stopped at the track to train for the rest of the morning. We did it one more time in the afternoon, this time with him in a chair and me riding top, and I was able to control my own pace, speed, everything. That was incredible, and I experienced my first anal O with ejaculation. My entire body was sore by the time he took me home. I didn't even go to school the next day; I just pretended, then came back home, soaked in the tub, and slept the day away. The next Tuesday, it was business as usual. I thought he was going to invite me back up that weekend, but he didn't. I ended up sleeping with Jesika all weekend out of frustration, confusing myself the whole time because I really liked doing that, too.

"Rem would invite me up once a month to train and I looked forward to those weekends. I found my voice more, managed to tell him what I needed, and he begrudgingly complied. I wrestled for months on what I liked more, being with him or Jess, and then I just decided I didn't want to choose. Being inside a woman is amazing. Having a man inside me is incredible. When I was 17, after my first trip to the States to see my dad's side of the family and fooled around with girls and boys there, I just decided I liked it all. I told my mum, she said, 'Of course you are,' so matter of factly. I told Sis, and she said, 'Great, now we can compare notes on cock sucking.' I told Clary, and she said, 'Don't tell Dad.' So none of us did.

"Anyway, it continued in college with Rem and I thought since I was now going to school in Tirana that it was going to be easier to meet and it was going to be a real relationship. But it was just more of the same. He would invite me over once a month for sex and train me three days a week, nothing in between that. So I started seeing others and having other experiences, Nico, during freshman year for a couple of months, some others until I started being exclusive with Samara, a trans woman, then Rem popped back into my life. I told him nope, I was with a cool chick that was comfortable with me and I with her, and it was all good for a few months.

"Then we got the news that Mum was sick and then she died. And instead of going to Samara, I disappeared from everyone and ended up at Rem's flat for about a month. I let him fuck me and degrade me any way he wanted to until he got bored and kicked me out. I broke up with Samara and started fucking ... everybody, really. I tried to settle with Natalis, but I told you how that ended up. After that I ran into Rem at Nemo's one night; I hadn't seen him since I graduated from Uni and he was with this twink and I couldn't help but to go over there and taunt him. He took me into the bathroom and fucked me with his toy at the bar. After that, we fell back into our old ways again, but now I was bottoming for him weekly instead of monthly for a few months until he got bored of me again.

"When I met Onyeka, she was giving me so much and I realized I didn't want the scraps that Rem was offering me anymore. I went to his place to tell him it was over. He held me hostage for 24 hours, fucked me hard, beat me down, and when I was allowed to leave, he told me I would be back. When Onyeka and I broke up, I had no intention of going back to Rem, but we ended up seeing each other at Nemo's on some random night. And like an idiot glutton for punishment, I followed him back to his place and let him dominate me. But it really got to me afterward, him gloating. 'I told you you would be back. I'm all you got,' he said. And I thought, *Fuck him. There has got to be something out there better than this shite.* And then I said those same words to him, and I meant it when I walked out of his door. That was eight months ago."

Ciaran was speechless. The only thing he could say was, "What a bloody arsehole."

Chris laughed. "Too right you are."

"Chris..." Ciaran tried to find the right words. "You don't feel like Rem took advantage of your age and vulnerability?"

"No," Chris said. "I told you, I fantasized about him. He was what I wanted at the time. I just didn't know how dominant and controlling he was. If I had known that, I wouldn't have willingly walked into that situation."

"But... you were fifteen. Fifteen. Did you *willingly* walk into it?" Ciaran was trying to get Chris to see what he understood about the dynamics of their so-called relationship and Rem's sexual grooming of him.

But Chris didn't. "Yeah, I did," he said confidently. "I figured out as I got older we had this Dom/sub relationship going on. But I chose to go back every time."

Ciaran decided to let that part go for now. But he asked, "Do you love him?"

Chris's eyes went wide. "Love? As in currently? No. I'm not even sure if love is what we ever had. Maybe I did when I was much younger. Infatuation, more like it. But if I did love him, I have not for a very long time."

Ciaran was quiet again, then asked softly, "Do you miss him?"

Chris thought about it. "Sometimes," he said honestly. "But not right now." He kissed Ciaran's head.

"So now I understand why you were so afraid to have a go at me," Ciaran said. "You were afraid I would have the same horrible experience."

Chris shook his head as he spoke. "There was no way I would ever hurt you like that. Or anyone. But especially not you."

"You wouldn't," said Ciaran. "Definitely not in that way that you were hurt. Not with another consenting adult." He paused and waited for Chris to get it. Chris stared at him blankly. Ciaran sighed. "And for the record, you were gentle and thoughtful and patient and loving. I felt pleasure from the first moments and today there was no pain, just you."

Ciaran moved his face closer and kissed Chris sweetly. Chris returned the sweet kiss. "I have another question," said Ciaran. "How come you haven't asked me to blow you?"

Chris laughed. "Dunno. I figured we'd get there when you were ready. It's no big deal to me."

Ciaran didn't believe him for one second. "But it is. It's something you like, that you want."

"Yes, when you are ready. Really, it's not that serious to me as long as I keep getting to do what we've been doing." He chuckled.

Ciaran looked him in the eyes and said, "I want to know what you taste like."

"Really?" Chris stopped laughing at Ciaran's seriousness. "Okay. Give me a second."

He went into the bathroom and cleaned himself up with soap and water. He wet the cloth again and came into the room. Ciaran was standing up. "What are you doing?"

"I'm getting on my knees," Ciaran stated. He knew how these things went.

Chris laughed despite himself, but then cut it quickly to not embarrass Ciaran. He told him, "No. Get back on the bed." And Ciaran did. He cleaned Ciaran up as well, then sat with his back to the headboard, legs open, and motioned Ciaran to sit in between them.

He said, "Just do what you would want done to you. Don't try to make me cum. That's not your goal right now. Relax your jaw, all mouth and tongue, and no teeth. And take your time. We have all night."

Ciaran sat there, kind of frozen. Chris sensed Ciaran's hesitation and said, "Hey, you don't have to do this, you know."

Ciaran snapped out of it. "No. No, I want to. I just don't want to embarrass myself. This will probably be the worst blow job in the history of blow jobs."

"No, I did that, remember?" Chris laughed. "Just do it a few times and see how it feels. And when you don't want to do it anymore, stop. We'll do something else."

Ciaran nodded. He started stroking Chris, then opened his mouth, took a deep breath, and took his head in. He tasted like skin and maybe soap. He moved his tongue around and came up, then did it again. He started applying more suction with his lips, discovering that it was a lot more work than eating pussy. Ciaran bobbed his head up and down a few times until he got the rhythm. He heard Chris's breathing change, but otherwise, he made no sounds.

He remembered Chris saying to do what he would want done to him and he started circling the head with his tongue. That got a moan out of Chris and it turned Ciaran on so much that he made him do that. He started licking the head and the length of his penis all around, then went back to sucking, applying more pressure with his lips and squeezing in his facial muscles on the way up.

Chris's moans became audible. "You are … a lot better … than what … you thought… you thought … you … would be… Don't stop… fuck… don't stop…"

Ciaran felt Chris grow in his mouth, get harder and harder, and it was the ultimate turn-on. He had never felt more masculine than in that moment in his ability to bring another man to ecstasy. He wanted more. He realized he had only made it about halfway down, so he pushed himself to open up his throat and go deeper.

When Chris realized what he was doing, he lifted Ciaran's hair from his face so he could get a better look. *Ciaran Beals, my magical male human, is sucking my dick, and he is pretty good at it. Pretty fucking great actually,* he thought. He moaned encouragingly and massaged his head while holding up his hair.

Ciaran was concentrating on going deeper and deeper, moving faster and faster, bobbing up and down. Truthfully his jaw ached, but he didn't want to stop so he pushed through it. He started tasting Chris's pre-cum, which encouraged him to keep going.

He got about seventy percent down when it happened: Chris's cockhead hit the back of Ciaran's throat a little too hard and Ciaran gagged violently. He choked on his own saliva coming up. Ciaran started coughing and spitting, then dry heaving on the bed.

Chris was still holding up Ciaran's hair with one hand, rubbing his shoulder with the other hand. "Are you okay?" he asked concernedly.

Ciaran was too embarrassed to look up. Chris pulled Ciaran's head close and kissed him passionately, running his fingers through his long, fiery hair. He kissed his neck and ears and kissed his lips again. He started to pull Ciaran down on top of him, but Ciaran resisted.

"No," he said. "Let me keep going." He bent down and deep-throated Chris again.

Chris moaned and sat back while Ciaran sucked and licked. He started jerking Chris faster, using his spit as lubricant, and had the other hand on his balls, finger inching toward his hole.

He kept stroking until Chris moaned, "I'm going to cuuuuum," and then he poked his finger in Chris's hole and moved it around.

Chris let out a "aaaaoooooh" and came hard. Ciaran planned to catch it in his mouth, but froze instead and watched in awe as the first pump of cum went six inches in the air and landed on his cheek. The next couple of pumps did the same, landing on Chris's stomach. He had never seen a penis ejaculate from that angle, and it was so thrilling it made him breathless. He couldn't believe he made a man do that. Ciaran had the mind to keep stroking until every last bit was out. He licked the head and what was on his hands, still holding onto Chris's genitals.

Chris watched him and laughed. "What does it taste like?"

Ciaran moved it around his mouth. "Salty porridge." They both laughed.

"Ho. Lee. Shit, Ciaran. That was a nice surprise." Chris was grinning.

Ciaran moved closer and kissed him, letting Chris taste himself on his tongue. He took a pillow and put it under Chris's midsection, and lifted up his thighs as far as they could go. Ciaran put his head down and put his tongue on Chris's back entrance.

Chris moaned loudly, trying to get words out. "Ooooooohh. Ciaran. You are … really … going for it all today … aren't you, mate… ooooh."

Ciaran did not respond, as he was darting his tongue in and out of Chris. He could taste his own sex on him, and it made him incredibly hard. It had been over an hour since they last made love, and all he had learned about Chris made him want to bury himself all the way inside of him. Not because he wanted to dominate him, but the complete opposite: to hold him close, make him feel good, safe, and loved.

Ciaran grabbed the lube and prepared Chris, then put Chris's legs on his shoulders. They locked eyes and Ciaran entered him in one motion, and Chris groaned, "Fuuuuck!"

He closed his eyes and held onto Ciaran's arms, as Ciaran leaned him over to see how flexible he was. With legs still on his shoulders, and Chris's knees on his own chest, Ciaran thrusted into Chris. The only sounds in the room were thighs slapping ass, Ciaran's low grunts, and Chris's moans. Chris's orgasm hit first, taking his breath away, then wave after wave after wave sent shocks throughout his body.

Ciaran let Chris's legs go and pressed his body down between them. Chris held onto Ciaran's arms and moaned loudly, knowing they could not be heard because of the spell Ciaran cast. Ciaran felt Chris's ride into oblivion and rode it with him for a while until he felt his own waves begin forming. He pounded through it and came silently into Chris, listening to his lover's climax song of moaning.

It made him keep moving long after he came, until Ciaran collapsed, sweaty and exhausted, on top of him.

Chris had to maneuver and move off the pillow as Ciaran was trying to catch his breath and was little help to him. Eventually, Ciaran leaned up until Chris stretched out his legs and got comfortable. But Ciaran immediately laid back down between his legs, chest to chest, arms around him. With his face in Chris's neck, he closed his eyes.

Chris played in his hair and massaged his scalp as Ciaran's snores quickly rose, and he could feel his steady heartbeat. He surprised himself tonight with how open he was with Ciaran; he had never told anyone that much about Rem or even his first sexual experience. He was also surprised at how emotional he felt about Ciaran. And for the first time, considered that he could be falling in love with his best friend; and a Magus.

CHAPTER 16

Adult Activities

11:36 a.m.

Charity knocked, waited, and then used her key to enter her brother's flat. She walked in and heard nothing, so she proceeded to his room to wake him up. She busted open his bedroom door and said, "Chrissy, you missed breakfast and I wanted to hear all about your big dick fr—AAAAH!"

She screamed, shocked to find her brother naked and a red-haired man equally naked, scrambling for covers.

"Get the fuck out of here!!" Chris yelled and threw a pillow at her as she ran from the room, slamming the door behind her. Chris turned to Ciaran. "I'm so sorry. So sorry."

Ciaran, still half asleep, mumbled, "It's okay. Kind of funny if you think of it."

Chris looked at the time, and Ciaran's stomach growled. "Let's get up. I'll make you something to eat. And you can shower if you want."

Ciaran sighed, then rolled off the bed toward the door. But then stumbled back and pressed his lips against Chris. "Good morning," he grumbled out, his voice still heavy with sleepiness.

"Good morning," Chris responded as butterflies rolled around in his stomach. Ciaran left the room and slid into the bathroom.

Chris laid out a towel and one of his t-shirts, and folded up Ciaran's jeans from the night before, placing the clothes on the toilet while he showered. When he came out, Chris went to take a shower. Ciaran put on the new t-shirt and his jeans. He walked into the main room and found Charity in the kitchen making eggs Benedict.

She smiled at Ciaran. "Nice to meet you with clothes on."

Ciaran blushed. "I'm Ciaran." He held out his hand for a shake and she took it gently. Her hands were very soft and feminine.

"I'm Charity, the cute sister. Have a seat. You must be famished."

She winked her hazel eyes at him and made him go pink again. He sat at the far end of the table and looked at her. She wore a sweater dress with a black and gold pashmina scarf around her neck, black tights, and high-heeled boots. Her dark brown hair was down, wet, and curly, like she had just come out of the shower. He found himself thinking of how gorgeous she was, even more than what her picture allowed. And wanted to kick himself for even thinking it after he made love to her brother just hours before.

Chris came into the main room and gave his sister a light shove and a kiss on her head before he sat down next to Ciaran.

"Soooorrreeee," she sang. She put two plates in front of them and sat down at the table across from them. "Soooo? Good date, then?" Her light eyes sparkled with amusement.

"Don't be an idiot," Chris said with annoyance.

"Thanks for breakfast," Ciaran said and smiled at her.

Charity waited, then huffed. "No info? Ah, fine then." She stood up. "I hope to see you around more, Ciaran." She winked at him again, and he found himself watching her walk out.

"She is ... interesting," Ciaran said, putting his eyes down to his plate.

"That's one way of putting it," Chris said, watching Ciaran watch her.

"She looks just like you, except her eyes and her height." He put a mouthful of food in his mouth.

Chris was amused. "Ciaran. Are you attracted to my sister? Want to fuck her next?"

Ciaran almost choked on his food and went red very fast. "She is gorgeous, yes. But no, I do not want to bang your sister. It's more like you're my original and she is the smaller female copy."

Chris laughed. "Good answer." He turned his body toward Ciaran and locked his legs around him. "Just so you know, we don't share very well."

Ciaran laughed again and shook his head. "Regardless of what happens with us, I will never touch your sister. Never. Believe that."

Chris didn't say anything, just smiled and nodded. Ciaran finished eating first and went over to the entertainment center in the living room again. Chris had quite a music collection: British bands, Irish bands, American bands, French singers, and African artists. Ciaran found the remote for the stereo and pressed play, curious about the last song Chris listened to. Coldplay's "Viva la Vida" blasted loudly through the speakers, and Ciaran grinned with all he teeth.

Chris said loudly from the table, "It's kind of my theme song."

Ciaran said loudly, "It's kind of my favorite band!"

Chris smiled. "Well, you're a Brit boy, so that's not surprising at all."

Ciaran laughed. He turned the music down. "What's your favorite band?"

"U2, naturally."

"Naturally, the most famous Irish band out there." Ciaran smiled.

"Best band in modern history. But I'm quickly becoming a Script fan. I should have been listening to them in my youth like the rest of my friends were.

"I don't think I know them."

"Well, let me introduce them to you."

He came over and switched the CDs, started with "Breakeven," which Ciaran loved instantly, then a couple of newer songs, and Ciaran became a fan. They spent the next few hours going through a number of songs. Chris warmed up some leftovers around 3 p.m. and talked about how they all learned to cook from their mother and how some of their favorite times were being in the kitchen with her while she and he talked.

At 5 p.m. Ciaran broke the news. "I have to get going soon. I get into work hours before you, remember?"

"Okay. But I got something for you first." He went into the drawer in the kitchen and handed Ciaran a package with a prepaid phone inside. "I found myself frustrated when I had no way to contact you on Saturday. I know you Magi have ways to send messages to each other, but humor a Commoner and please call me?"

Ciaran chuckled. "Okay, no problem." He turned on the phone. "Can you believe I've never had one before? I don't have any Commoner friends. Before you, of course."

That made Chris smile. "Of course."

"Ted, my older brother, has one, though. He interacts frequently with Commoners in his line of work. He'll be thrilled that I have a number, instead of sending me his *Amina.*"

"His what?"

Ciaran smiled. "One day you'll see my *Amina.*" He was close to Chris's face, so he leaned in for a kiss. "Thanks."

Chris returned the kiss and said, "I can get used to spending more time with you, Ciaran Beals. Can't wait to do it again tonight."

"About that," Ciaran said. "No more fucking in the Tank."

Chris was taken aback. "What? *Why?*"

Ciaran said, "Because we are adults with jobs and responsibilities. If we ever got caught, that would be your job and career, and Dale would have my balls in a vice." Chris sat back. He knew Ciaran was right, but he was annoyed, anyway.

"So listen, come home with me tomorrow after work, yeah?"

Chris, still annoyed, said, "Yeah, okay. But what are we going to do tonight?"

"Same thing we've been doing. Patrol. Talk. Play games. Actually get some work done."

Chris sighed. "Fine. But you're gonna owe me for this."

"Name your price," Ciaran said.

Chris smiled and leaned into Ciaran's ear and said, "Suck my cock again."

Ciaran looked at Chris and said, "Go sit in the chair, then."

Chris was shocked that he so readily agreed. He happily went to sit on the couch. Ciaran kneeled between Chris's legs and they kissed. He rubbed Chris's imprint through his sweatpants and broke from Chris's lips first. He pulled down Chris's pants with his help to get them down to his ankles and started stroking. He was determined to do it right this time as he wrapped his lips around his cock. He alternated between licking and sucking, kept pushing himself down deeper and deeper, relaxing his throat a little more each time. Chris started moaning instantly and kept moaning throughout. When Ciaran felt Chris had reached max stiffness, he started jerking Chris harder and faster, watching for when he came.

Chris decided to stand up, taking Ciaran by surprise. He took his prick from Ciaran's grasp, held Ciaran's head, put his penis in his mouth, and thrusted into his face, slowly at first, then faster. Ciaran allowed it; he was shocked and thrilled, it instantly made him hard. He held onto Chris's bare bottom, kept his mouth open, his throat relaxed, and his eyes locked on Chris's intense gaze, hoping not to gag, hoping he was doing it right. But he couldn't help the gurgling sounds he was making.

After a full minute of non-stop face fucking, Chris pulled out of Ciaran's mouth and started stroking himself right over Ciaran's face, still holding his head steady. Ciaran, fully aware of what was about to happen, closed his eyes and opened his mouth. Chris let out a simple "ugh" as his eyes fluttered and he exploded all over Ciaran's face. Chris put it back in Ciaran's mouth, to which Ciaran promptly sucked softly. Chris fell backward onto the couch and looked at Ciaran, who was still kneeling with his eyes closed, cum streaks all over, dripping from his forehead.

Ciaran started laughing. "That was porn star worthy." Chris laughed back. Ciaran's eyes were still closed. "Now that you've dominated me, am I allowed to wash it off?"

Chris kneeled beside Ciaran and took his face in his hand, then began to lick his cum off him slowly, from top to bottom. Once done, he put his tongue in Ciaran's mouth to kiss him. Ciaran moaned, tasting Chris on his tongue again, then he opened his eyes.

"Now it's porn star worthy." Chris smiled.

"You licked all your cum off me," Ciaran said, surprised.

Chris shrugged. "I did. Won't be the last time, either."

Ciaran was in awe of him, and he was also incredibly horny. But he practiced restraint. "I really have to go."

Chris touched his obvious erection that wanted to punch a hole through his jeans. "No, you don't."

"Yes, I dooo," moaned Ciaran. "Because if I don't, neither of us are making it to work tonight."

They kissed; Ciaran broke away first and stood up. Chris reluctantly stood up as well, pulling up his pants. Ciaran went to the bathroom and washed his face before Chris walked him to the door to put on his shoes and handed him his coat. They kissed again and held onto each other for a moment.

"See you in a few hours," Ciaran said, opening the door and disappearing in the vestibule in a wisp of smoke.

Chris found himself standing there breathing it in until it was all gone. He had smelled that smell before, remembering the night he gave Ciaran a massage and picked up his tank top afterward, sniffing it. The scent was familiar to him now. It smelled like Ciaran.

***

10:52 p.m.

When Chris arrived for work, he half expected Ciaran to show up, but he knew he wouldn't. He was anxious to see him again, touch him, kiss him. This newfound territory with his best friend left him with feelings of excitement he had not felt in a long time. Despite what Ciaran had said, he was going to return the favor of a blow job tonight.

1:02 a.m.

Ciaran was waiting at Marker 1. Chris walked right up to him and kissed him on the lips, surprising Ciaran, but he welcomed the greeting. He slid his hand inside of Chris's and they walked, talking a little as they patrolled. It felt nice to be that close to Chris, an intimacy between them. Sex was easy for Christopher, but intimacy was what he needed. Ciaran was determined to be his guide in that.

When they got back to the Tank, Ciaran sat at the table and pulled out regular playing cards. Chris's eyes narrowed. Ciaran saw his reaction, but resisted the urge to laugh and instead ignored him, setting up the cards. Chris sat down at the table and began to play Gin Rummy.

"Okay," Chris started, "let's talk about this. When you say no fucking on the job, you mean no actual intercourse, right?" Ciaran gave him an exasperated look, but didn't respond. "Look, I'm just asking for clarification purposes. Like, for instance, can I touch you?" He moved his chair to sit next to Ciaran and touched his leg.

Ciaran did not flinch. "Anything that could get you in trouble by your own bylaws is out."

Chris smiled. "Well, there is nothing against touching another person."

"It's your turn," Ciaran said, pointing to the table.

Chris turned to the game. They played for a bit, but then he lost the hand. "Shit."

"That's because you aren't paying attention." Ciaran laughed.

"That's because there are other things I'd rather be *doing*," Chris retorted.

Ciaran did not respond. He knew that Chris would be disappointed, but he did not think that he would be that childish about it.

Chris began again. "Okay, when you say no fucking in the Tank, what about the woods? Technically, it would be off site." He grinned.

Ciaran smiled as well. "And how would that go over if someone catches their ranger with their pants down?"

"That's only if we got caught. I'm sure you have ways to conceal us, being a Magus and all." He winked.

"Chris. No."

Chris moved closer again. "Can I kiss you?" He leaned in for a kiss and Ciaran kissed him back, but was the first to break away.

"We are not having sex in here anymore. Your place, my place, anywhere in between. Just not here," Ciaran said.

Chris would not let up. "Any kind of sex? Oral? A quick knob slob? I owe you one."

Ciaran was trying to keep a cool head, but Chris was making it hard for him, literally and figuratively. "Do you want to play another game?" he asked.

"No, I do not want to play another game unless it involves penis play."

Ciaran sighed. "Why is this so hard for you, really? Simply being together isn't enough?"

Chris took Ciaran's hand and put it on his growing erection. "Because I like you and I want to be with you in other ways. I just want to make you feel as good as you make me feel."

He reached over and started rubbing on Ciaran's groin, glad that he, too, was getting hard. But Ciaran gave him no reaction in his face. Chris pushed Ciaran further. "Is it a crime that I want to make love to my boyfriend right now?" he said softly, innocently.

Ciaran became frustrated with Chris's statement and pressuring him, but he did not want to show it. Instead, he chuckled and said, "Oh, you are good. Really good." He kissed Chris, then stood up. "I'm going back."

"No!" Chris said immediately, standing up too. "Why?"

Ciaran decided to tell him the truth. "Because you are getting to me, Christopher. Because you know I want you too. And if I stay, I am going to betray my own words to you, my own integrity. You know what I'm saying to you is right, yet you are intentionally trying to push my buttons, appeal to the part of me that has real feelings for you, just so you can play tonight. And I don't feel like playing this game with you. So I'm going back to work."

Chris was stunned. He did not like the feeling of being read by him. Ciaran went to kiss Chris with a peck on the lips to which he returned halfheartedly.

"I'll meet you here at 7 a.m. I'm taking you home with me," Ciaran said. Then he left, leaving Chris with feelings of sexual frustration, annoyance, bewilderment, and admiration.

6:45 a.m.

Chris was at the table finishing up his log when Ciaran Wisp'd right in front of him. Chris ended up doing a second patrol, just to walk off his energy and frustration, and he was still annoyed at Ciaran. So when Chris saw the smoke of the Wisp, he barely looked up.

Ciaran took a seat opposite Chris and waited. Chris finished his log, got up to put it in the cabinet, and then busied himself around the room. Ciaran tried hard not to smile at his childishness.

"So you're angry with me," he stated instead of asked.

"Nope. Not angry." Chris wouldn't look at him.

"Annoyed then?" Ciaran leaned back and put his right foot over his left knee, and crossed his arms.

Chris let a moment pass, then said, "I'm not a child, you know. You don't have to talk to me like I am one."

Ciaran started, "When did I—"

"Earlier today. When you called yourself scolding me. Get over yourself, Ciaran. You don't have the moral compass in this relationship. Telling me how I am playing games."

Ciaran resisted the urge to roll his eyes. "I didn't say you were playing games. I said you were playing with my emotions and I wasn't playing *that* game with you."

"And how was I playing with your emotions? By saying I wanted to fuck?"

"Ah, but that's not what you said. You said you wanted to make love to your boyfriend. Like I was some silly little girl needing affirmations from her lover to be pressured into having sex. You don't even talk like that, especially not to me."

Chris decided to poke at him. "So, are you saying you don't want to be my boyfriend?"

Ciaran was getting annoyed again at the mind games. "Fuck, you are good at this. Does this shit really work? And if so, what kind of wankers have you been dating?" He chuckled.

"Oh, so now I'm a joke to you. My feelings, this relationship, all of it is just one big game to you," he said childishly.

Ciaran decided to get off the merry-go-round Chris was trying to drag him on. He said seriously, "No, I am laughing at your veiled attempt to get under my skin. Stop it. Nothing about any of this is a game to me. I don't like my emotions to be toyed with. Take note of that. You don't like your feelings to be ignored. Duly noted."

They stared at each other. Ciaran got up and stood in front of Chris, who was still frowning. He touched his waist with both hands and moved so close that his lips were almost touching Chris's.

"I'm an adult. You're an adult. We're going to be adults about this." He rubbed their nostrils together and said softly, "And if I'm your boyfriend, then treat me like a boyfriend, and not a fuck buddy." He looked Chris in the eyes and waited.

Chris sighed and put one hand on Ciaran's waist. "I don't kiss fuck buddies." Ciaran smiled and gently kissed his lips. Chris put his tongue in Ciaran's mouth for a deeper kiss.

"OH!"

They heard a voice behind them and quickly pulled apart and turned around. Bergina had just entered the tank for her shift; she was covering for Miche that day and Chris had forgotten. "I'm sorry, I didn't mean to … interrupt." She mumbled and went toward her locker.

Ciaran moved to the front door, unsure of what to say or how to feel. It was the first time someone had seen him and Chris intimate, seen him intimate with another man.

Chris quickly recovered. "Bergina, you remember Ciaran? He does some conservation work in the forest."

"Oh yes. We met a few months back one evening before Chris's shift, yes. How are you?"

"I'm fine, thank you, and yourself?" Ciaran said very politely.

"Very well, thanks." She smiled and Ciaran returned her smile.

He continued to stand awkwardly in the doorway while Chris gave his evening report. He then grabbed his backpack and walked over to where Ciaran was standing, giving his arm a reassuring squeeze. Chris turned to Bergina. "I'll see you … tonight?"

"Yes, I am doing a double. I will see you tonight. Good to see you again, Ciaran."

They left and Bergina smiled. The truth was, she had seen the kiss last Thursday night under the lamppost and was curious if it was going to go anywhere. She was happy to see that it was.

CHAPTER 17

In My Place

Ciaran was quiet in the car. So quiet that Chris was sure if there was a saltshaker nearby, Ciaran would be playing with it. Chris wanted to reassure him that it would be okay that they were public, but he also knew that Ciaran needed to believe that for himself. Instead, he decided to put on Coldplay and not talk at all, but sing along to the songs.

Indeed, Ciaran was all in his head. This relationship he had dived into suddenly became very real, very fast, not just something to do on an overnight shift. And although he had never seen himself as someone who would be in the closet, he did think he would have kept it private and for himself a little while longer.

It had been about five days; just a long whirlwind weekend. But maybe he and Chris had been together in a sense all that time, which was why it had been so easy for them to fall into step with their new journey so easily. He thought of his parents again and how they would take it, him being with a pansexual, biracial, male Commoner. Would they be surprised? Or is it something they've always known about him? He didn't care so much about what strangers would think, but what would his brothers say? He considered calling Ted, his older brother. Or Sean, his womanizing brother. What would he think? He considered calling him too, then freaked out. *Maybe I'm just a coward.*

Ciaran's head was spinning, and he was grateful to not talk. Chris just seemed to get it, get him, and that's what made him feel good being with him. Even putting on Coldplay was intentional, and for him, he knew this. In spite of the thoughts running through his head, he had no regrets thus far about being with Chris, who was currently singing loudly and kept looking at him with a smile.

Ciaran smiled and thought, *God, I could love this man.* Then got flushed and freaked out in his head again over the thought.

When they arrived at The Atrium, Ciaran had Chris park closer to the alleyway next to the restaurant. They walked through the alleyway toward the back of the building and turned to a pair of dusty, frost-covered double doors with heavy chains on them. Ciaran put his hand out and the chains parted and opened for him. Chris grinned as he followed Ciaran over the threshold, and the doors immediately closed behind them.

They walked through an open area that could only be described as a true atrium and greenhouse. Chris was once again in awe of the world of magic. It was like walking into a secret garden. Birds, scurrying animals, and plant life, some regular, but much of it definitely moved as if it was alive. Bushes, small trees, butterflies, moths, and... *was that a fairy?*

Chris could not contain his excitement if he tried. They had to cross a small bridge over a creek going diagonally through the area. As they crossed through, a large wolf-like animal came up to sniff them and demanded to be petted. Chris stepped back in fear. But Ciaran bent down and petted him.

"Hey, Joey. Having a good day?" He stood up and pulled a berry off of a nearby tree, bent down, and gave it to him. To Chris's astonishment, Joey stood on two legs like a kangaroo, and barked appreciatively. He was nearly five feet.

"Meet my friend Chris," Ciaran said casually. The animal walked over to Chris on his two legs and stared judgingly. He started sniffing him, then sneezed.

"What is it?" Chris asked.

"An Emmth. He belongs to Earl and lives here in the atrium. He protects the building from Commoners and intruders."

Chris grabbed the same fruit and held it out. Still eyeing him suspiciously, Joey sniffed him a few more times before he took it, then went back down to four legs. Chris patted his head, and he made a small noise. Suddenly the Emmth leaped away, disappearing farther into the garden.

"It's a good thing he didn't bite you," Ciaran said, amusingly. "It means you have pure intentions."

They walked to another set of doors, this time wooden, and again Ciaran held his hand out and the doors parted. It was an entrance to a small apartment building of two levels, a large open foyer with high ceilings, rows of doors on each side, and a huge staircase right in the middle. Ciaran made his way up the stairs, and Chris followed. They stopped on the second floor and went to the left, walked all the way down the hall to a door with the number ten on it. Ciaran grabbed the handle and opened the door.

"Magi just leave their doors unlocked?" Chris asked, astonished.

"No. It only opens for me. And whoever else I allow."

Chris nodded. They walked into the flat together. Ciaran led him to the right into the living room area, which had a couch on one side, a large fireplace, and a TV over it. A bookshelf was in one corner and a door to what Chris assumed was the bathroom was in the other, since the entrance to the galley kitchen was behind the wall of the couch. Some kind of gold, furry animal skin rug was in the middle of the wooden floor of the living room.

Ciaran walked to the back of the apartment and came back with a pair of dark gray sweatpants and a red t-shirt. "Here, in case you didn't bring a change of clothes."

Chris assumed they weren't going to be wearing much clothes, but he took it anyway. He wanted to explore first. He went over to the mantel over the fireplace to look at the pictures. Ciaran came over and started pulling them down one by one to show them to Chris.

"This was us, the whole Beals gang. We took a trip to France where Ted was living with Elodie before they married and he moved back to London to settle down. I flew up to meet up with them. That's Dad, Mum, Diana the baby sister, Ted, the oldest, me in the middle, the twins Sean and Shane. Shane is gone now."

Ciaran stared longingly at the picture, and Chris knew he was thinking about his dead brother. Chris pointed to other pictures. "Who are they?" He pointed to an attractive brown-skinned couple.

"That's Selma and Andres, my best mates. We were at Campus together, played a lot of sports and duels with Andre, got into a lot of trouble with Selma. They are married and have two children. He plays football professionally now, always traveling and I barely see them, but we try to catch up at least once a year."

Chris pulled down a picture of a group of teenagers, Ciaran on the right. "Schoolmates?" he asked.

"Yup," Ciaran said. "This was our crew. Me, Selma, Andres, Tessa, Bo, Jimini, Magna, Lucy, and Darragh. Best mates ever. I still keep in touch with half of them. Other than Selma and Andre, I talk to Bo and Lucy for sure because we are kind of in the same field, caring for animals. Lucy works for Scholarly, teaching and researching magical creatures. Technically, she's Dale's boss as the Scholarly took over the Reserve about fifty years ago, but if you ask Dale, he has no boss. Bo also works for Scholarly, but he finds and researches magical creatures in the field. Magna works for the Council and manages and monitors Magi secrecy and security. And Darragh died in the war with Shane." Ciaran said the last part with stiffness. Chris touched his shoulder. Ciaran continued, "The others, I have no idea what they're doing. I don't even know if they survived the war."

Chris grabbed the next picture, four young teenage boys, Ciaran in the middle. Ciaran smiled. "My Campus dorm mates. Jesse, myself, Salid, Khalid, and Felix. We had six dorm mates, but Rory's parents pulled him out after he got trapped in the vortex."

Chris was confused. "Am I supposed to know what that means?"

"Oh, it was okay because Andre, Jesse, and Shane went in and fished him out with a Trident," Ciaran said seriously. Chris blinked at him and Ciaran laughed. "One day you'll hear all about my Campus magical adventures."

Chris shook his head and tapped the last picture, of Ciaran and his brother, which looked like it was taken recently. His hair was longer, and they both were growing beards.

"Yeah, that's me and Sean last year at the Campus in Cape Town, South Africa. We stayed there the longest, almost four months. Best part of our trip; we learned all sorts of *dulé-less* magic."

He held out his hand and a book came flying off the shelf behind Chris into Ciaran's hand.

Chris flinched. "Don't do that without a warning next time, mate," he said seriously.

Ciaran laughed. "Here. Your crash course to the plants and animals in the Magi world. If you were a Magus you would have been tapped for Scholarly or Novo, the way you gather knowledge and care for people, animals, and wildlife."

Chris smiled and turned around to peruse the bookshelf. Ciaran went into the back room to change, and Chris was still there when he came back, reading through a book of Latin spells and incantations.

"I'm going to run downstairs to get breakfast," Ciaran said. "You want to come?"

"Ah, no. Think I'm going to stay up here, snoop around, and go through your shit," he said without looking up.

Ciaran laughed. "Fair enough. I will tell Phoebe you said hello."

He left and Chris continued to go through his book-shelf, which was a combination of Magi specifics, such as the Dragonology Educator training manual, but also regular books about wildlife, topography of Albania, bird watching, and identifying certain herbs and their uses. In the far corner were the dragon fiction novels that he knew Ciaran had, *A Game of Thrones, Lord of the Rings,* and *The Hobbit* among them, like himself. Chris wondered how much of it was accurate in Ciaran's world, and if it really was fiction.

He grabbed the set of clothes Ciaran left for him and headed to the bedroom to change. Truthfully he did bring a set of clothes, but he liked the idea of wearing Ciaran's clothes better.

Ciaran's bedroom was simple: Black iron barred head-board, springy mattress in the middle of the room, with two end tables on either side. Large closet along one wall. A matching dresser with a large mirror against the wall opposite the bed. Chris went through the drawers and found it eerily organized; underwear and socks neatly rolled and lined up. T-shirts folded like they were on display of every color except white.

Interesting, he thought. On the nightstand was the bottle of almond oil that Chris used, making Chris smile. But there was also lube. That made him smile more.

He went over to the closet and it was also eerily organized as well. His jeans were hung, which Chris found funny for some reason. He had some dress shirts, again, none of them white, and other items on hangers such as Magi hooded cloaks. He wondered which ones made Ciaran fly.

But the surprise was the rows and rows of footwear. Ciaran apparently had a shopping fetish for his feet. Chris had only seen Ciaran in his black boots and the loafers he wore on their date. But Ciaran had sneakers for days, all brands and colors, including white, which he found very amusing. He also had casual footwear, loafers, oxfords, and toe boots.

Chris could not help himself; he knew he and Ciaran wore the same size. He got dressed in Ciaran's clothes, then picked out a pair of black trainers and walked back into the living room.

Chris went back to the bookshelf. He looked over the books again and saw some sticking out of the top. Chris reached up to grab them and his hand folded around another thin, cylindrical object. Chris wrapped his fingers around the stick. He pulled it down, but he already knew what it was. It was about ten inches long, dark brown, and rough, as if it was a branch pulled directly from a tree and shaved but not smoothed out.

But Chris was unprepared for how it felt. Heat spread from his palm to his fingertips as the *rodulé* vibrated in his hand. Then, just as suddenly, it stopped.

"Whoa," Chris said in shock. He switched hands but could not recreate the feeling again. "Interesting." Chris gently put the *dulé* back on top of the bookshelf. He figured that it was hidden because it was stronger than Ciaran's normal one, and it wasn't something he wanted to mess around with. Instead, Chris grabbed a book and got comfortable.

Ciaran found him lying on the couch with his feet hanging over the side, reading the book on Magi wildlife. He laughed. "Went shopping in my closet, yeah?"

Chris shrugged. Ciaran motioned for him to come to the table in the kitchen. He bought steak and eggs with hashed potatoes and black pudding. They ate and talked about Ciaran's organizational skills, "The *rodulé* does it all, trust me," and his shoe collection, "Trainers are for running or causal dress wear, shoes are for going out, boots are for work," and his lack of white clothing, "I'm a *Nigri Veneficus*, we don't do white."

As the conversation died out and they were sipping tea at the end of their meal, Chris said, "Hey, Ciaran?"

"Yeah?"

"Can we have sex now?" asked Chris with a straight face.

Ciaran decided to also keep a straight face. He took a moment, then said, "Come take a shower with me."

"Tooooo ... have sex there?"

This time, Ciaran laughed. He got up and walked to the closet near the bathroom, pulled out two towels and washcloths, then walked to the bathroom. Chris followed.

Ciaran stripped Chris, and then Chris stripped Ciaran. He turned on the shower, asking Chris what his temperature preference was and then Chris got in. But Chris watched Ciaran open up his medicine cabinet and take down a small package from the highest shelf. It was in the shape of a soap bar, wrapped in dark red tissue paper. There was a small round sticker holding the packaging closed. Before Chris could get a look at the writing, Ciaran ripped it open. Chris didn't know what he expected, but it was indeed a simple white bar of soap.

Ciaran stepped in, lathered up the cloth with a soap bar, and began washing Chris's body. "I don't hate this at all," Chris said. "This soap smelled amazing. Sweet, but not too sweet. Inviting. Soothing."

"My sister makes these," said Ciaran, "for the apothecary shop. She's an actual wiccan. It's infused with herbs and oils to heighten the senses and bring forth virility."

That made Chris grin. "So we *are* going to have sex," he deduced.

Ciaran smiled as he scrubbed Chris's back. "It's not that I don't want sex. I just want a little intimacy."

Chris said, "Intimacy leads to sex."

"Not necessarily, not always. Intimacy is about being close to someone. Sex is just one way to reach that goal. Standing here with you like this is another way. We're touching, but we aren't pounding each other. We talk about personal things all the time. We can be close without actually having sex."

Ciaran grabbed the shampoo and started washing Chris's hair. Chris had never had anyone wash him down head to toe before, and it felt good.

"Is this one of those relationship things you are teaching me?" he asked, amusingly.

Ciaran did not answer, but smiled again. Chris grabbed the cloth and did the same to Ciaran, cleaned him up from head to toe with the same virile soap.

When they were done, Chris came out of the shower first and went to grab his towel, but instead, his eyes went to a black, fuzzy-looking robe on the back of the bathroom door. It had a red patch of a fist holding a *rodulé*. Chris reached out, and it was just as soft as it looked, if not softer.

"Whoa!" he exclaimed. "You're holding out on me." He took it down and put it on. "It feels like being wrapped in a black cloud."

Ciaran chuckled. "You can borrow it, but it stays here." Ciaran wrapped a towel around his waist and they walked to the bedroom.

Chris went to admire himself in the mirror on the dresser while wearing Ciaran's robe. "It even looks good on me." He posed a few times. "Do they give these to everyone at Campus?"

"No, only a few Magi enforcers got one. For special services for fighting in the civil war. The last battle for Commoner freedom." Ciaran leaned against the dresser with his arms folded. "Talindra was a powerful sorceress and a mega bitch who believed that Magi should not be living in the shadows, but ruling the world. And she had a strong following. They orchestrated a coup and tried to take over the Scholarly and Magi Council at the same time. But we stopped them."

Chris sat on the dresser next to him. "Want to talk about being there?"

"You mean being there super late?" he deadpanned.

"How late were you?" Chris asked. It was the closest Ciaran had come to talking about the day that changed everything for his family. He doubted Ciaran had ever really talked about it. He wanted to keep Ciaran talking.

Ciaran took a moment, but then started talking. "By the time we got there, the sun was up, and so many people had already died, including Shane and Darragh. But the battle was still fierce, so, me and the other Reservers just jumped right in. There had to be at least eighty of us men, and it didn't seem like much. But maybe because we were all experts in dueling, we tipped the scales. They weren't just dealing with desk pushers, researchers, and elder Magi anymore. We were trained mercenaries. We managed to push them back, giving the Magi enforcers and NV's a chance to do what they needed to do, which was band together and destroy Talindra's front line and capture her."

Ciaran sniffed. "The thing is, I had been considering leaving for months before that. I left the Magi enforcers because I was tired of fighting, of killing. For three years, I was essentially a child soldier, and that's not the way it was supposed to be. After Campus we dedicate at least one year of service to the Magi council, training, learning about secrecy, and defending our community. But by the time we graduated, the tension was brewing, so my generation was trained to spy, torture, and kill."

"Whoa," Chris breathed out.

"Yeah," Ciaran said sadly. "And I was great at it. But that's not the life I wanted. I wanted to protect life, not end it. So at nineteen, I told them I wanted out, and Grandminister Graham pulled some strings and got me and my friends an official release. But the moment I left my *Nigri Veneficus* post, it seemed like the whole world had gone mad. The propaganda that Magi should be superior to Commoners seemed to grow overnight. Suddenly blue-marked Magi were everywhere, and it was open violence on Commoner men, women, and children. Entire families slaughtered. Presidents and ministers dying mysterious deaths only to be replaced by a Magi, the bad kind. It was a scary time. I began to feel restless and hopeless, like I made the wrong decision. Especially after Chitra left, moved her whole family back to India to get as far away from the deaths in Europe as possible. But we had our own problems here, like trying to keep CVs from infiltrating the Reserve, as they had tried many times already, so there's that. So I had one foot helping out there and the other antsy to get back to England."

"How did you know what was going on to join the fight?" Chris asked.

"Ted sent me a message. I was in the breakroom with about twelve other men, including Dale, on the overnight shift, and his *Amina*, his creature spirit, came to me. He said, 'Ciaran, listen. Magi warlocks are trying to take over Scholarly in London, and the Council is ready to make its last stand. We're all here, Mum, Dad, Shane, Sean, and Diana. We might make it out alive. If we don't, I love you, little brother. You've been my best friend my entire life.'

"I turned to Dale and said I'm going. I knew it would take me the rest of the night, but there was no way I was sitting there. Not surprisingly, all the other men in the room said they were leaving, too. Dale didn't say anything at first, but then touched the tip of his *rodulé* and sent out the Reserve wide emergency signal, so that all the Reservers within a hundred-mile radius got it. The day crew, and the night crew that weren't there, started coming onto the grounds. He had me repeat the message to everyone, then said he was pulling out the Flyers—the transports we use to go on missions— and it was battle-bound. No shame if we didn't want to go, but if you did, it was leaving in twenty minutes. Told us to send out goodbye messages just in case.

"It didn't matter what Campus we were from, we were fighting not just for our world but for your world too, for Commoners to live in peace. Everyone except a couple of younger Dungers that Dale forbade, one Novo, and Dale signed up. Even Sarah, our lead Novo, came back dressed in all black, her hair in a bun, looking fierce and ready to battle. She and Dale got into a fight over it, but she won.

"Dale pulled me aside and said he couldn't go. His brother was fighting for the wrong side and he had told him the next time he saw him he would kill him on the spot for what he did, putting an unspeakable hex on their parents. There were only five dragons at the time, Ben, Anna, Rehoboth, Hina, and Hansel, so he was going to take care of them. So we left, about midnight. It took us about four hours to get there. I was late and my brother died." He sniffed again.

Chris let a moment pass, then said quietly, "You're a hero, Ciaran." Ciaran scoffed. "No, really. Think about it. If you would have left months before, you would have been with your family during the entire battle, possibly died there—"

Ciaran cut him off. "I wouldn't have died. I know advanced magic."

Chris said, "You know advanced magic now, but at that time, almost three years ago, at twenty-four years old, you didn't. So let's just agree that death for all of you was very possible." Ciaran nodded begrudgingly.

"Right, so if you had left, the message would not have gotten to the Reserve, and there would have been no reinforcements to turn the battle around. So, yes, it's the fucking worst that you couldn't save your brother or one of your best friends. You'll carry that with you forever. But if I were you, I wouldn't want to change how you got there. Or when. You saved a lot of lives. Helped to end the war in a massive way. Like you said, gave the Council and Magi Enforcers a chance."

Ciaran sniffed again. Chris reached around Ciaran's shoulder and pulled a little, motioning for him to come closer, and when he faced him, he wrapped his arms around Ciaran's neck.

"I'm not going to fucking cry," Ciaran said, muffled in his shoulder, but held him back.

Chris laughed. "Well, you wanted intimacy. What's more intimate than two naked bros hugging?"

Ciaran didn't laugh back. He lifted his head up and kissed Chris gently on the lips, then more passionately. Chris wrapped his legs around Ciaran while they kissed each other's lips and neck. Then Ciaran pushed Chris farther back on the dresser, opened the robe, and grabbed his waist to pull it toward the edge, so his butt was half hanging off. He got down on his knees and put his tongue in Chris's freshly washed anus. He licked softly and lightly, increasing pressure with every lick. Chris moaned loudly with pleasure and put one leg on Ciaran's shoulder. Ciaran licked his balls and the soft area between his balls and anus, and traced the rim of his anus with the tip of his tongue, then put his tongue in again.

"Fuuuuck yeah," Chris moaned encouragingly.

Ciaran found he really liked doing it a lot, maybe because it was like cunnilingus, maybe because it didn't make his jaw ache like a blow job did, maybe because of how it made Chris tremble, maybe all of the above, but he was happy to continue to pleasure Chris that way. Especially since the smell of Chris's natural musk went right to his brain and held him there.

Eventually, he stood up, took off his towel, and started stroking himself while fingering Chris with two fingers. He looked behind him and quietly summoned the lube to him. He poured lube on himself, then shifted Chris down a bit more so he could enter him standing up while Chris was still on his dresser. Chris wrapped his legs around Ciaran again, and inhaled sharply as Ciaran entered him slowly, holding on and filling him up. Ciaran kissed him, while thrusting.

Chris cried out, "Ooooohhh fuck meeeee." Ciaran smiled and obliged.

Ciaran moved rhythmically in full strokes, kissing him every so often, breathing in his scent. The scent that was slowly making him feral. Chris moaned at each thrust in between kisses. Then Ciaran pushed all the way inside again and lifted Chris off the dresser by his ass cheeks, surprising Chris with his strength. Chris immediately wrapped his arms around him and held on as Ciaran turned around, carried him to the bed, and laid him back down again. Ciaran proceeded with his task, grunting in sync with Chris's moans.

Chris couldn't think. There were no thoughts in his head. Every stroke Ciaran gave him was like a loud drum. Or rather, he was the drum and every time Ciaran's cock banged, his body vibrated. All he could feel, hear, smell, and taste was Ciaran. He turned his head and Ciaran's wrist was there, his palm flat on the bed. Chris stuck out his tongue and licked it. Why, he didn't know.

He turned to Ciaran, and there was fire and determination in his eyes. Chris reached out and grabbed Ciaran, pulling him close. But he didn't kiss him. Instead, he licked Ciaran's neck. It was sweaty and dewy, and the taste went right to Chris's brain. He did it again, and again, dragging his tongue across Ciaran's neck, his ears, across his face. That simple act drove Ciaran into overdrive. Ciaran banged harder. Chris licked more.

Eventually, Ciaran rolled over, pulling Chris on top of him. Chris immediately took control. With Ciaran's hand on his waist to gently guide him, he gyrated slowly back and forth, then faster, making sure he hit his spot repeatedly until he felt his first orgasm radiate through his body. It was so intense that Chris couldn't get a sound out. Ciaran could feel Chris tighten and shake from the inside as he came. He sat up on one elbow and pulled Chris closer to him with his free hand.

"Cum. Again," he told him.

They kissed and Chris moved again, slowly at first, then faster, and eventually moved into a squatting position on Ciaran, sending wave after wave of orgasmic pleasure. Ciaran, in turn held onto Chris's waist. When Chris wanted to slow down, Ciaran gripped him tighter, moving him faster against him.

"Ciaran... Ci... Ciaran," Chris tried to tell him to slow down, that the intensity was too much. But he didn't know if he really wanted it to stop, and all he could get out was moaning Ciaran's name in his ambivalence.

Ciaran again felt Chris trembling from the inside and felt his body trembling in sync with him. Chris managed to cry out this time as the corner of his eyes began leaking with tears and his penis leaked with cum. Ciaran thought for sure he was going to cum too, and surprised himself with how focused he was. But it wasn't easy. His brain was swirling with Chris's scent, touch, and feel. He felt like an animal wanting to break Chris in half. So Ciaran had to stay focused and not let the magic get to him.

Chris collapsed on top of him, landing in Ciaran's underarm. He had no idea what possessed him to do it, but he moved his face closer and began to lick Ciaran right there. The sensation again sent Ciaran into overdrive. In all his dating experience, no one had ever, *ever*, licked his armpit. And Chris was savage, the way he dragged his teeth through Ciaran's red armpit hair, his entire face smothered in the smell of Ciaran. He could have stayed there forever, licking, biting, nibbling. But Ciaran needed to kiss him. So he roughly pulled Chris by his hair out of his shoulder and forced his tongue into Chris's mouth. They kissed for a while, hungrily, tongues battling, teeth clashing, lips biting, yanking hair, cocks in a sword fight.

Ciaran needed, *needed,* to be inside of Chris again. "Turn around."

Chris turned his back to Ciaran. Ciaran brought the lube to him again and glistened himself up, then turned Chris to his side and entered from the back, this time forcefully, and Chris screamed out and nothing in his life had ever felt more right. He lifted one of Chris's legs and held it by his thigh, moving slowly this time, all the way in, out to just the tip, then back in again. Chris leaned his head back, and they kissed.

Then Ciaran said, "Again."

"...What?"

"You're going to cum again. And again."

"I can't..." Chris said breathlessly. "Twice is all I got right now."

Ciaran, still pushing deeply in and out, took Chris's own hand and put it on his penis. Together they stroked, and it took no time at all for his cock to harden. Ciaran moved his hand away. Chris continued stroking.

Ciaran kissed the back of his neck and said, "You will. Cum. Again." He started licking and nibbling and kissing Chris's neck, ears, back, shoulders, and neck again, then pulled his face back for a kiss. "Cum again. For me," he said.

Chris's whole body was on fire, inside and out. He wanted to cum again and badly now. He stroked himself, thinking it would take longer since he had climaxed twice in the last thirty minutes, but his penis responded, like his dick had been waiting for that moment. Ciaran reached over and pinched his nipples, still deep stroking from behind, grinding against his prostate.

He had never experienced sex with anyone like that before. It was needy and primal, and he had no control over any of it. His senses were indeed heightened, and the physical sensation Ciaran was giving him sent Chris over the edge. After another five minutes of stroking, he felt his orgasm hit him, sending a shock of electricity to his front. Chris's whole body jerked.

Chris's voice caught in his throat mid-moan as ropes of thick white cum shot out of his penis. His body continued to spasm, and he found his voice. "Fuuuuuck Kiiirrrroooonnnn fuuuuuuck."

Ciaran pumped hard against his prostate, and did not stop until Chris's "aah" became higher in pitch and tears leaked out of his eyes again. Ciaran almost lost sight of it. But he didn't cum. Not yet. He gave Chris a moment to catch his breath, then changed position to put Chris on his back.

Ciaran lay between Chris's legs, and Chris held them up by his arms. Chris thought he was going to get pounded again, but Ciaran surprised him by entering him slowly, leaning down and kissing him, running his hands through his hair. Chris held onto Ciaran's back and Ciaran penetrated deep again, but moved more rhythmically, at an even pace. They kissed and moved together until Ciaran felt his own orgasm, that he had been pushing back the whole time, begin to rise. He moved faster to ride it out with Chris's cock trapped between both of their abs. Chris felt the build-up and had no willpower to fight against the tidal wave that was coming. He threw his head back and blacked out as his cock twitched and three ropes of cum shot out of him. His body shook, and Ciaran's did, too.

Ciaran also did not fight against it. The smell of Chris's sperm was all it took. He let out a soft but long "aaaaah" in Chris's ear as he came and came in abundance. Chris felt every single shot deep within him, the force and strength of his spunk making his body jolt.

As Ciaran's ejaculation waned, Chris reached between them and jerked himself hard and fast. Ciaran lifted up slightly and watched. With Ciaran still hard inside of him, it took nothing, no time, for Chris to cum. Again. Ciaran looked into Chris's eyes, which were wide with astonishment. They kissed and moved together until Ciaran unexpectedly released again.

When Ciaran was done, finally, he rolled off of Chris and lay on his side of the bed. He knew they needed a moment to come down or they would never stop. The potion infused in the soap was that strong. Chris was still feeling electricity radiate through his body and didn't know which way was up, what day it was, or how to spell his own name. When he remembered who he was, he looked over at Ciaran, who was also staring at the ceiling with all smiles. Chris moved closer and put his head on Ciaran's shoulder.

"Ho. Lee. Shit," Chris said, bewildered at what had just happened. He had the urge to lick Ciaran's armpit again, but it was not as intense as before. Whatever was in that soap had successfully done its job.

Ciaran turned to him and smiled. "And that's how you make love to your boyfriend."

CHAPTER 18

London Down

As the first days of April came in, Chris and Ciaran had settled into a routine. They patrolled together almost nightly, Ciaran would stay for an hour, then go back to work. In the morning they would alternate flats to go to and eat breakfast – Chris would mostly cook but sometimes they would eat at The Atrium. They would make love, then sleep into the afternoon. Then they would spend the day together listening to music, arguing about sports, watching movies, or talking about magic until it was time for Ciaran to start his shift. If they were at Ciaran's house, Chris would leave with him and drive back home where Ciaran would Wisp to work. If they were at Chris's, Ciaran would Wisp to work from there. Then they would meet for patrol and do it all over again.

Chris was steadily going through all of Ciaran's books about magic. Ciaran still rarely did magic around him except for the same few incantations, but if he asked him a question about something he read, Ciaran would talk about it. Ciaran, likewise, was going through Chris's music and book collections. Chris would take Ciaran through songs and lyrics and the ones that made him feel happy when he was down, or matched his intensity when he was upset, or would read him his favorite passages from his beloved books.

Sunday nights, Ciaran's only night off since he worked six nights a week, were date nights, and they would go out to dinner at different places. On one of those Sundays, they had dinner upstairs instead and Ciaran met Clarissa and her son Rudy. She was more stunning in real life than her picture could ever show. She also had a very motherly way about her, the way that she spoke to her siblings and the way they gave her respect.

Rudy was a ball of energy, and Ciaran enjoyed playing video games or football with him. Ciaran actually preferred being at Chris's house. It was lively and there was never a dull moment with Charity entering in unannounced with stories from her work as a nurse, or Chris unexpectedly having to babysit Rudy because Clarissa needed a break. And Chris loved the way Ciaran was with his nephew. It made him wonder how Ciaran would be as a dad.

With every letter that came from home, Ciaran was tempted to add in his responses about his relationship with Chris, but the words never made it to paper. *Next time,* he thought each time. He knew his sister Diana's and her fiancé Quentin's wedding was coming up in a few months and he wasn't sure if he was ready to invite Chris just yet. Not because he didn't want him there, but because it scared him to think about his family's reaction to it.

Chris, on the other hand, preferred the quiet of Ciaran's place. Living in the house with his family for all his life made it almost impossible to have quiet moments, which was why he enjoyed the night shift as a ranger so much. Now he had a place to go and think, without Clarissa's nagging, Charity's talking, and Rudy's whining.

Chris was surprising himself not just that he wasn't getting bored with Ciaran, but that he craved his constant presence. Chris found that he liked the intimacy between them just as much as everything else. They could lay side by side and not talk, and it brought him comfort like no one else had before. The Saturday nights when Ciaran worked felt the longest and the loneliest. Ciaran, in his life as a partner, was changing him and he felt it. He realized that it was his first adult romantic relationship, and he reasoned that had a lot to do with it. He felt like he needed an alpha male to put him in his place from time to time, not in the dominant, abusive way like Rem had, but in a loving, patient, understanding way. Ciaran had no problem calling him out when he was being immature ("Go apologize to your sister for being an arsehole") and pushed him to do things like care maintenance on the car he just bought and opening a real bank account.

And they both agreed the sex was out of this world. For Ciaran, it continued to be an adventure as Chris found new areas of sensitivity on him, like licking his armpits. For Chris, he didn't know how he ever thought he would have the upper hand sexually; maybe for the first day or two, but Ciaran was a quick learner and did everything with passion and sensuality. Ciaran learned all the erogenous zones on Chris's body before he learned Ciaran's, and made it a point to make sure he was sexually satisfied, daily.

Chris knew he had strong feelings for Ciaran, but kept them buried just beneath the surface in case Ciaran ever wanted to talk about it. Because of the many deep conversations they had had about life, worldly politics, religion, magic, or culture, they never talked about how they felt about each other. And Chris understood why: Ciaran was still struggling with his sexual identity. And to bring up feelings was also to bring up his feelings about being with a man, being public, and having friends and family members know. Chris understood the unspoken silence on the issue and was in no hurry to push Ciaran along. As Ciaran had said to him many months ago, when he was ready to talk about it, Chris would be the first to know.

7:48 p.m.

Ciaran came into the Reserve and automatically felt something was wrong. It was eerily quiet, no hustle and bustle of the day's events. He quickly went up the hill to see half of the day crew milling around with the night crew.

Sarah came up to him. "London died a few hours ago. The boys wanted to start the funeral march, but Dale won't come out of his hut. No one knows what to do, so we're just waiting."

Ciaran sighed deeply. Remembering the loss of Kumoi seven years ago, he understood all too well how Dale was feeling. Dale had been through many dragon deaths, but Ciaran knew how close he and London had gotten in a short period of time.

Ciaran started walking toward the hut, but Bruno stepped in his path. "He is just going to curse you out. Let him be," Bruno growled at him.

Ciaran did not appreciate being stopped by the large man. He gave him a hard look, stepped around him, and kept going. He did not knock when he got there, just opened the door, and let himself in. Dale was sitting at the table, a glass of bourbon in front of him, with a bottle halfway done. He didn't look up when Ciaran came in. Ciaran sat at the table across from him and poured himself a glass, drank it quickly then held out his glass. Dale looked at him, then poured him another glass, filled his own glass halfway, and they drank in silence.

Dale then asked, "Those daytime fuckers still out there?"

"They are," Ciaran said.

Dale snorted. "Tell them to fuck off. Their shift is over."

"And they will, right after the funeral march. They are waiting for you."

Dale took another sip and took a long moment to respond. "I can't do this one, Ciaran. I'm too bloody angry. He didn't even have long with us. Barely three years? That wasn't enough to get over the damage they did to him. Fucking cunts."

"Well," said Ciaran, "It was probably the best years of his life, innit? He was free. Slept when he wanted, ate what he wanted, flew when he wanted. He had a best friend too, someone to look after him and care for him. To love him." Dale snorted again, then took another sip. "He deserves a proper, magnificent funeral, Dale, worthy of his life and his service."

He grumbled, "Fuck off. I'm not going out there. I'm not."

Ciaran stood up. "Okay. I'll do it."

Dale laughed. "You just learned how not to shit your pants, and you're going to lead a dragon funeral?"

"Somebody has to do it and I sure as shit aren't letting Bruno take the lead on this. Besides, I've been a part of three already."

"Yeah?" said Dale. "The first one you cried so much I was ready to send you back to your mum with nappies.

The second one you set off the wrong damn fireworks and almost took half the canyon out."

"And I did fine with Dani, sweet girl she was."

"That's because I had you in the back with the Shitheads," retorted Dale.

Ciaran rolled his eyes and looked at his watch. It was minutes to eight o'clock. "I'm going to do a roll call and assign roles. We're lining up at 8:45 p.m. and we're leaving exactly at 9 p.m. Come or don't come, but London's going in the ground by midnight. And it would be nice if the one person he loved and trusted the most was there to see him off."

Ciaran left Dale's hut and walked back over to the field where at least sixty men and Sarah were waiting. He started giving orders.

"I need about twenty men to levitate him; London is huge. Fifteen diggers and another ten, just in case. The rest will stay back and take care of the dragons. Sometimes the dragons follow, either on the ground or in the sky. If they do, let them, just keep an eye on them. Especially Hansel, he—"

Bruno cut him off and said loudly, "Who the fuck made you Lead?"

Ciaran said just as loudly, "If you wanted the fucking job, then you should have stepped up, Shithead. Why am I coming in doing it when he died hours ago?"

"Because we were waiting on our actual leader, not some ginger-haired dragon fucker playing dress up!" Bruno yelled at him.

Ciaran took a step toward him, and Sarah got in the middle with her hands outstretched to both of them. "Whoa. How about we do what Ciaran is asking so we can get this over with, Bruno? No one is leading here. We're a team. And Dale needs us to pull together right now."

She turned to the other men. "Lifters over here. Diggers over here. Back up over there. Let's go." She clapped her hands and people started moving. Bruno glared at Ciaran before he moved to where the lifters were.

Ciaran went to check on London's body. When he got into the valley where London was, he found a Fixer already there, eyes red like he had been crying, sitting on the ground near the dragon's face.

"Hello?" Ciaran called as he came closer. The young man looked up. He looked familiar, but Ciaran couldn't place him. Ciaran didn't know a lot of the guys on the day crew unless they were still in training.

"I'm Ciaran," he said, holding his hand out for a shake.

The young man stood up and took it. "I'm Vladimir. Vlad, really. I know who you are, Ciaran. You're the Senior Tamer," Vlad said in his Russian accent. Vlad was short but burly, with a face full of black, curly hair that matched the hair on his head. Ciaran remembered him from the night Betta escaped. But he did not mention it.

He looked down at London. The dragon was at least twenty-nine feet long, with brown scaly skin and pink scabs here and there. He looked like he was sleeping peacefully. Vlad spoke again. "It's my fault, you know. I didn't watch him properly. If I did, I would have seen the signs." He choked up.

Ciaran put his hand on Vlad's shoulder. "He's been sick for a while. Dale noticed he had been eating less in the winter. I too noticed he had been losing weight and sleeping restlessly at night in the last month. Something internally has been piercing him. There was nothing you could have done to prolong his life. He was old, he lived a hard life, and he got to die in peace. He was grateful. And we should be too." Vlad sniffed again. "Have you done this before, Vlad? How long have you been here?"

"Two years this past January. Sven tapped me after six months to move to Fixer."

"Like me, huh? You must be something special."

Vlad smiled at him. "I'm skilled with my *rodulé*. And I just have a way with animals in general. I would like to be a Tamer sooner rather than later, so I'm studying all I can."

"Who's your coach?"

"Tendai, under Hina, but also he has me as a Fixer under Anna. He said if he had room on his team he would take me, but he doesn't."

Ciaran nodded. "Tendai is good. He was my coach, too, under my first dragon. You'll be a Tamer before you know it. Come with me, Vlad." Ciaran motioned for him to follow him while they checked on the other dragons.

Hansel was restless, making weird noises and pacing. Ciaran told him, "He's distraught; he knows London has died. We will need to keep an eye on him for the next couple of weeks." They checked on Ben and Anna, who seemed fine. Ciaran told him, "They will probably take flight and follow us. That's okay, that's how they show tribute."

They went to Betta, and Tommy was trying to coax her out of the corner. "She's confused," he told Vlad. "She was not close to him, but she knows something is wrong. Tommy is trying to reassure her and he'll do this all night if he has to."

"But I won't have to, right?" Tommy said to Ciaran expectantly. "Because you're going to step in here, aren't you, *el jefe*?"

"Nope," Ciaran said, shaking his head. "I have a dragon funeral to lead. You'll figure it out."

But Ciaran walked over to Betta, touched her face, and spoke softly to her. She grunted, then closed her eyes and allowed him to pet her. He walked back to Vlad.

"I don't spend a lot of time with her," said Vlad. "Since she ran out on me that night, she eyes me suspiciously. I don't think she likes me."

"This dragon bitch doesn't like anyone," said Tommy. "It's her normal way. Now, if she tried to bite you, then she hates you. But regular dislike is normal for her."

Vlad chuckled. "I'll take note of that and won't take it personally."

Ciaran said to Tommy, "Stay here and keep her company. Feed her venison if she wants to eat. If not, keep her hydrated. I will take over when I get back."

He motioned for Vlad to follow him. "You're on digging. It's where you need to be tonight. There is no *Vis* in the digging, to remind us that magic doesn't solve all of life's problems. It's also a reminder of how precious life is, and the work we do here." Vlad nodded.

They walked back over to London where the rest of the Reservers in the funeral march were waiting. He saw Bruno with the diggers instead of lifters and that was surprising, considering his utter disdain for all creatures, much less dragons. Ciaran remembered Chris at that moment for some reason and was grateful for the phone he had given him. He walked back over to the barracks for some privacy.

"Hey," Chris said, surprised at the call. He was about to take his shower to get ready for his shift.

"Hi, Chris. Listen, I don't think I will make it to patrol tonight. London died today and we're giving him a proper sendoff. The dragon march usually takes four hours minimum, so…"

"Oh. Okay." Chris and Ciaran were rarely apart, so this would be one of those rare days. "So the morning, then? Your place?"

"Yes. If I'm going to be late, I will let you know."

"Okay. Ciaran? I'm sorry about London. I know he wasn't yours, but it still affects you. It's okay to feel. Just a reminder."

"Thanks for the reminder," he said softly. "Until then."

"Until then." Chris hung up first, glad he got the heads up so he could prepare himself for another lonely night.

CHAPTER 19

Funeral March

By the time Ciaran had gone to change into his work uniform, made it back to London, and got everyone lined up with their assignments, it was ten minutes to nine. The men were chattering softly when someone noticed Dale coming down the hill into the valley. A hush fell over as he walked down in the only Magi cloak he owned—black with gold stars that twinkled every time he moved, and gold buttons down the front. He walked slowly and Ciaran knew it was because he was shitfaced drunk and trying not to show it.

Everyone was silent as he went to stand beside Ciaran. Ciaran looked at him for direction, but Dale gave him no indication that he was leading. So Ciaran called out, "Lifters!"

Seventeen men pointed their *rodulés* at the forever-sleeping dragon. He lifted about thirty feet in the air, with all four wings spread out like he was flying. Sven, who pulled five men for drumming, began the slow pounding of the drums and they began to walk in silence, with London floating right above them. About two kilometers of nothing but drumming into their walk, Ciaran started one of the dragon funeral choruses:

"Oh Jenny, oh Jenny, why did you go?
My heart will never be the same.
Oh Jenny, my Jenny, you left me alone
And now there's no one to tame.
Oh Jenny, oh Jenny, you told me you'll stay
But then you took off and you're gone.
Oh Jenny, my Jenny, I thought you would stay
But left me to sing this sad song."

Those who knew it joined in, the rest learned it along the way and sang. Dale was the only one not singing. A few more kilometers, the song died out, and someone started another funeral chorus, then three more after that. After walking for almost two hours, they made it to the edge of the valley below the mountains where the dragons were laid to rest. They stopped while the diggers scouted for a good spot, conjured shovels together, and stood in a semicircle.

Surprisingly, it was Bruno's voice that called out, "Heave!" Together, they dug the tip of the shovel into the earth. "Hoooo!" he called out again. In unison, they lifted up the shovel, carrying dirt with them, and tossed it behind them. Bruno called out again, and the diggers continued to dig.

The rest formed a line behind them as they dug. After a while of watching them, Dale left the circle, conjured up a shovel, and joined them. Ciaran did as well. Someone started up the choruses again, and Sven and the drummers drummed while the others either sang or dug. Suddenly, a shadow passed overhead, then two more. Hansel, followed by Ben and Anna, had followed the funeral march and circled above, with Hansel continuing that terrible cry like a chicken being strangled.

Two hours later, the hole was ten feet deep and 30 feet wide and the levitators lowered London into the ground. Everyone waited, but Ciaran did not move. It was tradition that the leader of the march started the covering. But he looked over at Dale and waited.

Dale grunted softly under his breath. Then he walked over and climbed into the grave on top of London. He petted him and whispered in his ear for a couple of minutes before he climbed back out.

Dale lifted up his *dulé* and said, *"Humo."*

Wind dusted up the dirt that they had just dug up and everyone hid their faces as it engulfed them. More than half of the dirt ended up on London, coating him completely. Some others mimicked Dale, including Ciaran and Vlad, and in minutes London was buried, his final resting place coated with pink tulips courtesy of the backup team.

Ciaran turned to the group. "Okay, you can start to Wisp back. But remember, it will only take you about two kilometers away; you will have to walk in. Or you can walk back the whole way. It's up to you. Day crew, find a spot in the barracks. You're staying overnight and will start your shift an hour after sunlight. That's when the night crew can leave."

Ciaran looked at his watch. It was five minutes to 1 a.m. He might have made it back in time to patrol with Chris if he Wisp'd just then. Then he glanced around as others were either Wisp'ing on the spot or walking back through the valley, and Dale was sitting on a nearby boulder staring at the flowers. *Chris will just have to wait until the morning,* he thought to himself. He walked over and sat next to Dale, waiting for everyone to leave.

When they were alone, he put his hand on Dale's shoulder and said, "It's okay, you know. I'm here for you, the same way you were there for me when Kumoi died. This is hard, but just know if there is someone you can talk to, it's me."

Dale slowly turned to Ciaran. "Get your paws off me before I curse them off. Don't know where they've been. Probably up someone's arsehole." Ciaran smiled and took his hand down.

They sat in silence for a bit. Then Dale said, "Speaking of hands in arseholes, how is it going with you and the cocksucker? The literal cocksucker?"

Ciaran laughed. "You just had to go there, didn't you? Always the unrefined Dale."

Dale shrugged. "I just assume there is a whole lot of cock sucking going on. No need to deny it now."

Ciaran shook his head with a smile. "We're fine. We're really, really good, actually."

Dale grunted. "Still confused about it all, I reckon."

Ciaran sighed. "It's been so crazy. When I'm with him, there is no confusion at all. It's pretty perfect how well we fit together, how good we are. It's when I'm not with him, which is rare, by the way, because I never want to be away from him. But when we aren't in the same space, I'm so in my head over it, Dale. I spent almost nine years on this Reserve and never looked at a man, never. Now I'm wondering if I'm actually gay or do I just like this bloke. And I really do like this bloke. Wondering how I'm going to tell my parents, and if they will accept me. Wondering if or when I should go to the Council over being with a Commoner. If it's even worth it at this point."

"It's not," Dale said. "Fuck that last part. We both know the damage has been done. Going to the Council now will just get you a one-way ticket to Claustra. He already knows you're a Magus. Just let it be."

Ciaran didn't speak for a moment, then said, "How did you know?"

"Ha! You didn't *abscondo* his arse from moment one, and that's not like you, Ciaran. You think I believed you used *abscondo* on him later on? Especially since you came back with this 'patrolling for safety' horseshit excuse to see him again and every day after that. No one spends that much time with someone unless you want to be close to them. And no one continues to spend that much time with someone and they don't know who you are. I married a Commoner once, remember?"

Ciaran did. Dale's first wife, the one he loved the most, was a Commoner. She passed away unexpectedly from an undiagnosed brain tumor. They were quiet for a moment, then Ciaran sighed. "So what do I do?"

"End it now, *abscondo* him, and move on," Dale said matter-of-factly. Ciaran looked horrified. Dale chuckled. "Ah, can't do that, can you? Then keep it to yourself. Do you know how many Magicians are married to Commoners pretending they know nothing? Fuck off with that honesty shit. The Magi Secrecy Unit don't want to hear it, anyway. Literally, they don't. Do not tell them; they are cursed and forced to tell if a Magi law is broken, or they descend into madness within twenty-four hours. Unless it's a major infraction, they live by the 'Don't ask, don't tell' rule, and you better do as well."

Dale stood up. "You love him yet?"

Ciaran's heart skipped a beat. "I don't know."

Dale grunted, not believing him one bit. "Well, when you do, make sure you hold on to him tight. You can be a real arrogant pain in the arse, so if anyone is willing to put up with you, you should keep them around."

"Thanks, Dale," Ciaran said sarcastically.

Dale lifted up his palms. "Well, hey. I say it because I care."

Ciaran laughed. Dale started walking, and Ciaran followed. They walked the two hours and talked about the trainees and Fixers and who was next to be moved up. Dale said that Vlad was next in line to be a Tamer out of everyone, even the ones that had been Fixers longer, despite his immense fuck up with Betta last summer. He told Ciaran that Vlad was smart, gentle with the animals, and had a way about him, and Ciaran should take him under his wing.

When they made it back, Dale went straight to his cabin and Ciaran went to check on the dragons. Ben and Anna were back, but Hansel was not. Betta was still in her corner and Tommy was lying next to her, asleep. He knew Betta was not sleeping, although she did not move; he could tell by the way she was breathing.

Ciaran went to lay on the other side of her head and thought about what Dale had said. He knew he was right about his relationship; he had already fucked up and broke secrecy, but he couldn't imagine regretting it. Chris had already changed his life for the better.

CHAPTER 20

The Mission

Dale spent the next three days in the cabin, leaving Sven, Ciaran, Khalid, Bruno, and Sarah to make sure things went smoothly on the Reserve. That also meant Ciaran could not leave the Reserve and worked round the clock. He and Chris spoke every morning, and he snuck out every night at 11 p.m. for a kiss, and again at 1 a.m. to patrol, but had to get back right afterward. Sleeping alone was torture for the two of them.

On day three, Sarah went in there and stayed until the morning of day four. Whatever she said or did worked because Dale came out of his hut that afternoon and resumed his duties. And it was a good thing because, during those three days, Hansel had become whinier and more aggressive. Dale demoted his lead Tamer Vincent to second in line, reassigned his Fixers, and took over, which appeared to be all Hansel wanted because he got happy having Dale's full attention. And Dale was happy to have a dragon to focus on again.

Ciaran, practically living on the Reserve, left little to no time for his relationship and they both felt it. But Chris was practicing not being selfish and immature and tried not to make Ciaran feel bad about things beyond his control, like work duties, so he held his tongue. So he was surprised when Ciaran showed up on his doorstep four days later on a Saturday early afternoon. He and Charity had just settled in for a movie marathon when his doorbell rang.

His eyes went wide as Ciaran said, "Got the next three days off. I don't go back until Tuesday!" They kissed and embraced as Chris led him inside.

Charity said upon seeing him, "Guess that's it for me then." She started getting up.

"No, stay," Ciaran said. "I'm intruding. I can come ba—"

"How about we all stay and watch a movie?" Chris suggested.

So they lay around and watched movies: Chris on the long couch with Ciaran on the floor next to him, and Charity curled up on the loveseat. Ciaran quickly fell asleep. He had been unable to get a good night's rest the last couple of days, having to be alert on the Reserve. He was awakened hours later, Charity gone and Chris's wet lips around his penis. Chris's blow job was always intense and precise, making Ciaran cum hard. Ciaran happily returned the favor, making Chris squirm underneath him until he, too, came.

Afterward, Ciaran came up for a kiss. He thought it was going to be simple and sweet, but they kissed for a while, savoring each other's tongue and lips. Ciaran came up for air first and put his face in Chris's neck. "God, I missed you," he murmured.

Chris caressed the nape of Ciaran's neck. "I don't like it when we are apart," Chris said softly. "It just feels weird now, not being by your side."

"I don't either. Every day it felt like something was missing," Ciaran said, nuzzling his nose deeper.

He thought about what Dale had asked him, if he loved Chris, and remembered how his heart skipped. It scared him to think the real possibility in such a short period of time was that the answer was yes.

A couple of weeks later, Ciaran came to work, and a translucent tiger approached him. He smiled at Dale's *Amina*. "Yes, Dale?"

The tiger opened his mouth and began to talk, but it was Dale's voice. "Come meet me in my office."

Ciaran was confused. Dale rarely used his office. But he followed the tiger up the hill and to the right of the barracks to a smaller building that held official offices on the third floor, and was used for training on the lower two. They went up to the top floor, and the tiger went through the closed door. Ciaran knocked.

"Come in."

Ciaran opened the door. The tiger had disappeared, but Dale was sitting behind his desk with his notes. He looked up and got right to it. "We received a message from a village in Chad, North Africa, the Sahara region. A boy found a dragon egg three years ago and hatched it. Turns out it's a Krekardron, a tail-whipping dragon."

"Oh," Ciaran said. He sat in the chair in front of the desk.

"He thought he could raise it on his own in the nearby mountains, but it's proven too much for him now. The villagers got a hold of the dragon and put an invisible cage around it, afraid it's going to burn the village down. They want us to take it away, as soon as possible. I'm giving you the mission."

Ciaran tried to keep his face stoic, but inside he was shocked, nervous, and very excited. Ciaran knew he was next in line to head a mission, but he didn't think it would happen anytime soon. He had only been on one other mission, and that was to bring Hansel there years ago. At the time, he was a guard in Squad B, and it was simple and easy enough. But being in charge of the mission was completely different than taking orders. Ciaran would be the one giving them. He was honored that Dale had that much trust in him.

"Pick your team, no more than twenty men," said Dale. "Bring it back alive if you can. If not, bury it out there."

"You're not going with us?" Ciaran asked.

"No. Sven will, if you ask him."

Ciaran nodded. "When do we leave?"

"Thirty-six hours. It's urgent but not high-critical. It's been there a few days already, so a few more won't hurt. And we need to do it right, so take your time and pick carefully. Krekardrons are Class C and can be nasty beasts. So create your team, go kiss your beau, and be back here by 7 a.m. Wednesday morning sharp. The Flyer is leaving at 8 a.m."

Ciaran nodded again, but he wasn't listening to the last thing Dale was saying. *Chris was not going to be happy about him going away,* was his first thought. And he also thought about how dangerous this mission was. While he was eager to go, a part of him realized he had something to come back to, which made the stakes higher. And for the first time since working on the Reserve he was afraid for his own life.

Dale watched him intently. "If you don't want it..."

Ciaran said quickly. "No, I want it!" He stood up and shook Dale's hand. "Thank you. I am honored that you trust me with this. I won't let you down."

As he turned around to leave the office, he heard Dale mumble, "Yeah, well, just don't die."

Ciaran went downstairs to one of the training rooms. He grabbed chalk and walked over to the blackboard, thinking about who he wanted on his team. Out of twenty men allowed, he knew at least seven of them had to be Hunters. *Which means Bruno.* He groaned audibly at that thought. But if he was going to lead a successful mission, he knew he needed the best on his team, and Bruno was the best, hands down. Also, Bruno's unflinching willingness to protect human life above all else was counter to his desire to protect humans and creatures. He realized exasperatingly he needed Bruno not just on his team, but as part of his leadership. He sighed and picked his Hunters: Sahid, Gideon, Jamie, Ismael, Axel, Mike, and Bruno.

He needed a Novo and naturally he chose Felix, one of his best friends, who had come over with him from Campus and the Magi military. And Felix was probably the smartest man he knew.

Tommy knocked, then came in as he was still staring at the board. "Oy Captain, my Captain, I was looking for you… What are you doing?"

Ciaran said, "Close the door." Tommy did and looked at him curiously. "Don't say anything yet, but… I'm tapped for a mission."

"Bloody fucking brilliant, mate!!!" Tommy yelled.

"Shut the fuck up, Tommy, sheeesh!" Ciaran scolded. "The last thing I need is people finding out and begging to be a part of the mission."

"Oh yeah, right. Because that would be awful." Tommy let one second pass, then said, "But you're taking me, right?"

Ciaran smiled and shook his head. "If I take you, who is watching Betta? Don't you have a responsibility right now?"

Tommy looked crestfallen. "You... You're really not going to take me, Ciaran?"

"I can't do this based on favorites, Tommy. I have to do this smart and pick the best of the best, make sure this goes well. You understand, right?"

Tommy nodded, but still looked sad. But then perked up. "Can I at least help you pick? I know more of these guys than you do. I work days and nights."

"Sure, Tommy. I could definitely use the help."

Tommy walked closer to the board with his hand on his chin and went through what Ciaran had done so far. Then threw a hand in the air. "Bruno! Fuck all hell, you can't take him with you! Switch him out for Ned. He's been here longer."

Ciaran shook his head. "Bruno is sharper. I told you, I'm not doing this based on favorites. I need the best."

"Well, then, now I'm glad I'm not going," Tommy said curtly.

Ciaran laughed. Bruno had broken his nose a few months after Tommy arrived on the Reserve for being Tommy, saying something inappropriate and weird. And Ciaran swung a tree branch over Bruno's head for it, knocking him out cold. Tommy had been scared of Bruno ever since and kept his distance. That was the real reason he stayed so close to Ciaran, because he knew Ciaran would never let Bruno put hands on him again, and Ciaran knew it, too.

"Tell me which Fixers and Dungers I should take," said Ciaran.

Together they created the list: five Fixers that he could trust to follow his orders—Jesse, who was his other friend from Campus, Demitri, Ollie, Lucas, and Vlad. Then he picked four Dungers that had been in training the longest. It would be an opportunity to prove themselves and get picked for paid assignments. Together, they decided on Dylan, Greyson, Mateo, and Lee. The latter two guys he did not know, but Tommy swore they were good. Along with the seven Hunters, plus Sven and Felix, he was feeling confident about his team.

Ciaran looked at his list and realized he had all of his Campus chums there except Khalid. He wrote his name down. They stood back and looked at the list of nineteen men.

Tommy said, "This is good. You'll do well."

Ciaran looked at him and smiled. "Not quite. I need one more." He wrote Tommy's name down next to Vlad.

Tommy looked stunned, then screamed, "HOLY FUCKING HELL I'M GOING!!!"

He jumped in Ciaran's arms and wrapped his feet around his waist, making Ciaran laugh. "Get the fuck off me, you brainless cunt!"

Once Tommy settled, they created the four standard squads: Squad D, The Perimeter monitored from outside and around the village, keeping everyone safe. He put five people there: Hunter Jamie, Hunter Mike, Fixer Ollie, Dunger Lee, and Dunger Dylan. Squad C, The Corral, kept everyone calm and happy. Their job was to spend time with the villagers, get to know local customs, and gain their trust. He put five men there with the most outgoing personalities, Hunter Sahid and his brother Khalid, Fixer Lucas, Fixer Demetri, and Dunger Grayson. Next was Squad B, The Preservation. They were Ciaran's immediate security team, the ones he would rely on to take orders from him and execute the plan. He chose his seven: Tamer Jesse, Tamer Tommy, Fixer Vlad, Dunger Mateo, Hunter Ismael, Hunter Axel, and Hunter Gideon.

And last was leadership, Squad A. Along with Ciaran, it would be Sven, Felix, and Bruno. Of course, Tommy begged to be on leadership. "I can help, honest!" But Ciaran told him no about five times before he threatened to take him off altogether, and that shut him up. Then Ciaran waved his wand and concealed the board.

He sent a signal through the *rodulé*, yellow light instead of red, and nineteen men showed up. Everyone was surprised that it was Ciaran who had sent for them, and not Dale. More than half of the mission crew were day Reservers, so they had to wait until everyone arrived before Ciaran started talking. Sarah, who was on site, came in with Felix to find out what was going on as well.

When Ciaran told them about the mission, a hush came over, then a buzz of excitement as they all started talking at once.

He told them, "You can say no, or you can agree to go, but I need to know before you leave this room if someone else is to take your place."

Not one person refused. And even Sarah said, "I'm going, too. Felix is great, but I want to go on this mission and you can't stop me."

"Well, that would make you number twenty-one, and Dale specifically said no more than twenty. I'm not canceling one of my men because you want to take the ride," Ciaran told her sternly.

Sarah got up and stood in front of him. Everyone knew not to make the small Scottish Mage angry, and they all watched quietly to see what she was going to do. But Ciaran crossed his arms, looking down at the short older woman in defiance.

"Ciaran Beals," she started in a condescending tone, "I am forty years older than you and have more experience in my pinky than you have in your left or right testicle. You will not stop me from going on this mission and neither will Dale.

And if you try, you will wake up with those same testicles glued together for the next six months. Dale told you twenty men. I'm a *woman*. I'm going."

And with that, she left. Ciaran shook his head, but didn't say anything else about it. He liked the feel of his testicles being separated. Ciaran turned back to the men.

"It's now," he checked his watch, "10:02 p.m. Everyone, go home, including the night Reservers. Get some much-needed rest, practice your incantations if you need to. Be back here by 7 a.m. sharp Wednesday morning. I will give you your assignments and last-minute instructions, then we are in the skies no later than 8 a.m."

Everyone started filtering out excitedly. Bruno walked over to Ciaran, and Tommy instinctively stood at Ciaran's side with a scowl on his face. Bruno looked at Tommy and scoffed, then said to Ciaran, "Call your mutt off, will you?"

Ciaran resisted the urge to say something nasty. Instead, he exhaled and asked, "You need something, Bruno?"

"Yeah. What are you playing at? Why did you pick me on your team? Plan on leaving me in the Sahara there?" he deadpanned.

But Ciaran said, "No. I picked the best. You lead the Hunters because you're the best Hunter. I need you on this mission."

Bruno continued to eye him suspiciously, so Ciaran gave him all of it. "You're in Squad A. I need your leadership. It's not about me or you. It's about making sure these men in my care come back safe and alive. Can you put your feelings aside and do that? Because I can. If you can't, then walk out and I will put someone else there."

Bruno stared at him intently. Then nodded. "See you the day after next," he said and left.

As soon as he did, Tommy puffed out air as if he had been holding it in. "Whew. I really thought Bruno was going to say something to make you hit him. Then I'd have to jump on his back and bite him like an alley cat, then he'd beat the shit out of me, but that's okay because I would be honored to get my arse beat for you, oy Captain, my Captain."

He smiled at Ciaran, who looked at him in disbelief. "You're so fucking weird, Tommy."

CHAPTER 21

Thirty-two Hours

10:57 p.m.

Ciaran left as well to catch Chris at the beginning of his shift. He Wisp'd to the bottom of the steps, then walked up. Chris was surprised to see him in the doorway.

Elijah, the newest ranger, hadn't even left yet when he saw his lover still in the street clothes he had on when they left his house that evening and not in his DRA coveralls. Ciaran and Elijah greeted each other, then Elijah went back to giving Chris the rundown of his shift. Ciaran loitered by the door, patiently waiting. Chris was barely listening, but nodded accordingly, with his thoughts focused on Ciaran.

Once Elijah left, Chris turned his attention to his boyfriend. "Well, this is a surprise. What's going on?"

"Sit down, I got some news," Ciaran said, and sat at the round table.

"What, you're pregnant?" Chris joked as he sat down as well.

Ciaran smiled. "Not at the moment." He cleared his throat. "There is a mission that I've been asked to lead. As the Senior Certified Dragonologist—"

Chris cut him off. "Wait, did you say Dragonologist? Is that a real degree or a made-up one? Like, do you have an actual certificate that says Masters in Dragonology? Because if so, I need to see it for clarification purposes." Chris laughed.

Ciaran didn't. He ignored Chris's last statement and started again. "As the Senior Certified Dragonologist on the Reserve, I have been tasked with the responsibility of leading a crew and containing a dragon needing preservation and bringing it back to the Reserve in one piece. I have already assembled my team. We leave approximately thirty-two hours from now." Ciaran waited.

Chris finally realized what Ciaran was saying. "So, you're leaving?"

"Yes."

"On..." Chris did the math in his head. "Wednesday morning?"

"Yes."

"To capture a dragon that is hurt somehow?"

"Contain. We do not *capture* dragons. We contain them and bring them to a safe location. Most likely the Reserve."

"Okay, contain a dragon. Where are you going? I don't think you said..."

"I didn't. Northern Chad in Africa."

Chris nodded. "Ah-ha. And for how long, I don't think you said that either...?"

Ciaran hesitated. "Normal reconnaissance takes three to five days, more or less. Sometimes more."

Chris felt his chest squeeze slightly hearing the time they would be apart, and decided to make another joke. "Ah-ha. Is this your way of breaking up with me, Ciaran?"

"Bloody hell, Chris, can you just be serious right now?" Ciaran said, annoyed.

"Okay, okay!" Chris relented. Ciaran sat back and didn't look Chris in the eye. Chris asked, "So how dangerous is this mission?"

"It's … nothing I haven't done before," Ciaran said, still looking away.

Chris didn't say anything. He knew it was far more dangerous than Ciaran let on. He decided to joke again, hoping it didn't anger Ciaran too much. "Will you bring me something back from your trip?"

Ciaran looked at him and smiled. "Sure. I'll bring you a key chain."

Chris smiled. "So. What are you going to be doing for the next thirty-two hours? I'm assuming not working on the Reserve but getting ready for your mission?" Ciaran stared at Chris and let his eyes answer him. Chris understood and nodded slowly. "Well. Make yourself comfortable. I got a shitload of incident reports to archive into the system."

Chris got up, sat at the desktop computer near the switchboard, and opened up the folder to start data entering. Ciaran took off his shoes and lay in the bed. They didn't talk as Ciaran lay there thinking about the mission and Chris tried not to think about it, so he put on music, instead. Two hours later, they patrolled together.

On the walk, Chris asked, "So tell me about your team. Who's on it? Tommy?"

Ciaran smiled. "Yes." They talked about his decision to add Bruno, how Sarah got around the twenty men rule by being a woman, and how he accidentally added all of his friends to be a part of his crew as well.

"That's okay," Chris said. "You need people who you can trust with your life. Those guys are it."

When they got back to the Tank, Ciaran went to the bed again and Chris lay beside him. They turned to lay on their sides and face each other, legs entwined. Ciaran reached over and traced Chris's lips with his finger. Chris opened his mouth and sucked his finger seductively.

Ciaran laughed. "Do you have to be lewd all the time?"

Chris said, "And you wouldn't want it any other way."

They lay together another few moments and then Ciaran said, "Tell me something you've never told me before."

"Like what?"

"Tell me ... about your first girlfriend."

Chris laughed. "Ah well, I can't tell you about my first girlfriend without telling you about my first boyfriend."

Ciaran laughed. "Only you would have one in the same. Okay. Tell me."

So Chris told him about Ramesh Ang, the Bangladesh boy he met freshman year of high school. They were on the same track team with Cristobal Hajdini, who he called Other Chris, Jaxon, Flakrim, and Ezekiel called Zeke. The six of them became fast friends, being all freshmen and the youngest ones on the team, paying their dues and proving their worth together. But he and Ramesh became closer, being the darker brown kids on the team, and two of four in their entire grade. They would hang out at each other's houses, play video games, and practice running and timing each other.

"One day after practice, we found ourselves alone in the locker room and I don't even remember what we were talking about, but he was looking at me all funny. Then he asked me out of nowhere, 'Do you want a blow job?' I was shocked. If he liked me, he never showed his hand until that very moment. But I said as calmly as I could, 'Yeah, okay.' And he just got down between my legs, pulled out my cock, and bobbed his head up and down until I came."

Ciaran asked, "Were you attracted to boys by then?"

"Honestly, I don't know," Chris said. "I found him to be handsome, I guess; he reminded me of Aladdin, which was my favorite Disney movie at the time. I found people in general attractive, or body parts really are what attracted me: lips, hands, shapes of bottoms, you know. I had seen a porno or two by then courtesy of Other Chris, and I would watch both partners move and both turned me on. I mean, I had a crush on Mr. Xhepa, but who didn't, with that olive skin, jet-black hair, and hazel eyes. I'm sure half the faculty wanted to fuck him, men and women.

"But Ramesh and I, we never flirted, not once. No sexual jokes traded between us. Nothing. So I really have no idea where it came from and I don't know why I readily said yes either, but I did, and then he did, and it was soooo much better than jerking myself off. He jumped out of the way when I came, but I didn't care. I didn't know swallowing was a thing at fourteen, anyway." Ciaran laughed.

"So naturally I said afterward, 'Let me do you.' And honestly, to me, it was better than getting an actual blow job. I felt him grow in my mouth and I didn't do anything but bob up and down and squeeze my cheeks in from time to time until he came in my mouth. I spit it out, but not before I moved it around in my mouth a bit. I couldn't believe I did that for him. Everything about it made me feel so..." He trailed off.

"Powerful," Ciaran finished for him.

Chris smiled. "Yes. You would know what that feels like now, wouldn't you?" Ciaran smiled back. Chris continued, "Well, after that, it was on. We would find reasons to be alone and then blow each other. At school, at my house, at his house, in the park, in these woods. Didn't matter. Then this fucker ups and gets a girlfriend on me! Right before Christmas break, he starts talking to us about how he asked out Nami, one of the cheerleaders. I think that was his way of telling me, because he said it nonchalantly as we sat around after practice, but he looked at me. I was fucking pissed, but I never brought it up the whole week we were off.

"The first day back to school, I walked right up to Jesika Bladvik, head cheerleader, tall, blonde hair, icy blue eyes, Icelandic goddess, kind of a bitch, but she was so beautiful she got away with it. I walked up to her and said in French, because I knew she spoke it, '*Will you be my girlfriend?*' And she says back to me in French, '*What took you so long to ask me?*' I kissed her right on the field in front of everyone. And just like that, I had a girlfriend out front and a boyfriend in the closet. For the next year and a half, through the rest of freshman year and sophomore year."

"Stop it!" Ciaran laughed. "That sounds wild."

"I'm serious," Chris confirmed. "And it was. Jesika and Nami became best friends because of how much time the four of us hung out. Then, Other Chris nabbed Emiranda, Emi, right after that and it was a new group of six that did everything together. By the time the summer hit, we were inseparable. We spent a lot of time in these very woods by the lake, breaking into cabins on the Northside where we would eat up all the food, watch movies, and sometimes porn, again courtesy of Other Chris. But any time we were alone, Ramesh and I would blow each other. Everyone would be downstairs or on one side of the woods and he and I would be on the other, face fucking each other.

"By sophomore year, Ramesh and Nami started having sex, so that was annoying. But he knew not to fuck her and then have me blow him, though. That was like our unwritten rule. We kept the girlfriend stuff separate. I wasn't sexing Jesika yet, though; I was still a virgin in the purest sense of the word. She would let me touch her but she was not giving it up, and honestly, I was still getting my nob slobbed at least twice a week so I wasn't too pressed to pressure her, which she really liked about me.

"But then he drops a bomb on me toward the end of sophomore year. Again he says it after a track meet when we're all together, track team, cheerleaders, at a celebratory dinner. He says his grandmother is sick and the whole family is moving back to Bangladesh to care for her, right after the school year is over. And he's looking at me when he says it. I'm fucking crushed. We had all these plans to go to college and get an apartment together. Obviously, the girls could come too. We needed a cover. But now he's going and didn't know if he could or would ever come back. As time got closer, we both were antsy. We were either fighting or blowing each other, but we weren't talking about him leaving.

"Two days before he had to get on a plane, we threw him a party at his house, Other Chris's idea of course. His parents had left a couple of days before that and left his older sister in charge, who she said to us, 'Do what you want.' And half the school showed up, definitely everyone in our year, and it was like a rave. We trashed the house so badly. By 3 a.m. it dwindled down to just the three couples, the six of us again. First, the girls left together, then Other Chris who lived a block away, headed out. Ramesh asked me to stay the night, and I said yes.

"We went upstairs to his room and started making out on his bed. Then he told me he needed a favor from me: He wanted me to fuck him. He took out a nine-inch dildo and some anal balls, said he had been practicing for months so it wouldn't hurt."

Ciaran started laughing loudly and Chris had to quiet him down to continue the story. "Listen, listen!! So I said okay, got the lube he had, and basically poured the whole bottle on him and me. I tried to get it in a few times but apparently, he wasn't practicing right because my head wouldn't fit. Or maybe because the dildo was straight and not shaped like a dick I don't know, but it wasn't going in at first. Then I just lost a little patience I think and just rammed it in there and he screamed so loud and clamped on my dick with his butt cheeks that when I pulled out, I ended up cumming all over myself. And the fucker laughed at me! I was so pissed and embarrassed..."

But he stopped telling the story because Ciaran was laughing so hard tears were coming out of his eyes at this point. "Oh God, oh God, that is fucking hilarious!" he continued to laugh.

"Fuck off, Ciaran, I want to hear about your first time next," Chris said, laughing with him.

When Ciaran regained control of himself, he said, "You know, when I asked you about your first time, you told me about Rem, not this one."

Chris shrugged. "I guess I didn't consider this losing my virginity. I feel like this is more Ramesh's first time, his story to tell."

Ciaran nodded and Chris continued, "So after he stopped laughing, we just lay in the bed and held each other. I think he was afraid to go. Afraid of never having what we had again with a boy. You can't be gay in countries like Bangladesh you know. So we kissed and held each other and listened to his sister fuck her boyfriend's brains out until it aroused us again and we ended up 69ing, then fell asleep.

"The next morning, Other Chris and Jaxon came by to help Ramesh finish packing up his room and I'm still there in the same clothes I had on last night. Jaxon had no clue but I found out later on that Other Chris knew almost the whole time, but at that time he made no mention of it. We helped him pack and his dad came home that night so I wasn't staying over. And that was that; he got on a plane and I never saw him again. I did find out he keeps in touch with Jaxon, which should annoy me but I get why he doesn't talk to me. I know he's married to a woman and has four kids. And he probably has a boyfriend on the side."

Ciaran asked, "Was he your first love?"

"I don't know. We never said it to each other."

"So what happened with Jesika?"

"Oh, I popped her cherry about two weeks later. Hers and mine." Ciaran laughed and shook his head. Chris smiled but said, "I kind of feel bad now because after Ramesh left I did start putting pressure on her and she gave in. Or maybe she was ready too. She was already sixteen and waiting for me to catch up. We had sex all summer and I am still shocked I did not get her pregnant, but she was probably on the pill or something. Then I met Rem in the beginning of my Junior year and I started pulling away from her. We broke up by the start of winter."

There goes that name again that keeps popping up, Ciaran thought to himself. But he let Chris continue.

"I still see her once in a while. Her and Emi are still best gals and Emi and Other Chris are married and still my best mates. Jesika is married and has a beautiful daughter."

"Did you love her?"

"Oh yeah, I loved her for sure," he said with a confident head nod. "I said it first, no hesitation, before we had sex. She was an amazing girl, and I cared for her a lot. I also really liked being with Ramesh. Which, I guess, made it hard for me to love her completely."

Ciaran smiled at him. "You know, when people ask you about your first time, you should tell them that story, not the Rem one. This is so much better."

Chris smiled. They lay in bed in silence for a few moments. Then Chris spoke. "I should have said it earlier, but I'm proud of you, Ciaran. You worked hard to achieve leadership status, proven yourself over and over again, and Dale finally rewarded you. You deserve to lead this mission. And you'll do great. I believe in you."

Ciaran touched his face in gratitude. Chris took his hand and kissed it, then pulled Ciaran closer to kiss him. They kissed and groped each other until Chris got on top of Ciaran, moving his groin back and forth.

Ciaran came up for air. "Uh-uh, no fucking in the Tank." Chris groaned and got off him. Then Ciaran said, "I know it's your turn, but come home with me. I want you in my space today."

"Okay," Chris agreed.

He turned his back to Ciaran, and Ciaran draped his arm around him. They spooned and talked until the sun rose, then moved to the table for Miche's arrival. They left holding hands, Ciaran having long since lost his embarrassment and shyness, and made their way to Ciaran's place.

CHAPTER 22

Magician and Man

When they arrived, Chris said he would cook breakfast rather than buy at The Atrium and Ciaran said okay, but he still needed to go downstairs for something. He returned thirty minutes later, as the food was almost done with nothing in his hands.

"Where did you go?" Chris asked curiously.

"I had to pick something up."

"Liiiiiike?" Chris raised an eyebrow.

Ciaran didn't answer and sat at the table. Chris brought over the plates and they ate in silence. As Chris sipped his tea toward the end of his meal, Ciaran took something out of his pocket and held it up. It was a mini key chain that resembled a *rodulé* attached to the ring. Chris was confused at first.

"It's a magical key-fob tied to me that will let you into the Atrium and my place," Ciaran explained. "So you can come and go as you please. When you approach the outside door in the alleyway, hold up the *rodulé*. The chains will part, and the door to the residence will open too. So will my front door with your touch on the knob."

Chris's heart caught up before his mind did. "Are you asking... you want me to... move in?" He slowly took it from Ciaran and twirled it around in his fingers as Ciaran talked.

"I want you to have access to my place, whether I am here or not. If you want to move some of your things in, or all of your things, either way, it's fine by me. As long as you know, it's your home, too." Ciaran shrugged.

Chris was speechless. He knew it was a big step for Ciaran and their relationship. This was the closest he had ever come to telling or showing Chris how he felt about him, and it meant everything to him that Ciaran cared that much to essentially ask him to live with him.

He got up and straddled Ciaran, and they kissed. Chris gyrated against his groin and sucked his neck until a big purple bruise showed up. Then Ciaran tapped Chris's leg so they could get up and take it to the room. They made love and fell asleep.

Ciaran woke up first a few hours later and straddled Chris as he lay on his stomach and fucked him awake until he came, then rolled over and went back to sleep like a bear back to hibernation. Chris, who couldn't go back to sleep after that, got out of bed and started making dinner. He decided to stay naked just in case Ciaran wanted him again. He showered and cooked lamb chops in mint sauce, Mediterranean pasta and a carrot and peas vegetable blend, Ciaran's favorite meal. While cooking, Chris called out of work for the evening. Elijah agreed to take a double shift in exchange for him working Saturday afternoon, and Chris agreed.

Ciaran woke in the late afternoon and laughed at Chris cooking with nothing but an apron on, bare bottom poking out the back. He went to take a shower. They ate dinner and talked of exotic animals and Ciaran's rug, which Chris had never asked him about until now, and about Chris's track record in high school and college. As night fell, Chris let Ciaran know he called out of work.

Ciaran gave him a look. "You can't call out of work just to be with me. It's not responsible."

"Ciaran," Chris started annoyedly, but then took a deep breath and said, "In less than twelve hours you leave, and I won't see you for days. So I'm here with you all night," he said.

As much as Ciaran didn't want to be selfish, he was grateful.

Ciaran turned off all the lights, put on instrumental music, lit a fire in the fireplace although it wasn't cold outside, and floated candles all throughout the apartment so they only saw each other by the light and shadows of candles and fire. He took off his clothes and said to Chris, "Join me by the fireplace," and Chris obliged. Ciaran showed him what else he bought: a massage oil, a new lube, and a sensual elixir infused with lavender, jojoba, cedarwood, and guarana extract for intensity and stamina.

"Is it going to be another night like that soap gave us?" Chris asked in amusement.

Ciaran smiled. "Not as strong. Diana's potion was like having mind-numbing Viagra in your system. This is more like drinking a mild aphrodisiac."

He drank from the small, nondescript, five-milliliter bottle and handed it to Chris. Chris happily drank the rest. "Now what?" Chris asked.

"Whatever we want. I got you all night," he told his lover. Chris grinned.

Ciaran began by giving Chris's body a sensual, lengthy massage on the colorful rug, from scalp to heel, leaving his genitals untouched and aching. Then he had Chris do the same for him. But Chris could not help himself and licked his entire groin area from front to back, never finishing the massaging of his legs. That was all it took. Ciaran happily faced the rug and let Chris inside of him.

For most of the night, they took turns entering each other in front of the fireplace, alternating positions, slow and intentional, the feel of the slipperiness of the massage oil making it easier for their bodies to mold together in any position they ended up in. Giving each other waves of orgasmic pleasure, edging but stopping just short of ejaculation as neither of them wanted—or could, thanks to the potion—to be the one to end their marathon lovemaking session. They would pause, touch, and kiss, until one needed to be inside of the other again.

Hours later, they came together, with Chris on top of Ciaran and Ciaran's hand wrapped around his shaft firmly, moving as Chris moved. Their bodies agreed for them. As Ciaran felt Chris's rectum close tightly around him and he knew he was on the verge of climaxing himself, he stroked him faster and held his own release until he felt Chris's penis begin to spasm in his hand. They moved into a blinding climax as one, the outward cries of pleasure harmonizing Ciaran's deep "aaahh's" to Chris's higher ones, then held each other as they came down together.

Chris lifted himself up to remove Ciaran from inside of him, and then lay on top of him, where their soft groins touched. Ciaran slowly turned Chris on his side, still holding him, and Chris buried his face in the crook of Ciaran's armpit, his favorite place. They lay there silently, the love swarming between them, but neither dared to say it first, for fear that the other's feelings would not match the intensity of their own. Instead, they fell asleep by the fire, leaving the question and the answer to linger in the air.

They rose around 6 a.m. and showered together. Ciaran could have Wisp'd to work, especially since time was of the essence, but wanted to have those last few moments with Chris and he knew Chris needed them.

Chris drove them to the forest and parked near the Tank, then they walked to the Reserve entrance hand in hand. When they arrived, Chris thought he was going to make a "don't die on me" joke but couldn't find the words. So he stood there with his heart aching. Ciaran likewise felt his chest constricting, and he pulled Chris into a tight embrace. They put their heads on each other's shoulders. After a couple of seconds, Chris started singing a song he had made up.

"Me and you, time stands still.

Magic and man has no will.

When it's me and you, and no one else,

The heat that you feel, it's all so real between us.

You and me, fingers entwined,

You and me, hearts aligned.

When it's you and me, and no one else,

The heat you feel, it's all so real between us.

Ranger and Magi, Magician and man,

Hold my hand, hold my hand.

Magi and ranger, your Commoner understands.

Just hold my hand, hold my hand.

When it's me and you, and no one else,

The heat that you feel, it's all so real between us."

It almost brought tears to Ciaran's eyes, and he had to swallow them away. He realized how truly beautiful Chris's voice was. How beautiful a soul he had. And how lucky he was that he found him in the woods that night. He held him tighter.

They both heard the sound of a breaking twig at the same time and lifted their heads.

Vlad was standing a few feet away, looking sheepish. "I'm… I'm so sorry, Ciaran. I was… I was just trying to get in without… without disturbing… you… and…" He trailed off.

Chris started to pull away, but Ciaran held onto his waist with one arm. "It's okay, Vlad. Tell Dale I will be up in a minute."

Vlad nodded and quickly disappeared into the tree.

Chris said, "Well. If your friends and crew didn't know before, they will know now."

"I don't give a toss," replied Ciaran sternly.

Chris smiled and turned to face him. "Ciaran? Please be safe. Don't be a hero if you absolutely don't have to. I need you back in one piece."

Ciaran pulled him back into an embrace with both arms around his midsection and said, "It's just a couple of days. I'm coming back home to you."

Ciaran checked his watch. 7:15 a.m. He knew he had to go now, and so did Chris. He touched Chris's head with both hands. He kissed Chris on his eyelids, forehead, nose, left cheek, right cheek, softly on the lips again, took both of his hands from around his waist and kissed them separately, touched his face gently with one hand, and kissed him passionately on the lips pulling his bottom lip. Then Ciaran turned around and quickly walked into the tree without a goodbye, knowing he didn't have to say the words. Chris walked toward the tree and touched the solid wood before him. And only then did Chris let the tears he had been holding back fall from his eyes.

Chris drove back to Ciaran's flat and parked near the entryway. He walked toward the frosted doors and the chains fell by themselves. The door opened and Chris walked in. He went over the bridge to the wooden doors and held up his hand with the key fob. The doors opened for him. Chris mindlessly walked to Ciaran's apartment and turned the knob. It opened with no issue.

It was quiet. Chris closed the door behind him, walked into the living room, lay on the rug that still smelled of the night before, and closed his eyes.

CHAPTER 23

Relationship Advice

Ciaran was trying to get focused as he walked up the hill, but his head was spinning. All he could think about was Chris. His team was milling around the Flyer when he walked up. Vlad was trying to catch his eye, but he ignored him.

Before he could say something, Dale barked at him, "Ciaran! You're fucking late!"

Ciaran lost it. He whipped his head around and yelled, "Is it eight o'clock, then? Then I'M NOT FUCKING LATE!"

Everyone froze as Dale jumped in Ciaran's face in a couple of strides and they stood nose to nose. They all knew Dale had no issue pummeling Reservers and Ciaran like-wise thought Dale was going to punch him. But he refused to back down, staring him right in the eyes. A part of him wanted Dale to hit him, to feel something other than the emptiness that leaving Chris out there had left him. But instead, after a few moments, Dale sniffed, spat on the ground in front of Ciaran, then walked away. Everyone was shocked, even Bruno, whose wide eyes betrayed him. Ciaran closed his eyes and took some deep breaths before he turned back to his crew.

"Everyone on the Flyer, now," he commanded. "We have a four-hour flight ahead and if everyone is here, we're taking off. I will give you your assignments on the way."

He went to the back of the Flyer to take inventory of food and supplies, and got on the transport last, taking his seat behind the driver, Silas. Sarah and Felix sat across from him on the other side and they rose in the air by 7:30 a.m.

Ciaran was grateful for the silence as they started their journey. He assumed that he was going to start thinking of strategies to put in place, but of course, his mind kept wandering to Christopher Jennings and the last thirty-two hours. *Was it love?* he pondered. He didn't know, but he knew Chris was deep under his skin now, and he couldn't let him go even if he wanted to.

After thirty minutes, he leaned his head back and closed his eyes. He honestly did not care if Vlad told the whole Reserve. He couldn't imagine hiding his relationship or holding back his feelings for Chris anymore.

As if on cue, Ciaran felt someone slide into the empty seat next to him. He opened one eye, looked at Vlad, then closed it again. *Great*, he thought.

"Can I ask you a question, Ciaran?" he asked quietly.

Here we go, thought Ciaran. "Speak," he said without opening his eyes.

"I mean... I don't want to pry, but I happened to notice your..." His voice trailed off as Ciaran opened one eye again to look at him. Vlad found his voice again. "Um... your friend and you are ... close. And I have a similar type of ... friend ... and... and we're close. Just... just not ... openly ... close..." His voice trailed off again as his eyes pleaded with Ciaran to understand, which he did.

So Vlad is gay, great, Ciaran thought. He asked, still looking at him with one eye, "What's your question, Vladimir?"

"I just wanted to know if you had any advice … on how to be more open with… with my *friend*," he whispered the last word.

Ciaran laughed out loud and closed his eyes again. "Well your first step is to probably stop whispering about it like you're going to die if you say it out loud."

Vlad went pink. "No one knows about me. About us. My father's side, the Commoner side of my family, is very religious and they would kill me, disown me. I don't know which would be worse. And his family… they are wealthy and snobbish Generational Magi and have to keep appearances. Even if I were a woman, I wouldn't be good enough for them because of my Commoner blood and wealth status. Or lack there of. So when it started, we just kept it to ourselves. And now… now he wants more. And I don't know if I am capable of giving him more than what it is right now." Vlad sighed in sadness.

Ciaran could not believe someone was asking him for same-sex relationship advice when he barely knew what he was doing himself. But he opened his eyes and turned to him, deciding to give him practical advice instead.

"Two questions: First, do you love him?"

"Yes," Vlad said automatically. "I couldn't imagine my life without him for a second."

Ciaran said, "Okay," thinking about his own feelings for Chris. Then asked, "Second question: What do you want?"

Vlad sighed. "I want… I want to live in a world where I didn't have to worry about what anyone thought, and we could just be together."

"And why can't you have that now?" Ciaran asked.

"Because our parents won't allow it," he said factually.

Ciaran was confused. "How old are you? I'm assuming you're of age."

Vlad answered, "I'm twenty, yes. He is nineteen years old, turning age twenty later on this year."

"So you are both adults. I'm going to also assume he has a job like you do? Neither of you are living off your parents?"

"Well no. He has his own flat, and he works, yes, but for his father. He does have a very hefty trust fund he is supposed to inherit at twenty-one. But he already said he would give it all up for me. A couple of million euros, I think. And at least five million Sagems."

Ciaran watched through his peripheral vision as Felix lifted his head from the book he was pretending to read, but stared straight ahead. Sarah absentmindedly scratched her head.

Ciaran raised his eyebrow at Vlad. "Really? When did he tell you that?"

"Last night. When he proposed."

"Whaaat?" Ciaran exclaimed.

Over Vlad's head, he saw Sarah lift her head from her book. She and Felix looked at each other. They were definitely listening, and he had a feeling a few more guys were listening as well.

He said to Vlad, "He asked you to marry him?"

"It's not the first time," he said dismissively. "It's probably the third time, really."

"He asked you to marry him three times, and you told him no?"

"I didn't say no. Just ... let's wait and see."

"Wait and see? What are you waiting for?" Ciaran asked in disbelief.

"I... I don't know... We don't even live in the same country right now. He's in Moldova back home at his parents' mansion, and I'm here on the Reserve. He wants to move here, but I just moved up and only a year ago could afford to move out of the barracks, and now I'm in Jesse's house full of men and I got some money saved but it's not enough because he comes from a life that I could never give him and maybe I don't think I'm good enough for him either," Vlad said in one breath.

Ciaran understood. "So it's not just the coming out part. It's not feeling worthy of him. Has he ever given you a reason to feel that way? I doubt it if he's giving it all up for you."

"No… it's me, I know it's me. And we've been together for too long for me to feel this way, but saying you want to be together forever when you're a teenager and then actually doing it no matter what may come… it's scary, you know."

Ciaran nodded. "How long have you been together?"

"Five years in September."

Ciaran's eyes went wide again as Sarah and Felix exchanged looks a second time. "Five years, Vladimir? Bloody hell, Vlad, will you marry the poor fucker already?"

Vlad smiled. "Well, when you put it like that—"

Sarah looked over and cut him off. "You know if I had a beau for five years that asked me three times to marry him and he's giving up his inheritance for me to come here so I can live out my dream of riding dragons, I would jump on that in a heartbeat. Love like that doesn't come around too often."

Vlad looked at her, terrified that someone knew his secret. But others were chiming in with advice as well. Ollivier from a Campus in France, who was sitting behind them and also lived in Jesse's five-bedroom house, said, "Yes, it sounds like it's more of a, what you think of you, problem, not what your parents will think."

Lucas, who came into the Reserve with Vlad, was sitting right next to Ollie and lived with them, agreed, "*Dah*. And you know I understand why you would keep it a secret as teens. Especially at our Campus. There is this image of men and masculinity, so you have to keep up appearances all the time. If you are gay, you shut up about it or you get beaten up, literally. You and Alexi aren't the only ones, Vlad. Trust me. But you aren't at Campus anymore. Be who you are. Fuck societal norms."

Vlad gasped that Lucas knew who he was talking about. Ciaran touched his shoulder in support as others spoke up.

Axel, who also went to the same Campus but years ahead of them, was a couple rows back and spoke up. "I got a cousin like that, also went to school with us. We all know he likes men, but he won't even admit it to himself. He plays rugby, burliest man you'll ever meet. But he's never been in a relationship because he feels like he can't do that living in Latvia. He's not happy a'tall. Don't be like him, Vladdy. Life's too short to not be happy."

Vlad, who was growing red at first, felt calm and encouraged by his crew members. It was silent for a moment then Sven yelled out from the back, "Marry the fucker, cum buckets, and keep your cock soft every night, unlike the rest of us with blue balls."

The men busted out laughing. Ciaran and Vlad turned around to kneel in their seats to look back, also laughing.

Bruno called out, "Speak for yourself, Sven. I got me a lady to keep me warm. You got Dale. And who would want to fuck that!?"

Everyone laughed again as Sarah blushed. No one noticed but Ciaran.

Bruno continued, "Seriously, Vlad. You're gonna lose him. You're gonna lose him to someone less worthy of him if you don't get out of your own head and join with your mate. Fuck the parents. Why do they get a say in your life, in your happiness? Life's too short. Spend it happy."

Ciaran turned to him. "Everyone is right. Life is too short. We just went through a war, a fucking pointless, shitty civil war where people died over power and discrimination. Generational Magi versus Commoner Magi. Magicians versus Commoners. Who gives a shit? We're all human. We all can die the same way. More than half of us on this Flyer were out there fighting and we all bleed red. We almost died. Children did die. My brother ... died. Do you know what I would give to have my brother back right now? He could come back saying he was a cross-dressing elephant fucker and I would kiss him and encourage him to be the best elephant fucker there ever was."

Some laughed, and Ciaran smiled a bit. "Because I would rather have him back alive, no matter who he is or who he loves. He died never having experienced the love that you've had for years and you've taken for granted." Vlad nodded.

Sven said, "Not only just that, Ciaran, look at where we're at, what we do every day. What we do is serious work. We could all die on this mission today. Or you can die next week tending to a dragon. Before lovely Sarah came along and perfected the anti-fire serum, we were literally getting burned alive at this job. Life is short; spend it with someone who makes you happy. Be who you are, and if he's the one, be who you are with him. And do it today. Because you don't know what tomorrow will bring."

Vlad nodded again. Mike, their American Magus from Brooklyn, New York, said plainly, "Ay yo, Vlad, fuck your family. We're your family now. And fuck his family, too. We'll be his brothers. Don't be afraid to bring him down here with us. We got your back, both of you."

"Here, here!" Jesse called out. And others echoed, "Here, here!"

Vlad stood up in the aisle. "I really, really appreciate all of you. Thank you for ... accepting me."

Mateo from Argentina said, "*Aye dios mio* what's to accept? We get it. Everyone on this bus likes to get their cock sucked, *bueno*."

"Here, here!" Silas the pilot called out and everyone laughed again.

Then Sarah called out, "Or their cunts licked!"

The men cackled, some saying "ooooh!!!"

"Sarah!" Sven said, shocked. "And here I thought you were a lady!"

"You men! You think you're the only ones who love sex. Campus girls like our insides camped in as well," Sarah said smugly.

The Reservers went crazy with their laughter and hooting until Ciaran said, "Alright, alright, settle down."

He gave Sarah a wide-eyed look of amusement, and she laughed out loud. People started moving into their side conversations as Ciaran sat back down, and Vlad sat with him.

"Thanks, Ciaran," he said sincerely.

Ciaran shrugged. "No need for it, really, we're family here."

Vlad nodded. Then he asked, "So, what about you? When are you getting married?"

Ciaran laughed. "You are light years ahead of Chris and I. We've only just started seeing each other in February and who knows where this will go."

Sarah, who was still listening, chimed in again. "Uh-uh, it's been a lot longer than that. It's been since last summer you two have been inseparable."

"Maybe. Or maybe Dale talks too bloody much." Ciaran wanted to add "in bed" but didn't want to blow her secret out of the water. She laughed and winked at him.

Ciaran gave out assignments an hour before landing, putting them in their squads to begin strategizing their role.

Sven was listening closely. He had led several missions over his fifty years at the Reserve and knew what to expect. When he didn't call out Bruno for a squad, he was curious. It was worrying because Ciaran and Bruno didn't get along even under the best of circumstances.

"Ciaran?" Sven called out. "Do you want Bruno leading the Preservation team?"

Bruno looked at Ciaran and raised one eyebrow and narrowed the other eye. Ciaran said confidently, "No, Bruno will be with you, me, and Felix in leadership."

A murmur passed through the group. Bruno folded his large arms and waited for the fallout.

Sven looked at the Hunter first. "No offense, Bruno, you know I love you like a son. But Ciaran," he said turning to the other man, "there is a reason we don't put Hunters in leadership."

"Yeah, and what's that?" challenged Ciaran. Everyone got quiet again.

"Because our instinct will always be to protect human life. To never forget that dragons are dangerous and deadly creatures," Bruno responded with his sector's code.

"Thanks, Bruno. I know the playbook," Ciaran said sarcastically. Bruno scowled at him.

Ciaran addressed Sven. "And so why wouldn't I want someone to advise me on what to do if shit starts to go sour?

You think I want a bunch of Yes Men on my team, when I know my instinct is to keep a dragon alive at all costs? I need balance. Bruno will give me that balance."

He turned back to Bruno. "Are you really going to have a problem telling me I'm fucking up if I am?"

"You mean *when* you fuck it up? Not at all," said Bruno. Ciaran's eyes narrowed at him, but he didn't respond.

Sven tried again, "But Ciaran, that's not how it's done."

Sarah chimed in from the front. "Yeah, Dale is going to be upset by this."

And just that quickly Ciaran was done with people challenging his decisions. "Well, Dale isn't here, innit? I am. This is my team. He told me to pick my crew, not how to arrange it. So I'm doing it my way and fuck off anyone that has a problem with that! Fall in line!" He glared at Sarah and Sven, who stayed quiet.

Then he turned to Bruno again. "Do you want leadership or not?" he barked at him. Bruno nodded once.

"Good. See you all on the ground." Ciaran sat down.

It was quiet until Tommy said, "Is it just me, or was that the sexiest thing you've ever seen? I mean. Not that I'm gay or anything. Not that there is anything wrong with being gay! It's good to be gay. It's gay to be gay. Not that I know what being gay feels like, like Vlad does. I was just saying, in a very nongay way, that that was very profoundly sexy."

Vlad went red again, and Ciaran shook his head as people started to snicker and giggle. Jesse yelled out, "Tommy, mate, why are you always such a fucking wanker!?"

CHAPTER 24

The Krekardron

Silas landed about a quarter of a mile outside the village and everyone exited. Squad D, the Perimeter, followed Lee's lead to spread out and circle the village, then set up a five-point radius surrounding it. It was where they would be the whole time. The rest followed Ciaran, Sven, Bruno, Felix, and Sarah into the village where the elders greeted them. The five of them continued to the canopy they had set up for the initial meeting while the rest of the team went to greet the villagers and find out where they could set up their camp.

Only the elders of the village and their descendants had magical abilities and were considered royalty by their people, and their magical children were revered. Their interpreter, Haziz, who was a cousin of one of the elders, spoke English pretty well. He led them to the seats in front of the seven elders of the community. Through Haziz, they learned the details of what happened.

A boy named Malechi, who was the son of Chief Elder Bocari, found a dragon egg almost three years ago in the mountains. He told no one and hatched it. He had been secretly raising it there, where it used the caves as its dwelling and hunted animals on its own, about three miles north of the village. Another person witnessed them two weeks ago and came back and told his father. Chief Elder Bocari was furious and banned his son from going back there, but of course, the boy didn't listen.

After Malechi snuck out for the third night in a row, he decided enough was enough. The chief wanted it dead, but other elders saw no cause for that since it had brought harm to no one. So the elders took a vote and decided it was best to trap the dragon at the base of the mountain in an invisible enclosure and sent word to the closest reserve, the DRA.

Haziz continued to translate for everyone. Ciaran asked, "How is its temperament?"

Elder Teslimi said, "It has been shooting flames and flipping its tail around day and night trying to get out. It has grown increasingly angry as the days go on."

Bruno asked, "How long has it been in there?"

"A week today," Elder Omoro said.

"How is it eating?" Felix asked. Everyone hesitated. He barked at them, "You're not feeding it!!??"

Elder Bocari answered, "We send it one cow a day. But we cannot continue to do so; it is taking away resources from our village."

"How big is it?" Ciaran asked.

"Ten, maybe fifteen feet?" Elder Teslimi answered.

"Okay," Ciaran said. "One full-grown cow a day isn't bad for a three-year-old dragon. It's not starving, but I'm sure it's accustomed to more since it was able to hunt on its own." He was thoughtful, then said, "I want to speak to the boy."

"NO," Elder Bocari said curtly.

"If you want our help, I have to know everything there is about the dragon. And he knows this dragon inside and out. I need to talk to him. Now. Someone go get him." Ciaran stood up and crossed his arms to show he meant business.

The elders argued among themselves, then Elder Omoro left. He returned with a tall, skinny boy no older than sixteen, who looked miserable. He had on a red Manchester United hat and jersey, and traditional African printed slacks. Ciaran sat down and the boy sat in front of him cross-legged on the floor and, at first, wouldn't look at Ciaran. Haziz said it was the first time he had seen white-skinned people before, and he was scared of them. Other than Mike, who was African American, Khalid and Sahid, who were Black African Brits, and Mateo, who was a brown-skinned Hispanic, the rest of the team were white.

Ciaran told him through the interpreter, "Malechi, I am not here to hurt you. And I'm not here to hurt your dragon. I just want to get him someplace safe. Do you want that for him, too?"

Malechi started crying in front of them, with his head down. "Malik is my best friend," he said in his language while Haziz spoke for him. "He's my best friend, and he's the most gentlest thing ever and he wouldn't hurt a fly. He's kind and smart and playful and I love him. Why can't he stay with me?"

Ciaran sat on the floor with the boy, motioning for Haziz to come close too, so Malechi understood him. "Because he doesn't belong here," Ciaran said gently. "You know that. He's getting big, and he's going to grow bigger, double his size. You're going to have to feed him more and give him more exercise and you just can't do it here. And if a Commoner sees him, the whole Magi community will be alerted and your entire village will be in trouble by the powers that be on this continent. You don't want that either. He needs to be in an open space with dragons just like him. I didn't come to hurt him. I came to help him. Can you help me do that? Get him someplace safe where he will be well taken care of, and loved just as much as you love him?"

Malechi looked at Ciaran for the first time and nodded. Ciaran asked him, "Will you take me to Malik? I would like to meet him." Malechi smiled and nodded again.

Ciaran stood up. "We're going to see the dragon now." Elder Bocari scowled at him, but the others were agreeable.

<hr>

Ciaran and his leadership squad set out with the Preservation squad: Jesse, Ismael, Gideon, Mateo, Axel, Tommy, Lucas, and Vlad; followed by Malechi and four of the Elders: Bocari, Omoro, Teslimi, and Embina, the only female Elder. They walked northwest through the desert, the three miles to the mountains. They heard the dragon before they saw him, roaring savagely.

"That's not good at all," Bruno murmured.

The dragon was jet black with a hint of gray in his scales, red on the underside of his wings and underbelly, and a very long, spiked tail. He had two long legs and two shorter arms, and his two wings were extremely lengthy. He was pacing and thrashing about, trying to find a weak point. As he noticed the big group walking toward him he started shooting flames at them. It stopped at the invisible wall and extinguished on its own, making the dragon even more upset.

The group stopped about a hundred feet from the dragon. Malechi started yelling angrily at his father. Haziz turned to the Reservers. "He is telling them that they did the wrong thing by trapping him like that. He can't even fly upward into the cave, his home, and has to cower on the underside of the mountain for shade. This has made his beloved Malik angry now. He has never seen him angry or aggressive."

"He's right," said Bruno. "That dragon has 'kill' written all over its face." He looked at Ciaran knowingly.

Suddenly Malechi broke from the group and ran straight for the dragon. Some called out, "No" but most just watched in horror as he ran top speed, saying, *"Malik! Malik, doa ov eme! Doa ov eme!"*

The dragon surprised everyone but Ciaran, as it stopped thrashing completely. Instead, he lowered his head at the sight of his guardian and friend who he had not seen in over a week, as if to prepare for a petting.

Unfortunately Malechi, who completely forgot, ran face-first into the barrier and fell backward.

The dragon flared its nostrils again in anger, but Malechi got up quickly, and started talking and cooing to it, rubbing on the barrier like he was rubbing the dragon. Malik responded by rubbing against the invisible wall right where Malechi's hands were. As the boy kneeled down and sat on his legs, the dragon likewise sat down and lowered its head down. Malechi started singing to it and the dragon was soothed.

As everyone continued to watch in amazement, Tommy said, "Make sure we recruit that one in a year, yeah?"

Vlad started walking toward them slowly. Ciaran looked at him sharply. "What the bloody hell are you doing?"

Vlad did not look back. "It's okay. I know what to do."

He continued to walk slowly until he was right behind Malechi. The dragon tensed again and looked at Vlad, but Vlad kept full eye contact with him and kneeled down slowly next to Malechi. He motioned to the boy to introduce him.

He pointed at himself and said, "Vladimir. Vladimir."

Malechi understood. He spoke to Malik in his language and took Vlad's hand to show they were friends. Then Malechi took his hand and placed it on the barrier with his. As Malechi said some words, Vlad repeated them. When Malechi cooed, Vlad cooed as well. And when Malechi started singing, Vlad listened for a few lines to make sure he got it, then started singing, too. And the dragon responded favorably to it all.

"Smart fucking lad," Felix said to himself, but Ciaran nodded anyway.

Ciaran took a few steps and joined them, kneeling on the floor, singing Malechi's song. Sven, Felix and Sarah followed together. Jesse, Lucas, and Tommy came last, and soon they were all sitting around the dragon and singing to it.

Bruno looked at his Hunters and said, "Take one step toward that dragon and I'm drowning you in the lake when we get back." So Ismael, Axel, and Gideon hung back with Mateo and watched.

Malik started loving all the attention, grunting and moving his long tail around. He tried to lick the wall a couple of times making them all laugh. Only Malechi and Vlad used the native tongue. The rest spoke to it in English, getting him used to the sound and words.

Chief Elder Bocari, who wanted the dragon dead, did not like what was happening and walked over briskly. Haziz followed and interpreted. He started yelling that the dragon would kill them all and he would show them how ferocious his temper was. He put his hands together and started rubbing them until orange sparks formed. He created a ball of fire and sent it hurling toward the dragon right over their heads. It was so close, they could feel the heat.

"What the fuck!" yelled Ciaran as he ducked.

The fire penetrated the barrier and struck Malik in the back. The dragon roared and rose up, breathing fire along the way. Ciaran and all the rest of the crew ran back while Mateo and the Hunters ran forward. Vlad had to pry Malechi away, who was hysterical, as the dragon would not respond to his voice either. The Hunters covered Ciaran and the rest, and they all walked back over to the elders.

Ciaran was pissed. He took out his *rodulé* and pointed it at Elder Bocari, crying, *"Quod electrica!"*

A white beam like a bolt of lightning shot out of his *dulé* directly at the elder's chest. The force was so strong it seized him for a moment, then flipped him high in the air, hurdling backward twenty feet from where they stood. Elder Bocari landed on his back in a daze.

The three other elders started conjuring balls of fire with their hands and did a defensive stance while the Reservers, with the exception of Vlad, Sarah, and Felix, drew their *rodulés* and stood beside Ciaran defensively as well. No one moved while the dragon roared behind them. Elder Bocari slowly walked over to them and glared at Ciaran.

Ciaran said coldly, "If you ever put my crew in danger again, I will release that dragon myself and watch as he burns your entire village to the fucking ground." He turned to Haziz and said, "Now interpret that shit word for word."

He lowered his hand, and the others followed suit. Then he walked around the elders back toward the village and the Reservers marched behind him, along with Malechi.

CHAPTER 25

Initial Thoughts

At dinner, he motioned for the Leadership Squad to meet in his tent. He wanted to hear their pros and cons of bringing the dragon back to the Reserve. Tommy, upon hearing this, followed Ciaran back to his tent and refused to leave when they met. Ciaran let him stay, too tired to argue.

"Initial thoughts?" he asked.

Tommy spoke first. "We can do it. We can bring him back. You saw how he responded to Vlad, and when it was just us and the boy. He was agreeable. We can tame him."

But Sven said, "Yes, but unless you are planning on taking the boy with us, I don't see him staying tame. He only really understands the boy's tongue."

Felix agreed with Tommy. "Vlad can do it. He was already mimicking Malechi, and it was working. We just need to learn some key phrases—"

Bruno cut him off. "Are you all mad!? That beast could kill us all. He was raised in the wild and belongs out there in the wild, not with our tame dragons."

"But our dragons came to us wild," said Tommy. "Except maybe Hansel, and maybe Betta. Both had humans looking after them. With the right team, he could be agreeable."

"And who would that be?" Sven asked. "Ciaran, maybe, but he has his hands full with Betta and Reserve duties. Dale has Hansel. And I don't tame dragons anymore. Maybe Vlad, and only because he was the smart one to get a warm hand-off from his owner."

"Vlad can do it," Felix said again. "He can be Malik's lead Tamer." He turned to Ciaran. "You know he can."

Ciaran turned to Tommy and asked, "Can you bring Vlad in here, please? I want to hear from him, too."

Tommy left abruptly as the group continued. "Bringing him back could go either way," said Sven.

"Oh, you mean either way like, maybe he'll be okay, or maybe he'll rain down hellfire on all of us?" Bruno deadpanned.

Bruno, Sven, and Felix continued to weigh out the pros and cons as Tommy and Vlad came back. Tommy took his place next to Ciaran again, as Vlad sat by the entrance and listened.

Sarah had begun to give her input, "Well, we can't just leave him with those cruel elders. Especially that Chief one. He wants him dead badly and they will kill him."

"Better they kill him than us. Or maybe it should be us," Bruno said.

"Oy!" Felix yelled at him. "We're not in the business of killing dragons."

Tommy muttered, "And this is why we don't put Hunters in Leadership." Ciaran really wanted to smack him.

Bruno said to Felix, "Yeah, when it's just you and Malik the Murderer in your face, ready to breathe fire on you, you'll be singing a different tune then." Felix and Bruno started raising their voices at each other, and Ciaran knew he had to calm it down.

"Alright!" He sighed. "We aren't killing him, for sure, and we aren't leaving him to be killed. But we aren't sure if we can tame him yet. What we need is more time."

"There's another solution," Vlad said quietly from his corner. They all turned to look at him. "We could let him go."

No one spoke until Ciaran said, "Let him go where?"

Vlad shrugged. "Wherever he wants to go. Although he was raised in the mountains, so he will probably stay up there. Either way, we set him free. We end the barrier and let him fly off."

Ciaran shook his head. "We can't do that."

"Why not?" asked Vlad.

Ciaran opened his mouth to respond, but Bruno answered, "Because, you horse's arse, what if he harms another person or a village? It would be blood on our hands."

"But I don't think he would," said Vlad. "He's only mad now because of being provoked. I believe Malechi when he says he wouldn't hurt a fly. He raised him to be a gentle giant."

Ciaran said, "Vlad, we'd be taking a huge risk on what we think, not what—"

Bruno interrupted him, "You don't know much about these Class C dragons, do you? Krekardrons are Class C dragons. They are naturally aggressive, with short tempers and memories as long as their tails. There is a strong possibility that he will want revenge on the villagers for trapping him all week."

"Not necessarily," Sven said, "Not if Malechi is still here. He sees him like a parent and a friend, and he would never harm the boy, nor let anyone else harm him. He showed that today."

"And if he doesn't fly off into the sunset to live his happily ever after, but instead turns around and heads for the village?" Bruno asked testily.

"Then we know that Malechi was wrong, and he is too wild, and we take him down, gently," Ciaran said with finality. No one spoke again, as his words sunk in. He turned to the healers. "Sarah, Felix, did you bring Dragonshade?"

"We did," Sarah said.

"We need to get the Dragonshade through his underbelly to put him down; the red skin is the softest," said Felix. "But Ciaran—"

Tommy cut him off by jumping up, and yelling, "Are we really talking about this!? Killing a dragon!? This is not what I signed up for!"

"What a naïve little shit you are," Bruno said nastily.

Ciaran yelled at him, "Bruno!"

But Tommy was upset and for the first time in his life stood up to Bruno and yelled, "Fuck off Bruno the Broken! You shouldn't even be in here!" Bruno smirked at him.

Ciaran tried to intervene. "Tommy, calm down..."

"No, you fuck off too, Ciaran!" Tommy yelled again, surprising everyone. "Fuck off for even suggesting it. What... what are you *saying*!? We aren't even going to try?" he cried.

Ciaran stood up and rounded on him. "We are going to try, Tommy. That's what we are here to do. But it doesn't mean we don't prepare ourselves for bad outcomes too. If you ever want to lead, you are going to have to understand that. Be all heart, but use your logical brain, too." He touched his shoulder and Tommy nodded.

Ciaran turned to the rest of them. "At sunrise, Vlad will go back with Malechi, since they have already formed a connection. Vlad, it will be your job to see if he is tamable, can follow directions, take cues, especially from someone other than Malechi. I don't want a crowd there again, so just the two of them."

Sven interjected, "Ciaran he can't do that by himself; you'll have to go with him."

Ciaran disagreed, Vlad seemed to be able to handle himself just fine around dragons. He reminded him of himself at that age. But he relented.

"Fine, the three of us will go... no, four; Felix, I want you to come too. Just in case we need a Novo he can trust. The rest of you come later and will stay all the way back, no less than half a kilo. Keep watch and if I need you, I will send up *scintillae*. We'll do it for two days. If by day three we've made good progress, we smoke Malik, load him up, and take him back."

"And if it all goes to shit?" Bruno asked sourly.

"Then we let him go and pray he doesn't attack another village or person," Ciaran replied. Bruno shook his head but kept quiet.

"He won't," Vlad said. "I heard you, Bruno. His nature might be aggressive, but his personality isn't. I can feel it. He's a good boy."

Sven said, "Let's hope you are right."

"So we aren't going to use force, then?" Tommy asked hopefully. "Or Dragonshade to kill him?"

"Only if it's completely necessary, like if he ever tries to harm the village," Ciaran said.

"Sounds like a good plan, Ciaran," Sven said. "Now, let's all get some sleep. If it all works out, we'll be home by the weekend."

They all walked out together. Vlad said, "Thanks, Ciaran. You're doing great by the way, for your first mission."

He smiled at him, and Ciaran smiled back before Vlad headed to his tent. Ciaran looked up at the clear night sky and all the stars, missing his best friend and lover. He turned to walk toward the desert to send a message to Chris.

***

11:03 p.m.

Chris woke with a start. The living room was supposed to be pitch black, but there was an eerily silvery glow next to him. He turned and yelped, "AAH!" and scrambled to the far side of the couch.

A translucent miniature dragon was sitting on the rug, like it was waiting for him to wake up. Chris watched it as it watched Chris.

"Ci... Ciaran?" Chris stuttered.

The dragon started to speak. *"Hey, Chris. Meet my Amina. My creature spirit. It's one of the ways us Magi communicate with each other. An Amina is a part of my essence that I'm now sharing with you. My Commoner boyfriend."*

It was definitely Ciaran's voice, and it made Chris's heart beat faster. He moved closer as it continued.

"I just wanted to check in and thought this would be the best way to do it. We arrived, and the mission is underway. If all goes well, I could be back in Albania by the weekend. Of course, I would have to stay on the grounds a few days more, make sure the dragon is well adjusted, but then I'll have a few days off so..."

There was a long pause, so long that Chris thought for a second that the message ended or Ciaran messed up somehow. Then he began to speak again.

"I miss you. A lot. This is the first time we have been away from each other like this, literally hundreds of miles apart, days without seeing or touching each other, and I hate it. I know you hate it, too."

Chris whispered, "I do."

"*I hope you're staying at my place while I am away. Eat break-fast at The Atrium on my tab after work today. Although... some-thing tells me you called out of work again and you're lying in my bed watching this. [Chris laughed] That's two days in a row that you haven't gone to work, all because of me. Go to work tomorrow so I don't feel guilty. Sitting around smelling my clothes is not going to bring me back any faster, mate. [Chris laughed again.] I'm going to go. I... You're in my thoughts. A lot.*"

Then the dragon lifted its wings and flew through a solid wall, leaving Chris in the dark smiling and feeling loved.

CHAPTER 26

Playing With Fire

The next day, Malechi, Vlad, Ciaran, Felix, and Haziz left at dawn, grabbing food and snacks to carry them through the day, and went to visit Malik. The interpreter translated Malechi's words to the dragon for them, so they could learn key phrases and words. They took turns talking to and playing with the dragon, who seemed to like the positive attention.

Vlad asked Malechi about the things they did together and they switched clothes so that Vlad had on his jersey and hat and smelled like him. Felix quizzed Malechi on Malik's favorite foods, sleep schedule, any particular smells, food, or items he liked, and if he noticed any illnesses he'd had, and he wrote it all down.

By midday, they knew what Malechi saw in him and kept trying to tell them: Malik really was a gentle giant. Their favorite game was when Malechi would say *"teswo eme"* which basically meant "copy me" and he would do things like pretend to faint and fall backward, then Malik would pretend to faint and do the same. If Malechi flapped his arms, the dragon would flap his wings and fly as high as he could go, then back down.

Malechi told them when Malik would get upset or frustrated, he would say, *"Voeli voeli ibi ubo"* which meant "hush, hush baby boy" or *"doa ov eme ibi"* which meant "listen to me, baby." Vlad and Ciaran both learned to say it with a perfect accent, and they would take turns getting him to respond to them as well. They stayed there the full day, and as the sun was setting, Malechi decided to sleep under the stars near his beloved dragon, and Vlad joined him to do the same.

Ciaran sent Chris another message through his *Amina* that night, *"Everything is going well, so keep your fingers crossed. Nights are terrible without you, you know. We really do sleep together every day, don't we? I don't think I realized that until now. I'm resisting the urge to jerk off thinking of you. Unlike you I am sure of it.* [Chris laughed out loud.] *Miss you, Christopher. A lot. I will be home soon."*

━━━◆━━━

Early Friday morning, Ciaran, Felix, and Haziz set out again. But as they got to the edge of the village, they were stopped by Chief Elder Bocari. He told them the elders met late last night and voted again. Haziz paused in translation, and his mouth dropped.

Ciaran looked at him curiously. "What did he say?"

Haziz managed to compose himself and turned to Ciaran. "They decided to end the dragon's life for the safety of the village." He looked at the chief who gave him a nod to confirm, as Felix and Ciaran were horrified.

Ciaran started yelling at the elder. "You can't do this! You called us! You gave us a job to do; let us do our jobs and take him with us safely. We need more time!"

But Elder Bocari was adamant. He said one word in perfect English, "No."

Felix was fuming. He looked at Ciaran and then Wisp'd away on the spot. Ciaran knew he had gone to Vlad and Malechi, so Ciaran grabbed Haziz's arm. "Close your eyes and think of Malik," he said quickly, and Wisp'd with the translator, too.

Vlad was quietly using his *dulé* to make a laser light through the barrier, watching the dragon's eyes dart back and forth while Malechi watched. He was startled by the sudden smoke around him as Felix, then Ciaran with Haziz, appeared. "What's going on?" he said, standing up, sensing trouble.

"They're coming! They're coming to kill him!" Felix said angrily. "Fucking arseholes want to kill Malik!"

Malechi understood and jumped up. He started talking fast in his language, his eyes pooling and tears falling.

Ciaran put one hand on Malechi's shoulder to calm him. He did not need to understand his words to understand his feelings. He looked into Malechi's eyes and said firmly, "They are not going to kill him." Malechi sniffed, then nodded.

Ciaran lifted his *rodulé* to the sky and murmured, "*Scintillae.*"

A red light started shining from his tip along with Vlad's and Felix's. Almost immediately smoke was filling the area around them as the Preservation Squad Wisp'd in, along with Sven, Sarah, and Bruno. When they were all there, Ciaran explained the elders' decision. Everyone matched his initial look of horror; even Bruno was upset by the decision.

Malechi started talking to them with intensity, gesturing upward. Haziz said, "He says, 'Let him go, let him go to the skies.'"

Ciaran turned to Vlad, who looked guilty. "I'm sorry, Ciaran," said Vlad. "I told him Plan B, to keep Malik safe, would be to open the barrier and let him fly back up to the highest mountains. We gotta do it, Ciaran, we gotta let him go now!"

Ciaran turned to his Leadership Squad. "We'll take a vote."

"Ciaran, god dammit!" Bruno yelled.

Ciaran yelled back, "I don't need your shit, Bruno! I heard everything you said the first night loud and clear. But I've been with this dragon all day yesterday and he is not what you think he is. Now, I need us all to consider the safety and health of the dragon, but also the risk to the villagers. So we either let him go or we try now to hold the elders back until we can get enough Sleeping Beauty in him to put him to sleep, subdue him, and take him back with us, which is also a risk, and possibly a fight. But either way, we aren't letting them put Malik down without good cause. So we vote. Let him go, or take him. Choose. Now."

Sven spoke first. "We don't have enough time. Let him go."

Sarah said, "I heard from Felix the progress that you're making. He's tamable. We take him."

Felix sighed. "Yes, but is it enough?" He thought for a moment. "I think we... we should let him go—NO keep him, keep him!"

Bruno growled, "Let him go."

Ciaran stupidly did not think the vote would come down to him. He looked at Vlad, and he knew what Vlad would say, but he couldn't risk it. Vlad was more sure about Malik's ability to adapt to life on the Reserve than he was. Younger adventurous Ciaran would have said to keep him, but the older wiser Ciaran instead said, "He'll be fine out there in the mountains. We'll let him go."

He turned to everyone. "We're going to end the barrier and let him go. Spread out and form a semicircle around the dragon."

The team did as they were instructed and pointed their *rodulés* out toward the barrier. Malik whined, unsure of what was going to happen, and Malechi cooed and soothed him. Ciaran counted them down from three and they said in one voice, *"Vis carmina omittere."*

Blue light came from their *rodulés* and stretched across the barrier, then rained down to the ground in glitters. Malechi ran straight for Malik and touched his nose, grabbed his ears playfully, and hugged his neck. They all watched as the two friends were reunited. Malechi continued to drag his hand across the dragon's mouth, down to the back of his ears, and rubbed them, and Malik responded with appreciative grunts and sounds.

Then the dragon lowered its head all the way to the ground. Malechi climbed onto the back of his neck and dug his hands into the grooves of his skin. He cried, *"Woerci!"*

The dragon lifted its head, stretched its wings, and rose upward. They flew in circles for a bit, then flew off toward the top of the mountains. Everyone was smiling, with Felix and Vlad hugging excitedly.

"Seriously, somebody, recruit this kid," Tommy said happily.

Even Bruno looked less sour. But he turned to his fearless leader. "Alright, Ciaran. I hope you know what you're doing."

Ciaran did not respond.

They walked back to the village and waited, wondering and debating whether Malechi was ever going to come back or if he was going to live out the rest of his days with his beloved dragon. Elder Bocari scowled at them, but the elders Teslimi and Omoro came over and thanked them.

"Chief Elder is the most powerful of us all," they said. "He threatened our families and our livelihood if we did not vote with him. This is for the best, even if the boy never comes back. Everyone is happier this way."

Everyone but Elder Bocari, who threw all of his son's stuff out of their home, and locked himself inside in anger. Chief Omaro and his family silently gathered his belongings and brought them to their bungalow.

They waited and waited, looking up at the skies, patrolling the village. It was Lee who spotted them first, coming from the Southwest side of the village. He sent his hummingbird *Amina* to Ciaran to say, "They are coming." And he led his team to be on guard for anything.

The rest of the Reservers ended up Wisp'ing to where Lee was. Malechi led the dragon to drop him off right outside of the village. Some villagers came out to watch in awe, but most stood back cautiously and in fear. Vlad ran right up to them and mimicked Malechi's petting behind his ears and dragging his hands across his face. The dragon stuck out his tongue and licked Vlad's whole arm which made the Reservers laugh.

Vlad told Malechi, "He has to go. *Woerci.*" He motioned for him to go to the skies again, pointing at the mountains on the northwest side where they had just come from.

Malechi nodded. He touched his dragon again and told him to go. The dragon gave one last lick on his friend's arm and began to take flight. As everyone watched the boy and his dragon, Ciaran saw the ball of light out of his peripheral vision and was powerless to stop it.

Chief Elder Bocari hurled a fireball toward Malik as he rose into the sky. It struck him on his side, between his wing and tail. The dragon roared a terrible roar and started falling sideways until he caught his balance.

"FUCK!" Ciaran yelled.

They all watched in horror as the dragon kept flying around and around, whipping his tail ferociously, growling, as if it was trying to decide what to do. "Keep going, keep going..." Bruno kept muttering.

Malechi ran to his father and started yelling at him. Elder Bocari raised his hand high, and it turned red, and he lowered it quickly across his son's face. Malechi let out a yell and fell to the ground. Bruno moved quickly and grabbed the chief by his collar, lifting him off his feet. Ismael, Gideon, and Axel had to grab his arms to keep him from snapping the man's neck. Chaos ensued.

No one except Ciaran noticed that the dragon had seen it all from above, heard Malechi's cry, and saw him on the ground. Not until Malik started nosediving toward them.

Ciaran screamed, "EVERYONE GET BACK!!" The villagers all retreated and scattered quickly, including the Chief Elder, with the Corral Squad trying to keep some order, pushing them toward the center of the small village.

Ciaran said to Lee, "Ash Burner Barrier, NOW!!"

Lee sent up a white streak high in the sky to the middle of the village. From four other parts of the perimeter surrounding the village, white streaks came up and joined with his then spread a white line from Lee's feet to Jamie's to Ollie's to Dylan's to Mike's and back to Lee's feet.

Ciaran yelled to his Preservation Squad, "Behind the white line!" They quickly got in order right as Malik soared over their heads.

Malik must have been watching to see where Chief Bocari went because he flew to the other side of the village and aimed for him. All the Reservers except the Perimeter Squad ran in the same direction, following Malechi, but the dragon was faster. As the Chief went into his dwelling, Malik opened his mouth and blew red-orange flames directly at the top of the bungalow. As the fire approached, the villagers screamed. But it turned to white ash as it went through the barrier and rained down on the people.

Malechi went to the front of his father's home, waving his hands furiously, green sparks emulating from them. Ciaran recognized the words, *"Doa ov eme ibi, woerci, woerci!"* He was telling the dragon to go. Finally, the dragon got the hint, roared, and glided upward, disappearing into the skies.

"This is bad, Ciaran, this is really fucking bad!" yelled Bruno as he stomped over to him, shaking ash out of his hair. "That dragon is going to come back and kill us all!"

"You don't know that," Tommy murmured.

He rounded on Tommy. "Oh really? Did your degree in Dragonology and fifteen years of experience working with them give you an informed decision on the attributes of a Krekardron dragon? No? Then SHUT THE FUCK UP!" he screamed, his face turning red with anger.

Bruno turned to Ciaran. "You know I'm right. Those sons of bitches are vengeful. So either we go after it and hunt it down or we wait for it to come for us, because *it will come back.*"

Ciaran indeed knew Bruno was right. "We wait for it to come back. Give it three days. If he doesn't come back in three days, most likely he has moved on."

"And... and when he comes back, Ciaran? What are you saying?" Tommy asked fearfully.

Ciaran did not respond, but instead looked around. "Where's Vladimir?"

They all looked toward the banging and saw Vlad punching and kicking the door of the elder's home, screaming in English and Russian, "Come out here you, motherfucker! You dog shit bastard! You ruined it, you ruined everything!"

The twins, Khalid and Sahid, had to lift him up and pull him away, with him screaming the whole time. He shook them off and started running out of the village and into the desert. Ciaran rubbed his temples; he would find and deal with Vlad later. For now, he had to strategize again and give out assignments.

"Corral, I need you to scope out the sand dunes on the southeast side of the village and create a cover cave. So that if we need to evacuate the village, they have someplace safe to go. Make sure there is enough food, water, and supplies for at least three hundred people, double the number of villagers.

"Preservation, I need you to patrol the outskirts of the village, eyes to the skies at all times.

"Perimeter is to keep the barrier up for the next 24 hours. The Preservation Squad will give you breaks and cover. Work out who is covering who. There are twelve of you until Vlad gets back.

"Sarah and Felix, prepare the Sleeping Beauty dragon powder and Dragonshade. If we are able to salvage the situation, we will. But right now, given the circumstances, our number one goal is to protect human life.

"Sven, go with the Corral, and Bruno, patrol with the rest. One way or another, this ends and ends soon."

Before anyone else could talk, he turned on his heels and left them standing there. Ciaran went to his tent, sat on the bed, and put his hands on his head, trying to figure out how he fucked up his first mission so badly and how to get out of it.

CHAPTER 27

The *Amina*

By the setting sun, the entire village was on edge, restless and nervous. The Ash Burner Barrier created a glow, so it continued to be bright, as if someone was shining a giant flashlight on top of them. After dinner, the women, led by Elder Embina, invited everyone into the circle in the middle of the village and did a dance and tribute to their ancestors, praying that their village and the people were spared. They went around to each Reserver and put a circle on their heads made from the dirt in their village, which they said gave them their strength and power.

It was deeply moving and spiritual, and made Ciaran think of Chris and his Catholic faith that he sort of practiced, but very much believed in. It was only during his trip with Sean around the world that he realized how many other Magi cultures equated their *Vis* coming from a Divine power or a sole Creator. His sister Diana was a practicing Wiccan, and even Sean gravitated toward the spirituality practices they learned in South Africa and their Campus in Cape Town.

Ciaran had been taught to revere magic, but never to think about the source of it all. He, too, began to see magic as part of the spiritual world and had a deeper gratitude for his ability and the source behind it. Whether he called it God or not, was still up in the air.

He glanced over at Malechi who had tears streaming down his face. His father was nowhere to be found, probably still hiding in his dwelling. He thought if he was closer, he would go hug him. Then decided to follow his instincts. He got up from his bench and came over to him, stood him up, and gave him a hug. The boy burst into tears in his arms, sobbing. Ciaran held him for as long as he needed to, while the women danced around them.

Chris had stepped out of the bathroom and there was his little dragon friend sitting on Ciaran's bed.

"Well... Hello there, Ciaran's spirit creature friend."

The silhouette of a dragon watched him intently. Chris sat in the chair and went closer to it. "Do you have another message for me?"

The dragon opened his mouth and began to speak.

"*Well. Things certainly took a shitty turn today. Looks like I'll be here another three days at least. The villagers did a prayer for us to their ancestors for the situation to end in peace. I don't know anymore... I just don't know what I'm doing. I'm going on instinct, hoping I'm getting it right. So if you got that rosary near you, send up a Hail Mary for us, yeah mate? But I think you're at my place, and going to work from there, so your beads are home. And you probably haven't been to your house in a few days, which makes me feel...*"

There was another long pause. Chris understood. "Me too," he said.

"*What I wouldn't give right now to be lying next to you, holding you. I'm going to stop talking now before I go down that path. Just know that I'm thinking of you every spare moment that I have, just as much and as hard as you are thinking of me. Maybe more.*"

"Definitely not more, mate," Chris said softly.

The dragon stretched its wings, flew over Chris's head and through the ceiling. "Until tomorrow, friend."

As Ciaran sent his *Amina* dragon up with a message for Chris, he watched Vlad walk toward the village from the desert. Ciaran sat down in the sand and waited for him. Vlad sat down next to him and was quiet for a long moment.

"I don't think I was ready for this, Ciaran," he finally spoke. "I'm so grateful that you asked me not only to be a part of your mission, and to have an input with your leadership. But I am way too emotional for this. I'm too attached to Malik now. I can't be a part of any harm coming to him, and I know that's the next logical step. I know he's dangerous right now, but I know in my heart he's not a dangerous animal. I just don't know how to separate the two thoughts." He sighed.

Ciaran let his words sit in the air before he spoke.

"I chose you, Vladimir, because you are strong and smart. You have good instincts and a big heart. I was just like you starting out, all instinct and heart. In some ways, I still am. And I agree with you, for what it's worth. I see what you see in Malik. I want you to keep following your instincts. But we also have to consider the damage he can do in the state he is in. Being a master of dragons also means understanding that we have to protect them from themselves as well. A vengeful dragon is not a happy, healthy, well-adjusted one. So if you really care for him, we have to do what's best for him." Vlad nodded with his head down.

"And just so you know, we prepared Dragonshade and Sleeping Beauty," said Ciaran. "I'm not heartless. If we can keep him alive and get him out of here, we will. I will look for any opportunity to do so, and you should too. But if it's too dangerous, if he is too dangerous to himself or anyone here, we will have to put him down, gently. Are you okay with that plan?"

"Yes." Vlad nodded again. "I want to be like you when I grow up, Ciaran."

Ciaran laughed. "And I want what you have, Vlad, a love of a lifetime. So we both have lots to learn from each other, don't we?"

Vlad grinned back.

The night passed quietly and without incident. As the day moved on, the villagers and Ciaran's team were less tense, and everyone moved about normally. Ciaran allowed the barrier to come down but said to them to stay alert, eyes on the skies at all times, day and night. He too fell in step to patrol the outskirts of the village with his team.

As night fell again and the village slept peacefully while the moon sat high in the clouds, Ciaran went to his spot to send another message to Chris.

1:02 a.m.

Chris walked up to Marker 1 and there was the *Amina*, albeit smaller, perched on the wooden pole with a phone attached.

"I need to give you a name, little guy," Chris said in amusement. "Or maybe he already named you Kumoi?"

The silver dragon opened his mouth and said, "*Let's patrol.*"

Chris let out a loud laugh. "Okay."

The dragon rose up and landed on Chris's right shoulder. He could not feel the *Amina's* feet, and could still see right through him, but there was a soft sound like leaves rustling near his ear. "*Tell me about your day,*" the dragon said in Ciaran's voice.

So Chris did. "Well, I still haven't been home. I've been at your place. I hung out in the atrium and observed a couple of other strange creatures. Found the fairy tree. They are interesting..."

Chris talked and patrolled with the dragon right by his side. When he got back to the tank, he said, "I guess I'll see you around."

But the dragon *Amina* went onto the bed and curled up, still watching him.

Chris smiled. "Okay then."

He went to the desk and started working, knowing that the dragon would be with him until sunrise, feeling like Ciaran was right there with him.

As Ciaran was watching his translucent dragon disappear into the night sky, Vlad came from behind him. "How do you do that?" he asked.

"The *Anima*?" asked Ciaran.

"Yeah. It's fascinating. I know what it is, but it's not something we learned at our Campus. Definitely didn't know you could send messages in its truest form."

"Well, if you've never done it before, you need to start with the basics, casting a Wisp outside of yourself."

"How's that?" Vlad asked.

"Well," Ciaran started, "Remember the science behind the Wisp is literally joining yourself with the air around you and directing it where you want to go. But a Wisp at its core is taking the very essence of your spirit, what makes you you, and combining that with the atoms in the air. The *Anima* incantation creates a Wisp, the essence of your spirit, taking on the shape of the creature that represents the spirit of who you are inside. Are you with me so far?"

Vlad nodded, hanging off his every word. "Yes."

"The *Anima* is a very thoughtful, intentional, advanced type of magic. You would really have to know all the parts of you, the things that make you happy, make you sad, what you love, what you fear. Then wave your *rodulé* in a circular counterclockwise motion directly in front of the center of your body, saying the incantation, until a dark mist begins to form. What comes out is a representation of you."

"But the *Anima* is silver, not smoky black like the Wisp," he questioned.

"Because a Wisp is just a void. We Wisp through a void from one place to the next. But the more of your essence you pour into it, the lighter it becomes."

"But how do I pour my essence into it?"

"That I cannot help you with," Ciaran said simply. "Because I don't know you like you know you. I know what makes me me. I know that when I envision myself, I am a fearless dragon. But I am also a young and scared one, trying to be brave. I know that my bravery comes from my courage, despite my fear. I know I like solitude, but I can be in the company of others, like most dragons. I know what I believe, what I value. I know I'm always growing and learning, and

I do the best I can with the knowledge that I have. I am a dragon."

Vlad smile. "I think I'm a dragon, too."

"Or you might be a pussycat," Ciaran said with a smile of his own, making Vlad laugh. "Have confidence in yourself. That's the most important part."

"Okay," Vlad said, excited to learn a new magical skill. "Show me."

Ciaran showed him the movement with the *rodulé* and gave him the simple incantation, *"Nantius animam produceré."*

After about an hour of practicing, Vlad was able to produce a black and silver, misty swirl. Ciaran was excited for him. "Excellent! What were you thinking of that last time?" Vlad just looked at him and smiled.

Ciaran laughed. "Okay, fair enough. Now, whatever it was, concentrate on it just a little more intently. The *Anima* is not a skillful sort of magic, it's internal. You can learn how to do it, but that doesn't mean you'll ever really be able to do it. Children conjure the *Anima* all the time without meaning to because it's concrete thinking and pure feeling. That's what people don't get. You have to feel it from deep within and allow yourself to let go and let it come out of you. No one knows what shape their *Anima* becomes until they do it, because it's in the deepest parts of you. Let it come out of you." He stood back again.

Vlad nodded. He closed his eyes and meditated, then smiled to himself. He opened them, pointed his *rodulé* at nothing, and said boldly, *"Nantius animam produceré!"*

A stronger ball of silvery blue came from his *rodulé* and it began to take shape, but not enough to form something. Vlad yelled excitedly, "AHA!!!"

Ciaran cheered and clapped for him. "Excellent!"

Vlad followed the light as it floated upward, feeling proud of himself. But while Ciaran was still celebrating, Vlad watched in horror as a black figure with a long tail flew in and out of the clouds in their direction.

"Ci... Ci... Ciaran, Ciaran! He's back!!" Vlad stuttered, then yelled.

Ciaran froze and looked up in the same direction. They looked at each other and simultaneously Wisp'd back, shouting for the Ash Burner Barrier to go back up and firing red sparks. But Malik was faster, and he flew over the village with fire already on his tongue. He went back to the chief elder's bungalow and shot a fireball of flames directly on it. At the same time every single Reserver that was nearby shouted a different incantation to subdue the dragon, but the damage was already done. The home burst into flames.

The dragon flew higher and disappeared into the clouds again.

CHAPTER 28

Dracoginus

Malechi came running from Omaro's dwelling a few doors down. *"Apa! Apa!"* he cried over and over again. Vlad had to hold him back from running inside the burning dwelling.

"Ciaran!" Bruno said, looking upward. "He's coming back again. He's not done."

"I know!" Ciaran snapped through his teeth. "We can protect the village with the *Ash* for now but... It's not enough."

Bruno nodded while keeping his eyes on the skies. "We need something stronger." Then he looked at Ciaran. "We need to fight fire with fire."

Ciaran nodded, knowing what he meant. He turned to Khalid, who was on the other side of him. "Corral, get the villagers out of here now!" He turned to the other Reservers. "Everyone else, who knows *Dracoginus*? Now is the time to step up."

"Dragon fire!?" Tommy yelled as the rest of the men with Sarah and Ciaran lined up. "He's just a baby; it will kill him!" Vlad looked equally worried.

"It won't," Ciaran said confidently. "Eyes on the skies. He's coming back. And when he does, we will do it simultaneously. Aim for his right wing on my go."

Tommy and Vlad joined the line. They stood in a semicircle and waited, *rodulés* poised, and no one spoke. They all saw the shadow of the dragon get lower and lower, darting in and out of the clouds.

"Ready..." Ciaran commanded. "Steady..."

Malik flew lower and lower, then dived toward them. "NOW!" Ciaran cried.

They flicked their *rodulés* in the same manner and cried in unison, "*DRACOGINUS!*"

Fourteen orange beams collided midair, forming one massive fiery dragon. Their dragon blew out a large ball of fire, hitting Malik directly in the uppermost part of the underside of his right wing.

Malik howled in pain and flew off course toward the left as the *Vis* disappeared. He landed about half a mile from the village on his right side, sliding across the sand, pushing up massive dust. The team covered their face as the gust of sand came toward them.

When it passed, they looked at Malik. Malik roared over and over again, then his roars became whines and whimpers.

"Is he okay?" Tommy asked softly.

"Only one way to find out," Felix said. He looked at Ciaran for direction. Ciaran nodded. He began walking toward the dragon. The men and Sarah followed, getting closer, but not too close.

"Line up again. Be ready for anything," Ciaran commanded.

They watched him, *rodulés* poised, as Malik whimpered and tried to lick his own wound. After a couple of minutes, Tommy said, "Now what do we do?"

Ciaran honestly had no idea, but Malechi saved him from answering. He walked up to Ciaran with a large blanket in his hand. He motioned toward the dragon.

"*Eme vomo*. Me, go," he said to Ciaran. Then he walked on toward his friend and pet.

They watched as he petted and cooed at the dragon first, sang a few lines of his song, then spread his blanket down. He created a greenish-blue fire with his hands and put it next to them. The dragon laid his head on the blanket and Malechi sat down next to his head, rubbing him. Calming him.

After a couple of minutes, Vlad broke the line and started walking toward them. But Ciaran said, "Vlad. No."

"He's not going to hurt me, Ciaran," Vlad said.

"You can't really be that stupid," Bruno said roughly.

"FUCK THE FUCK OFF, Bruno!" Vlad screamed at him, raising his *dulé*. "I'm not Tommy; I will fucking end you."

"Hey!" Tommy said, offended.

But Bruno also broke the line with his fists balled up, ready to raise his *dulé* too. Ciaran held his hand out on Bruno's chest and shook his head once, then turned back to Vlad.

"Bruno is right, Vlad. Be smart. Be safe. You cannot go over there. You don't know what he's going to do if you approach him. You were one of the faces that did this to him. They have sharp eyesight and long memories. He is still dangerous to us. To you."

"Well, there is only one way to find out," Vlad said and turned to walk again.

Ciaran was losing his patience with the kid. *Is this how Dale felt about me when I was young and reckless?*

"Vladimir Yaroslavich!" Ciaran yelled. "You are now disobeying a direct order! If you leave this line, there will be consequences!"

Everyone was silent as Vlad froze in the spot and was thoughtful. He turned around to Ciaran and said, "Ciaran, I need you to know that I respect your authority and your leadership. And I couldn't ask for a better friend or mentor at this point in my life. I am so grateful to you. But I have to do this, for me. I have to trust my instincts. And if you really meant what you said to me two nights ago, you know why." Vlad turned around and walked toward Malik and Malechi.

"What a dumb fuck," Bruno murmured. Ciaran watched Vlad make it about 3/4ths of the way there and then started following.

"Ciaran!" Bruno called out incredulously.

"I can't let him go by himself, Bruno. He's my responsibility, as are all of you. If something happens to me, you're in charge, and you know what to do." He looked at him knowingly and Bruno nodded.

He turned to keep walking, but Sarah called out, "Wait!"

She ran up to him and took off her satchel. "Sleeping Beauty is in there. And here is the Dragonshade." She handed him a needle the size of his shoe. "Either way, he's going to sleep tonight." Ciaran nodded.

He walked to the dragon to find Malechi and Vlad sitting on the blanket on either side of him, caressing his chin and singing softly to him. Vlad stopped and said, "He's really hurt, Ciaran. He's in a lot of pain. Can't we do something, please?"

Malik looked up at Ciaran with sad eyes and whined. Ciaran reached down and petted his wet nose and face. He whispered, "I got you, boy. You're going to be safe with me, I promise."

Ciaran set the bag of Sleeping Beauty down between the two young men. "Put him to sleep, Vladimir."

Vlad looked at Ciaran and mouthed, "Thank you." He dug in the bag and pulled out a handful of yellow powder and blew it softly in his nose. "Sleep, Malik," said Vlad. "You're safe now."

He motioned for Malechi to do the same. *"Lepese,"* said Malechi. "Sleep. *Lepese."*

Together, they blew handfuls of dragon powder into his nostrils and mouth. Halfway through the bag, Malik closed his eyes, but they did not stop until he was snoring deeply.

Ciaran turned around and gave Felix the signal. Felix walked over to inspect his wing. He ran back and got Sarah, who returned with some herbs to soothe his burning skin. Together, they worked to ensure his wound was treated and would be healed in a few hours. Bruno led the other members of the team slowly toward them.

Ciaran said to them simply, "We're taking him." He looked at Bruno first. Bruno gave one nod.

Sven, Bruno, and Tommy bound the dragon's legs with an invisible rope, and the other wing to his body, giving space for his burned wing to heal. Ciaran looked at his watch; it was almost 3 a.m. He turned to his team.

"If you are all in agreement, let's not stay another night. Let's get him on the Flyer and back to the Reserve by sunlight. That way, when he wakes up twelve hours later, it will be on our turf, with no ability to breathe fire. I like those odds a shit ton better than what we've been dealing with."

"Here, here!" Lee said, thoroughly exhausted from the last forty-eight hours.

And Bruno confirmed, "Let's get the fuck out of here."

"You have twenty minutes; say your goodbyes," Ciaran said.

He sent green sparks up in the air, and in moments, the Flyer came over and landed near the dragon.

Silas stepped out and exclaimed, "Woo wee! I saw all that drama from way over there. Everyone okay?"

"Yeah we are," Mateo said. "But *coño*, I don't think the village will be the same without their chief elder."

They all glanced back at the bungalow that was still quietly burning.

CHAPTER 29

Albania

Ciaran called a meeting with the rest of the elders, letting them know they were taking the dragon. Haziz told him that Omoro would take over as Chief Elder now that Bocari was gone. Malechi took Vlad's arm and led him to the home he was staying at, with Omoro's family. He gave Vlad his hat, three of his unwashed African print tops, and told him to take the blanket that Malik's head was still on.

Vlad told him, "We will take care of him, I promise. Come visit him in Albania. AL-Bain-Ee-Ya."

Malechi repeated, "Ah-Baaan-eee-yah!" They hugged.

By the time they got back, the crew had gotten Malik hoisted to the top of the Flyer and tied down, still in a deep stupor. Elder Embini and other women from the village came by with food for their journey and seeds from the flowers that grew in their region, especially near the mountain.

"So he always remembers his home," Haziz translated for them. And soon they were back on the Flyer, heading home.

Ciaran again took his seat in the front, and everyone was falling asleep from exhaustion. Ciaran's mind once again wandered to his happy place—Chris—when he felt someone slide into the seat next to him. Without opening his eyes, he said, "What do you want, Vladimir?"

"I just want to say how sorry I am for disobeying your order, and I really appreciate you and respect your leadership on this mission. We could not have done this without your cool head and logical thinking. And all things considered, I think it went really well."

Ciaran laughed. "Yeah? Let's see after I give my report to Dale."

"I also wanted to tell you that as soon as we get back, I'm flying to Romania to tell my parents about me, then flying to Moldova to ask Alexi to marry me."

Ciaran opened his eyes and looked at him with a smile. "That is an amazing plan. Congratulations. However, the mission is not over. I need at least six to eight people to stay on the Reserve another three days at least, to ensure the dragon is adjusting to his new life. And since you are his new best friend, sorry, but you have to be there to tame Malik and build your team, so your trip will have to wait."

"Okay, yeah sure I can do tha—waaaait!" Vlad said excitedly. "Does that mean I will be his *Lead* Tamer!?"

Ciaran smiled again. "Yes. You get to pick your second-in-command Tamer and a couple of Fixers, a minimum of four people, to assign to Malik. I suggest you pull from the group that came with us, people Malik is familiar with. I would pull the Dungers, all four if you can, or maybe three Fixers and one Dunger, then I can pull the other Dungers into Fixer roles. They all did brilliant, and it's nice to be rewarded with a promotion after a mission. Lee did extremely well these last two days, sharp and quick thinking. But it's up to you who you choose."

"Wow. And here I thought you were really going to punish me for insubordination."

"Oh yes, I bloody well am," Ciaran said. "There will be no Dungers assigned to Malik for the first sixty days. You will be on dung duty, Shithead." He leaned back and closed his eyes.

"WHAT!??" Vlad hollered, and a couple of people shh'd him.

"You heard me," Ciaran said, arms folded, and eyes still closed. "You will be cleaning up Malik's shit for two months, by yourself."

"Ciaran. Ciaran, you can't do that. My team will never respect me," Vlad pleaded. "Ciaran—"

"That sounds like a personal problem," Ciaran cut him off.

"Fuck," Vlad muttered. He went back to his seat next to Mike to complain to his friend.

Ciaran smiled. His mind wandered back to his lover, waiting for him back in his bed.

7:39 a.m.

The Flyer arrived in the Reserve Sunday morning, to Dale's surprise. The team moved Malik to the far side of the valley, away from the other dragons, and untied him. Vlad, Tommy, Felix, Lucas, Ollivier, Mateo, Lee, and Jesse agreed to stay on with Ciaran at the Reserve for an extra seventy-two hours to help with Malik's adjustment. The rest went home on a five-day paid leave.

Sarah, Sven, and Ciaran went with Dale to his office to update him on the events of the mission. Dale, as expected, cursed them all out for putting Bruno on the Leadership Squad and putting Vlad in charge of anything, giving him free rein. But the three convinced him that both decisions were right for the job; that they were impressed with Vlad's quick thinking and great instincts and Bruno's mostly cool head, but solid input and advice.

After an hour or so, Sarah and Sven went home, and Dale and Ciaran continued to talk about the mission, with Dale bringing out the bourbon, even though it was before noon. They talked for a bit, then Dale said to him what Ciaran never would have imagined.

"When I'm ready to keel over and die, you'll take my place here, leading this Reserve."

Ciaran was speechless. "Men have been here longer than me, Dale. I'm not next in line to be the Dragon Ringmaster. No way."

"Yes. But no one bleeds the Reserve like you do. You bleed this land like I do. You care about the dragons here, as well as the people and the work we do here. So, you'll get married, have children, but you'll die on this land just like I will. You know I'm right." He gave Ciaran a knowing look. "I won't pass it to anyone but you when you're ready. And if I die first, don't worry, I will leave instructions."

Ciaran didn't say anything, but he was thoughtful. Dale continued, "You should know, though, Bruno will be here too. Sven has been mentoring him into leadership."

That was surprising to him. "Oh. I didn't know."

"I thought that's why you asked him to join you."

"No, I asked because I needed the best on my mission. Bruno is the most skilled Magician on the reserve, besides me. And he's a Dragonologist; he understands dragons like I do. Even if he hates them."

"Hm," Dale grunted and took another sip. "You think he doesn't care about the dragons, but he does. He's just more logical about it where you are all heart. That's why you clash so much; you're different sides of the same coin. But I hope you see that now, now that you've spent some time around him, see his thought process, and can work with him. Because it will be the two of you here leading this ship, like myself and Sven, until the sun sets on us, and you bury us at the gravesite with our dragons."

"Yeah," Ciaran said. "I get Bruno a little more now. I hope he gets me, too, though. You should be having these same conversations with him."

"Who says I haven't been?" Dale gave him a stern look. "You're not my favorite, you self-absorbed cunt."

Ciaran smiled, knowing Dale was lying. He was definitely Dale's favorite.

Ciaran resisted the urge to call Chris right away when he left Dale's office, since he had a lot of work to do. He spent the next couple of hours writing up his report, highlighting key players and giving out recommendations and accolades for their records on the Reserve. He gave Bruno the Second in Command Honor for his leadership, Vlad received the Bravery Honor, Tommy received the Team Player Honor, and he gave out two Unsung Hero Awards to Felix and Lee. Then he joined the rest of the skeleton crew for Malik's awakening.

Malik started stirring a little after 2 p.m. Vlad was already next to him, wearing one of Malechi's shirts and hat, singing Malechi's song. Everyone stood at least ten feet back while he opened his eyes and adjusted to his new surroundings. Vlad petted him along his face and behind his ear the way he liked, and Malik responded favorably. But then he raised his head and looked around.

Het out a loud roar that echoed through the valley. Then a whine. Malik sat up and stretched his wings. He could tell that his right wing was no longer damaged. But he was afraid to fly. He gently closed them back. Ciaran and Felix came closer to assure him he was fine.

Bruno, Ollivier, and Mateo had left and came back with three venison carcasses, laying them a few feet away from the dragon. Malik opened his mouth to cook his meal, but only smoke came out. Sarah had subdued his fire ability while he slept. Malik whined again.

Bruno used his *rodulé* and called out *"Ignitus,"* setting the food on fire until crisp, then blew it out with a flick of his wrist.

Malik walked over and sniffed. He grunted appreciatively and ate. Ciaran and Vlad smiled at each other, knowing he was going to be okay. After he ate Malik, lifted his head, searching faces, and started walking over to Bruno. Bruno initially backed up, but then held his hand out as Malik came closer. He scratched the soft spot behind his ear. Malik grunted appreciatively again.

Suddenly a dragon flew above them and landed a few feet over. Betta roared. Malik looked at her for a moment suspiciously. He had never seen another dragon before. She went up and started flapping around him. At first, he looked annoyed that someone was disturbing him, but then was intrigued. She started circling him and he roared at her. But then he flapped wings and chased her into the sky. The Reservers stood and watched them fly around playfully, then land near the watering hole where Malik made his first monster poop.

Ciaran conjured up a shovel and handed it to Vlad. "Get to it," he said with a straight face.

Everyone snickered as Vlad gave Ciaran a deadly stare. Ciaran did not budge. Vlad snatched it from Ciaran and sauntered over. He pulled one of the barrels that they kept in the valley and started pulling up small piles of hot steaming dung and loaded it into the barrel.

Vlad slipped, then caught his balance and yelled, "Aaaaah, my fucking trainers!" making everyone laugh again.

"Awww, he looks like a baby," Mateo joked.

"You would have thought he hadn't done this just a year ago," Lucas said.

Vlad continued to struggle, slipping every few moments and cursing. Ollivier said, "Let's help this poor son of a bitch." He conjured his own shovel and started walking over. Lucas and Lee followed him, and Vlad looked relieved and grateful for the help.

"No fucking way I'm cleaning up dung," said Tommy, and walked away. Jesse and Felix laughed, but then followed Tommy back up the hill.

Mateo was standing there with the two older men watching the dragon, then turned to them. "I want to be a Hunter."

Ciaran looked at him in surprise. "Really? I thought you loved being close to dragons."

"I do. And I will ride a dragon someday. But I understand a lot more now. I thought Hunters hated dragons, but they don't. They preserve and protect life. All life, human and dragon." He looked at Bruno. "Will you train me to be you?"

Bruno raised his chin up with pride. "You start tomorrow right before dawn at the edge of the valley."

Mateo grinned. "*Gracias.*" He looked back at his friends cleaning up dragon dung, shook his head, and walked away.

Only Bruno and Ciaran remained, standing side by side, watching the dragons fly and play together. Bruno broke the silence.

"It's because they are both so young and about the same age. I think Betta has been bored with all the older dragons around who prefer sleeping to flying. Now they can keep each other company."

"I think you're right, Bruno." Ciaran paused, then said, "Thanks for deciding to come along. I appreciated your insight and your counsel. I want you to know that. I couldn't have done this without you. I appreciate you."

Bruno grunted. "Couldn't let you fuck it all up now, could I?"

Ciaran smiled and pushed him slightly with his shoulder. "So, I figured out you're not a complete arsehole."

"I am a complete arsehole," Bruno said back automatically. "Don't ever forget it."

"Didn't I just see you pet a dragon?" Ciaran said, amusingly.

"Fuck off, Ciaran," Bruno said with no malice, almost friendly. "Don't you have a boyfriend to make plans to fuck later on?" He gave Ciaran a wink and walked away.

Ciaran laughed, then pulled out his phone.

Chris was sitting at the top stair of the Tank when his phone rang. He smiled wide and said, "Well, look who remembered to use a phone rather than send scary but cute-looking shadow dragons."

Ciaran laughed. "They didn't exactly have cell phone towers in the middle of the Sahara."

"Didn't?" Chris asked hopefully. "But you do now?"

"I do," said Ciaran. "Albania has great reception service."

Chris stood up, his heart beating fast. "You're back? On the Reserve?"

"Yes. I will be here the next couple of days; I have to make sure my team is good, and the dragon is adjusted. But I am back in the place I call home. And will soon be with you."

"Ciaran, I'm here."

Ciaran's heart started beating fast as well. "Here … where?"

"At the Tank. As you rightly deduced, I did not go to work Wednesday night. Bergina worked a double for me and I took her Sunday afternoon shift. I'm here now until tonight."

Ciaran looked at his watch: 4:15 p.m. He knew he would not be able to disappear—Malik just woke up and anything could happen—he needed to stay close. But maybe later on tonight…

"You're off at eleven, then? I'll come see you."

"Okay."

Neither spoke for a moment, yearning in the silence between them. Then Ciaran said, "Okay. I will see you soon." He hung up first.

Chris's heart continued to beat fast as he held onto the phone, even with Ciaran no longer on the other end. He grabbed his walkie and patrolled, needing to walk off his nervous energy. He walked over to the Reserve entrance in hopes that Ciaran could see him, but logically he knew Ciaran would not suddenly appear.

He went over to the lake. Because it was already spring and the weather was nice, there were a few people out at the campsites, and some fishers in boats. But otherwise, it was quiet for a Sunday. He sat on a picnic table until dusk, then patrolled again before heading back to the Tank.

He thought of nothing but Ciaran and their last few months together, leading up to their last moments. Being with Ciaran continued to excite him, but also calmed him in ways that no one else had ever done. In the beginning, it was more about a balance between maintaining the friendship and building on the lust between them for him. But his feelings continued to grow deeper than friendship, deeper than lust. He had no idea what to do about it since he had no idea where Ciaran's feelings about him were.

10:57 p.m.

Chris gave Ulrick, who did the overnight shift on the weekends, the shift report and left, closing the door behind him. He stood at the balcony of the Tank, scouting the parking lot and grounds, and waited. He heard a small noise to his right and Ciaran appeared at the edge of the forest. Chris's plan was to play it cool, but Ciaran's was not, and he moved with urgency toward him. Chris noticed and abandoned his initial plan and started taking the stairs down two at a time.

They met a few paces from the bottom of the stairs. Chris also planned on making a joke or a funny remark, but Ciaran was all business. He grabbed Chris's neck and kissed him passionately, jamming his tongue into Chris's mouth. Chris moaned and returned the passion. In the middle of the parking lot, their hands were touching everywhere from face to bottoms, lips biting and tongue sucking, and neither could get enough.

After a few minutes, Chris said between kisses, "Ciaran … if you … don't stop … your … little rule … about no … fucking on the job … is going … out the window … not … not that … I'd mind…"

"Uuuugh!" Ciaran groaned and kissed him on the lips one more time, then stepped back, raising up both hands in surrender. He backed away about a foot and adjusted his erection. Chris laughed.

"Where are you staying tonight?" Ciaran asked him.

"Well, I've been summoned home since my family has not seen me since last Monday and Mummy Clary is about to put out a search party for me." Ciaran smiled, liking the idea of Chris sleeping in his bed this whole time. Chris asked, "Will I see you tomorrow?"

"Yes. I'm going to try to sneak out again. I have a new protégé to cover for me."

"Oooh, Ciaran is breaking rules for me. This is new," Chris teased.

Ciaran came closer and put his hand on Chris's waist. "For you, I'd rob a bank right now." They kissed again, softer, slower. Ciaran said in between kisses, "I ... want to ... make love ... to you ... so badly ... but I ... I have ... to get back..."

Chris rubbed Ciaran's obvious erection gently, then whispered, "I know."

Ciaran moaned until Chris stopped and moved his hand away, but held him close so that their erections touched. They stood there and embraced, chin on each other's shoulder.

"I will pop in in the beginning of your shift again," vowed Ciaran.

"10:57 p.m.," Chris said.

"And then again when you patrol."

"1:02 a.m. at Marker 1."

Ciaran smiled. "And I'll come by one more time before the end of your shift. Maybe about an hour before."

Chris smiled back. "5:39 a.m."

They held hands and Ciaran walked Chris to his car, kissing him again before he got in. He watched Chris drive away, remembering the times Chris would drive off, leaving him there in the parking lot with confused feelings.

Ciaran was not confused anymore.

Go deeper into the Magi world with Chris and
Ciaran as their soul-tie becomes stronger...

BOOK CLUB QUESTIONS

1. What is your initial impression of Chris Jennings? Of Ciaran Beals?

2. If there was a hidden world of magic, would you want to know or be a part of it? Why or why not?

3. Both Chris and Ciaran experienced the death of close family members, Chris's mother and Ciaran's brother. How do you think these deaths affected their personality?

4. What scene do you think changed things for Chris and Ciaran: their initial meeting? The encounter with the evil warlock? Their tender moment after discussing Chris's mother? The massage? Another key moment?

5. What are your thoughts about Rem's grooming of Christopher? Should Ciaran have pushed more for Chris to understand grooming?

6. Which Reserver would you like to know more about, or hang out with in real life?

7. Do you have a favorite dragon?

8. If you were to compare this MM Romantasy with others, how would it fair?

AUTHOR BIO

Wife, mother, partner, daughter, sister, friend, social worker, life skills coach, and part-time erotic romance novelist, Eskay Kabba finds the complexity of human nature and creates romantic and erotic love stories. The characters reflect the notion that no one is all good or all bad, but we are all just trying to find love in hard places. Eskay pens erotic romance novels that celebrate the LGBTQ community, people of color, and interracial relationships. When not writing about the throes of passion, Eskay finds joy in spending time with her family and loved ones, reading dystopia and fantasy series, and binging popular shows from a streaming app.

Eskay.Kabba@gmail.com

Discover more at
4HorsemenPublications.com

10% off using HORSEMEN10